INSIDIOUS

ALSO BY BRETT BATTLES

THE JONATHAN QUINN THRILLERS

Novels

Becoming Quinn

The Cleaner

The Deceived

Shadow of Betrayal (U.S.)/The Unwanted (U.K.)

The Silenced

The Destroyed

The Collected

The Enraged

The Discarded

The Buried

The Unleashed

The Aggrieved

The Fractured

The Unknown

Novellas

Night Work

Short Stories

"Just Another Job"—A Jonathan Quinn Story

"Off the Clock"—A Jonathan Quinn Story

"The Assignment"—An Orlando Story

Down

THE ALEXANDRA POE THRILLERS

(Cowritten with Robert Gregory Browne)

Poe

Takedown

STANDALONES

Novels

The Pull of Gravity

No Return

Mine

Night Man

Novellas

Mine: The Arrival

Short Stories

"Perfect Gentleman"

For Younger Readers

THE TROUBLE FAMILY CHRONICLES

Here Comes Mr. Trouble

INSIDIOUS

THE NIGHT MAN CHRONICLES

BRETT BATTLES

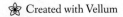

CHAPTER ONE

Miles Deveaux is a cautious guy. I would be, too, if I were like him.

Then again, I would never be like him.

Never.

Exhibit number one of his vigilance: his house's alarm system.

It's an expensive Kojima 33R.

That's the kind of system usually limited to supersized mansions or places you'd find expensive jewelry and priceless works of art. Deveaux's place is not a supersized mansion. It's not a mansion at all. It's a small, unattractive, two-bedroom house. And as far as any expensive jewelry or priceless works of art go, there is nothing like that inside.

The Kojima system has been tweaked in a way that is not unique but is certainly rare. If it's triggered, instead of alerting an alarm company or the police, it only notifies Miles himself.

Too bad for him, this is not the first Kojima 33R I have bypassed.

What am I doing in the house of a man I have never met? Especially here, so close to home?

A less than satisfying response to the first question is, it has to do with a hobby I picked up last year.

As for the second, that's equally complicated but let me give it a shot.

Right from the start, I made a rule not to take on any cases that fall within a couple hundred miles' radius of my townhouse in Redondo Beach. Deveaux's house is off a winding mountain road in an area known as Newhall, just north of the San Fernando Valley, putting it well within my exclusion zone. I know that doesn't really answer the question, but I guess what I'm trying to say is that this is not the first time I've broken the rule, nor, I suspect, will it be the last.

Perhaps it's more a guideline than rule. Though *guideline* might even be too strong a word. A suggestion? A hope? Maybe I should accept reality and forget about the rule altogether. Or maybe I should just stop doing all these little side projects.

You know you can't do that.

Heh. Of course Liz would say that. (More on her later.)

At least Newhall is far enough away from my home that it would be extremely unlikely for me to run into someone I know. And bonus, this little corner of Los Angeles County is far from where my other local rule-breaking activities have taken place, so the chance that what goes down tonight will be tied to anything else I've done is effectively zero.

I'm not going to lie. I'd been hoping for a few more days before I had to return here. That's right. I've been inside the house before.

Twice.

It was during my second visit—which happened just this morning—when I made the discovery that caused me to move up my timetable.

Right now it's almost 6:30 p.m., and given that this is

January, that means the sun's already been down for an hour and a half.

I'm sitting in Miles's home office, in the dark. There are only two lights on anywhere on his property, and both are outside—one illuminating the front porch, and the other the driveway, directly in front of the garage.

I have a set of night vision goggles in my bag on the floor next to me. I doubt I'll need them, but I'm good at what I do because I'm always prepared to improvise.

Miles is the kind of person whose life runs like clockwork. Today is Thursday, so he should be pulling into his driveway in fifteen to seventeen minutes. A normal evening would then unfold in the following manner: shower, fifteen minutes; dinner, twenty-five minutes; TV, sixty minutes; then office time until he goes to bed at eleven p.m. Two or three nights a month, there are exceptions. And thanks to what I discovered this morning, I know tonight is going to be one of those.

That is why I'm here.

I had a little prep work to do, so I've been in the house for about thirty minutes already. Another key to success: don't rush things when you don't have to.

I finished everything up about ten minutes ago, and am now in wait mode. It's something I had to learn to be good at in my day job. It took a bit of work; I wasn't always the most patient guy but I finally mastered it. If I hadn't, I'd probably be dead by now.

The hilly area where Miles lives is mainly occupied by large houses on one acre-plus plots of land, which means there's a lot of space between everything. Most of these big residences popped up in the past twenty or thirty years. Miles's house, however, is one of the few small legacy homes still standing from when this was a middle-class neighborhood pre-1990s. The vast majority of the other houses were torn down to make room for his new neighbors. He inherited the place when his mother died a few years ago. Not much changed for him, though, since he'd never actually moved out.

He has made a few improvements since the deed was transferred to him, however. The most obvious renovations are the office he created out of his former bedroom and the upgrades to the master suite. The not-so-obvious work was done in the kitchen, where he installed a secret compartment behind one of the lower cabinets. It's a convenient place to store things he doesn't want others to see.

If I was in a generous mood, I'd tip my hat to him. The compartment wasn't easy to find. I knew there had to be something like it somewhere in the house, but it still took me over two hours on my first visit to figure out where it was. With a careful guy like Miles, I have to believe he did the work himself, which would mean he's a pretty good carpenter, good with his hands.

Are you ready? Liz asks.

"As I'll ever be," I whisper.

Liz has been particularly anxious on this mission. I can feel the tension oozing off her as she stands—floats? hovers? —behind me.

He's coming.

I check my watch. It's 6:42. His normal arrival window will open in one minute. "I've got this. Don't worry."

I know she wants to say more, but she doesn't.

About Liz. She's my girlfriend. Well, *was* my girlfriend, right up until the moment she died a year ago. And yeah, I know, it can't really be her voice in my head. It's just my subconscious. And I also know I probably shouldn't be answering it. I try sometimes, but I can't stop myself.

When I look at my watch again, the display reads 6:44. Miles should be here any second. I turn my ear toward the street, as if that will help me hear his approaching car. But all remains quiet as my watch ticks over to 6:45.

This is unusual. I've spent a lot of time in the previous ten days spying on his place, plus two entire afternoons, watching four months' worth of stored security footage from a neighbor's gate camera, logging his patterns. Until tonight, there have been no deviations.

Is it possible he's proceeding directly to his pre-chosen spot for this evening's planned activities?

If true, it won't be a complete disaster. The notes I discovered this morning told me where he plans to be and when he's planning to make his move. I can get there in plenty of time to stop him, but I'd much rather deal with him here, where we won't be disturbed. Besides, I've put in a lot of work into setting the scene just right.

He left work late, Liz says. *He'll be here in three minutes.*

Okay, it's when Liz drops little info bombs like this that makes it hard for me to dismiss her as a figment of my imagination. Especially because she's usually right.

You're thinking that's got to be a coincidence, aren't you?

I hear you. I tell myself that all the time, but then something happens that makes me question the definition of reality.

Here's a perfect example. Exactly three minutes after she last spoke, the headlights of Miles's car swing into the driveway and the automatic garage door opens. I'm not as freaked out by this "coincidence" as I used to be, but I can't say I'm completely all right with it, either.

Miles pulls his vehicle into the garage and shuts off the engine. At the same time I hear his car door open, the garage door starts closing.

Are you ready?

"Asked and answered," I say.

Living Liz would have acknowledged a repeated question

like that with a whispered, "Just double-checking." Spirit Liz merely falls silent.

From the Kojima alarm control box in the kitchen, I hear a muted triple beep, indicating it has been remotely deactivated. The kitchen door opens and someone—Miles, I presume—enters. (Not once during my observations has anyone else been in the house. Granted, my sample size is small, but Miles does not strike me as the kind of person who entertains guests.)

I hear him set something down. Probably his briefcase on his dining table. Miles is an accountant at an equipment rental company in the Valley. Not sure what he carries in the case, but since he's leaving it in the other room, it's not something I need to worry about.

The footsteps continue out of the dining room and into the hallway that runs past the office. The hallway light clicks on and some of it spills through the room's open door. I'm sitting off to the side, and the only way I can be seen is if he sticks his head through the doorway.

I tense, ready in case that happens, but he walks right by and enters the master bedroom at the back without even pausing.

I've stood outside his windows while he was home, but this is the first time I've been inside the house with him, so I wonder if he's the kind of person who, despite being the only one here, closes the bedroom door when he takes a shower.

When I hear the sound of the latch clicking shut, I have my answer. If you ask me, it's probably a habit left over from when he lived with his mom. This thought morphs into an image of a forty-year-old Miles wearing a towel around his waist and screaming, "Mom! Get out!"

Ugh. I'm going to have a hard time scrubbing that image from my memory.

As soon as I hear running water, I grab the device lying on the floor next to me and stand up.

Be careful.

It's sweet of Liz to worry like this, but I'm in no danger. People like Miles are not even close to being in the same league as I am.

I make my way to the bedroom door. The sounds from the other side are distant and echoey, which tells me they're coming from the tiled bathroom.

I try the knob and am happy to note his closing-the-door habit does not include a turning-the-lock component. Not that I wouldn't be able to get through it, but I appreciate the time he's saved me.

The bathroom is off to the left, its door facing the back of the house, so it's impossible for him to see me enter. The sound of running water is from a faucet and accompanied by the *swish-swish-swish* of Miles brushing his teeth.

I walk toward the bathroom doorway until I can see his reflection in the mirror. Naturally, this means he can see me, too, but he has eyes only for himself. As much as I'd like to ignore it, there is one other detail I feel obligated to mention. He's brushing in the nude. If nothing else, the sight has freed me from the image of him in a towel yelling at his mom.

After a few more passes of his toothbrush, he spits into the sink.

And then, when he raises his head, he finally notices me.

For maybe three seconds he stares into the mirror, stunned, as if he doesn't understand what he's seeing. But his fight-or-flight instinct kicks in soon enough, and he jerks to his left, backpedaling toward the shower.

"Who the hell are you? What are you doing in my house?" This is the first time I've heard him speak. His voice is higher pitched than I imagined. I like it when little things like that surprise me. Keeps me on my toes. Big things, however, I prefer to know ahead of time.

Without saying a word, I stride into the room.

His back bangs against the shower door, and his breath catches in his throat as he realizes he has nowhere to go.

Not sure if I mentioned this or not, but I'm wearing a mask. It's a full head thing, a la Spider-Man or Deadpool. I received a pair of them for Christmas from a friend. Whether she meant it in jest or not, the mask is perfect for my needs and I've already used it a few times. This hood is black, except for the deep blue see-through material that covers my eyes and mouth. My clothes are all black, too. As are the gloves I'm wearing.

It's no wonder Deveaux is shaking.

"Get out of my house! Or-or-or I'll call the police!"

It's a bluff. The last people he wants traipsing through his place are the cops. I'm tempted to say, "Go ahead," but every second I'm here is another second I have to spend in his presence. I'd like to keep that to a minimum. So I pull my Taser out of its leather case on my belt, turn it on, and give the trigger a quick pull.

A sizzle of electricity sparks the air.

Miles's eyes grow wide enough for me to see white all the way around.

I feign a lunge to the left, and when he turns to block it, I shove the Taser into his back.

The shower door rattles as his body convulses against it. When I pull the device away, he crumples to the floor, moaning.

After returning my weapon to its harness, I slip a metal collar around Miles's neck and clip it closed. The collar is attached to a chain of five heavy-duty steel links. The chain in turn is welded to one end of the four foot long metal pipe I've been holding. I purchased it off a sex-toy website under the bondage section. You'd be surprised by the number of useful items I have found there. Or, I don't know, maybe you wouldn't.

Via the pipe, I give the collar a yank to get Miles's attention. He's still feeling the effects of the jolt, and it takes another pull to get him to look at me.

I motion for him to stand up, but his attention has fallen on the pole. The Taser must've dulled his mind, because he doesn't realize the pipe is connected to his neck when he grabs it, and ends up jerking the collar and causing it to dig into his neck.

"What is this?" he says, his panic increasing. "Get it off me!"

I rattle the chain connected to his collar, and motion again for him to stand.

He scrambles off the floor, his hands still on the metal pipe. He gives it a feeble twist, as if testing to see if he can free it from my grasp. He can't, but to make sure he understands that, I grab the Taser again. Before I even turn it on, his hands drop to his side.

"Please! No!" he says.

I keep the Taser pointed at him for another ten seconds before putting it away. I extend my hand toward him, palm facing the ceiling, and then curl my fingers toward my wrist twice, Bruce Lee style. Without waiting for a response, I head out of the room, pulling the pole.

When we reach his office, I maneuver him inside, around his desk, and into his chair. He stumbles more than once before he's seated, but I hold tight to the pole so the collar acts as a— albeit painful—steadying device.

His eyes have been on me the whole time so he hasn't taken in the room yet. If he had, he would've seen the bits and pieces from the memorabilia collection I found in his secret kitchen compartment. I've arranged them throughout the room. These include news articles Miles printed from the internet, each with some rendition of a headline like VALLEY HEIGHTS

RAPIST STRIKES AGAIN; twenty-three snippets of hairs, no two locks from the same person; and twenty-three sketches of women, also all different. Miles actually has some artistic talent, which is disturbing given the circumstances.

I've taped the articles and the sketches to the walls and laid out the hair trophies on the desk in nice neat rows. I probably could have matched each lock to a sketch, but that seemed an unnecessary step.

There are other items on the walls, items that have never been in Miles's possession. Specifically, photographs from the police files on the Valley Heights Rapist case. Pictures of each crime scene, and close-ups of bruises and other injuries his victims incurred. These came courtesy of my friend, colleague, and mask-gifter Jar, who knows her way around a computer better than most.

It takes almost half a minute before Miles finally notices I've redecorated the room. The fear on his face switches instantly to anger.

"Those are not yours to touch," he growls. "They belong to me. They are private!"

He reaches for a lock of hair. But before his hand can get close, I jerk the pole back and forth, rocking his head, then shove the pipe toward him until he's pinned against the back of his seat.

With my free hand, I remove two sets of handcuffs from one of his desk drawers. These are also from his secret stash.

"What are you going to do with those?"

If Jar were here, she would say something like, "That is an unnecessary question," because my intention is obvious.

I toss one pair onto his lap and point at his left wrist.

"I'm not putting this on myself," he says as if I'm crazy.

I set the other pair on the desk and grab my Taser.

"Wait, wait, wait! You don't need to—"

He's wrong. I do.

I shove the Taser into his leg, zapping him for a second time. As he convulses, the handcuffs fall from his lap onto the floor. I turn off the Taser, and while Miles is recovering, I scoot the cuffs over to me with my foot and pick them up.

As soon as he's breathing semi-normally, I throw them into his lap again. He jumps at the contact and has to scramble to keep them from falling back onto the floor.

"I'm doing it, all right?" he says as he wraps one of the cuffs around his left wrist. "I'm doing it."

After it's closed, he starts to put the other end around his right wrist. I stop him with a shake of the chain.

He looks up. "What?"

I point at the arm of the chair on his left. He immediately understands what I want—which is kind of creepy—and attaches the open cuff to the chair's arm.

I toss him the other pair. He attaches one end to his right wrist but hesitates to connect the other to the chair.

"I don't think I can do this," he says.

Sure, it would be a little awkward, but he *can* do it. What he's really saying is he doesn't want to. Can't blame him. Once he closes that last cuff, whatever tiny chance he thinks he has of getting away will disappear.

I switch on the Taser, and miraculously—with the help of Miles's thigh to steady the metal bracelet—the cuff finds its way around the chair's other arm.

His feet are still free, but I have a solution for that.

I move behind him, the metal collar twisting around his neck as I do.

He grimaces. "Stop doing that! Please! It hurts!"

I pick up the syringe I hid on the windowsill behind the curtain. He tries to see what I'm doing but the collar restricts his movements, so he's unable to witness me plunging the needle into his shoulder at the base of his neck.

He does scream, however, and say, "What is that? What did you do?"

What it is is a little thing in the business we refer to as the hobbler. For the next few hours, Miles will have no use of the muscles below his rib cage.

I wish I could have stopped him long before tonight from doing what he's done, but the police didn't link the attacks until recently and I was unaware a serial rapist was on the loose. When it did come to my attention—or, let's be honest, Liz's attention—I once more ignored my moratorium on local jobs and hopped right on it.

With Jar's help, we identified Miles as the probable perp. After that, it was up to me to secure the proof and deal with the problem. The reason I'm here tonight is that Miles was planning on attacking victim number twenty-four about two and a half hours from now.

At least that woman, and any others who would have followed without my intervention, won't fall prey to him. It eases my guilt a little but doesn't wash it away.

I move back around the desk and stand before him, motion-less, allowing the drug to do its thing. Miles prattles on during this, switching between wanting to know what I've given him and pleading for me to let him go. He even offers to give me a hundred grand in exchange for his freedom. Little does he know, every cent he has in cash and stocks—approximately $275,000—will be transferred out of his accounts before the night is over. The money will be distributed through various untraceable sources to his victims, in the forms of scholarships and grants and inheritances from unknown relatives. It can never erase what happened to them, but the money and news of Miles's demise should at least give them some relief.

The asshole's monologue stops midsentence, and his eyebrows knit together. He looks down at his lap, his breathing growing more rapid by the second.

"I can't move my legs. I-I-I can't move my legs." He looks at me. "What's happening? What did you do to me?"

I pull a lever on the pole and the collar pops open, allowing me to remove it. After laying the device on the floor, I deposit the empty syringe and the Taser in my backpack and zip the bag closed.

There's one more thing I have to do before I leave here. Well, two things actually.

I retrieve four coils of rope from where I left them against the back wall.

I can't take the chance that Miles might tip the chair over and break the arms, allowing him to drag himself out of the house. I use the first coil to secure his chest to the chair's back and two more to tie his forearms to the chair's arms.

I then turn the chair so that Miles faces the curtained window and drag it flush against the desk. I use the last coil of rope to attach the two pieces of furniture to each other. There's no way he'd be able to tip the chair over now.

One of the upgrades Miles installed when he converted his bedroom into an office was curtains that open automatically by a switch near the door.

I flick it on, and the drapes start to pull apart. As they do, they yank on the strings of two confetti poppers I attached to the top rod.

The timing is perfect. Just as the sign I taped to the window is revealed, the poppers pop, sending little pieces of colored paper raining down all over Miles as he reads my handiwork.

CONGRATULATIONS!
YOU'VE JUST CAUGHT

THE VALLEY HEIGHTS RAPIST

Maybe it's a little over the top, but I think it's a nice touch.

I exit through the front door, leaving it unlocked, and head around to the field behind the house.

Because only one road passes through the immediate area, my car is parked in a different neighborhood a mile away. I left it there so no one will connect it to what happened here tonight. I hike back to it, an unseen silhouette through the wilderness on a dark night.

Once I'm in my car, I call the Santa Clarita Valley Sheriff's Department, using an app that will feed whomever I call a false phone number and disguise my voice.

After a dispatcher answers, I give him Miles's address and say I heard screaming from inside, then hang up.

Thank you, Liz says.

Again, I'm struck by the wish I could have taken care of the problem long before now.

I know you do, she says. *But you acted as soon as you could. Thank you.*

Welcome to my life.

CHAPTER TWO

I could have called while I was driving home to let Jar know how things went, but I've spent too much time in that creep Deveaux's house. I want to shower first.

Unfortunately, washing off doesn't do as good a job as I'd hoped of removing the sense of disgust clinging to me. Perhaps I should have used sandpaper instead of soap. Then again, I'm not sure even that would have worked.

When I call Jar, she greets me with, "Sounds like everything went well."

I grimace. "Did it make the news already?"

"No. But there are reporters en route so there should be something on the ten p.m. broadcast. I have been monitoring law enforcement."

"Tell me they have him in custody."

"They do." A beat. "One of the officers mentioned something about...confetti."

I haven't told Jar about my little addition to the plan. It's something that came to me this afternoon when I was getting everything ready.

"Confetti," I say. "That *is* odd."

The pause that follows is deafening.

"I would like you to tell me what happened," she finally says. "Every detail."

Jar is not my boss. If anything, I'm one of her bosses when we're working our day job. But I quickly learned I can't do everything myself on these little hobby missions of mine, so I have often turned to her for help. I trust her. She's my best friend. (Though I've never actually told her that.)

What I'm trying to say is that anytime she asks for details, I give them to her.

When I finish describing the evening, she says, "The confetti and banner were not very professional."

"Professionals get paid. Last I checked, I am not." I say this with a smile in my voice. She doesn't laugh. "I'm beat. Can we talk later? I hear my bed calling."

"I thought we were going to play *Caverns of Exiles.*"

Dammit. That's right. I promised her we'd play tonight. Since we're not in the same city, it's one of the ways we stay connected.

Jar is Thai and is usually at her home in Bangkok when we play online video games together. For the last couple of months, however, she's been in San Francisco, staying with two of our other colleagues while she recovers from an on-the-job injury. A bullet smashed into a boulder she was hiding behind, and she took some rock shrapnel to her face that cut her cheek and damaged her cornea. Treatment for the latter involved several appointments and one minor surgery. It's my understanding everything's been going well, but she does have to wear glasses all the time now, and she still has a few follow-up doctor visits to make. That's why she hasn't left the States yet.

"You're right," I say. "We were."

"If you wish to cancel, we can."

"No, no. It's just...can I at least take a nap first?

"That is acceptable. How long do you need?"

Most friends probably would have insisted I get some rest and that we would play another day. Not Jar. To her, I would not have presented the option of a nap if I didn't mean that's all I need.

"A couple hours would be great."

"Midnight, then. That will give you three."

I'm awakened by my alarm fifteen minutes before the witching hour.

Jar and I end up playing *Exiles* all night. I'd like to say my pitiful performance was hindered by my lack of substantial sleep, but these multiplayer games are not my forté. I'm much better at the single-player ones that are more story based, like *The Last of Us* or *Horizon Zero Dawn*. I can make stupid mistakes in them and no one makes fun of me.

By the time I sign off, the night sky outside my townhouse is starting to lighten. I should probably go to bed, but I'm too keyed up from playing. Plus, I'd feel kind of guilty if I squandered what is shaping up to be a glorious Sunday morning.

January is one of L.A.'s coolest months, and true to form, we're in the middle of a cold snap. That means it probably won't get above fifty-four degrees today (that's about twelve degrees Celsius to pretty much the rest of the world). Right now, it's a bone-chilling forty-two (six).

Before you start cackling at my description, I realize a lot of places would call weather like this springtime.

My response: it's all relative. And if you don't believe me, ask anyone who moved here from the Midwest. Their first Southern California winter is spent laughing at everyone wearing sweaters when the temperature dips below sixty-eight. By their second, they're bundled up as much as the rest of us.

Braced for our arctic conditions in a stocking cap, knitted gloves, sweatshirt under a zipped-up hoodie, and sweatpants, I hop on my motorcycle, a Yamaha MT-07.

We had a few hours of rain in the middle of the night, but this morning the sky is crystal clear, and it's as beautiful out as the city ever gets. Wanting to take advantage of this, I head inland toward the Hollywood Hills, where the views are fantastic.

The early hours of Sunday are one of the best times to drive in Los Angeles. With the occasional exception of a Caltrans construction zone, you have the freeways basically to yourself. For me, it's freewheeling all the way to Hollywood and into Griffith Park.

I leave my bike near The Trails Café and start the climb.

Within the first quarter mile, I pass eleven other early birds who are taking their time on their way up. Me, I'm going for the burn, and I reach the Griffith Observatory in under ten minutes. Not my fastest time, but pretty good for having slept only a few hours last night.

I'm sure you've seen the observatory before. It's been featured in dozens of movies. The original *Terminator* for one, when Arnold arrives in a clap of thunder and a flash of lightning. It's also in *Rebel Without a Cause* if you've ever seen that. And of course, *La La Land*.

If you haven't seen any of those, the observatory is basically this long, art deco concrete structure, with telescope domes at either end and another dome in the center for...I don't know, aesthetics? (Actually, I'm pretty sure that's where the planetarium is located.) Anyway, there's no denying it's beautiful. But what's even more impressive is the view of the city from the walkway around the building. The panorama really hammers home the fact that L.A. goes on and on and on.

I'm not stopping there, though. I'm going all the way to the top of Mount Hollywood.

I jog through the parking area to the next trail. There are three times as many people up here than were on the lower path, which is annoying and also explains the several dozen cars I saw in the observatory parking lot. I was really hoping for a little more elbow room.

This is the reason that, when I near the peak, instead of turning onto the path that will take me to the top, I detour onto one that will lead me all the way to the Hollywood Sign. I have no intention of going the extra two and a half miles to get there. I just want some time alone on a quiet trail.

Almost immediately, I know I've made the right choice. No one else is around, and with the rises and dips of the terrain, I am also hidden from people on the other trails.

A little L.A. trivia for you. The Hollywood Sign is on Mt. Lee, not Mt. Hollywood. Why? I don't know. What do I look like—Wikipedia?

As I'm heading down one side of the ridge between the two mountains, I sense Liz's presence.

"Hey," I say.

Hey back.

I was hoping the hike would draw her out. It's something we always loved to do together, especially first thing in the morning. I know not to expect much, conversation-wise. Her presence is more than enough.

Still, I can't help but whisper, "I miss you."

I feel her hand hover over the nape of my neck softly, as if she's going to caress it like she used to.

That way, she whispers.

It takes me a moment before I realize what she means.

There's a trail ahead leading off to the right, toward the San Fernando Valley side of the hills. It's one I've never taken before.

I turn onto it, thinking she wants me to see something new.

Is anything really new to her now? I'd ask her, but I know she wouldn't answer. Besides, she's not real, remember?

When I was a teenager, at every opportunity my goal was to sleep in until ten a.m. on weekends, holidays, and summer vacations. If I woke up before that, more times than not I'd consider the day ruined.

I was an idiot.

There is something special about early mornings, magical even. It's in the light and the air and the smells and the sounds. It's as if when the majority of people are still asleep, their brain waves don't muddy up the atmosphere for those of us who are up. I know, I know. That sounds a bit like new-agey BS but I swear, as people start waking up, the magic fades.

Thankfully, the new trail is also devoid of other hikers, making it easy for me to pretend I'm the only person in the world. Don't get me wrong, I love the big city, but every once in a while it's nice to feel alone. I breathe it in, letting the sense of solitude replenish me. (Yeah, I hear myself, too. More new-agey crap. I'm a native Californian—what can I say?)

I'm getting hot from all the exercise so I take off my hoodie and tie it around my waist. As I look up, a blotch of purple just off the trail ahead catches my attention. It looks like a piece of cloth, maybe a T-shirt or something like that.

Whatever it used to be, it's litter now and I'm not a fan.

As I near it, I see the spot of color is farther off the path than I thought. For a split second, I consider ignoring it, but the voice in my head (the normal one, not the Liz-driven one) would never let me get away with that, so I leave the trail.

The ground is still moist from the rain, and my boots sink

into it enough to leave identifiable prints that would be unacceptable in my day job. When I'm only a couple of yards away, the hillside, which has been relatively flat until now, begins to tilt downward, forcing me to slow.

When I reach the spot of purple, what I find is not a T-shirt or a loose piece of cloth.

It's a backpack. Like the ones high schoolers and college kids carry, and like what I often use for work. It sits right at the top of a rocky chute that drops down at a pretty steep angle. One wrong step and I'd tumble over the side.

Since that's not in my plans for the day, I stop short of the bag and lean forward to grab it.

I expect it to be empty but it's not, and I have to give it an extra tug to free it from the bush that appears to have saved it from falling down the hill.

Something about the bag is setting off my caution alarm. It's a hazard of my job. When you spend your professional time in the world of secrets and deception, you're suspicious of pretty much everything. To that end, I've been trained to question both the expected and unexpected, a habit that often leaks into my downtime.

I set the backpack on the ground. Then, using the sleeves of my hoodie as makeshift gloves, I unzip the main pocket.

Inside are two books. I pull one out far enough to get a look at its cover and am immediately possessed with the desire to toss it down the hill.

Cooler instincts prevail, however.

The book is a textbook, specifically for college-level accounting. It's an updated version of the textbook I lugged around for an accounting class I took way back when I was going to UCLA. As you may have guessed, that's not a pleasant memory. The accounting part, I mean. Not UCLA. That was a blast.

Perhaps the owner of this book was having the same visceral

reaction I had to debits and credits and double-entry accounting and became fed up enough to fling the bag with the book inside into the brush.

I pull the other book out. It's a novel. *Jade City* by Fonda Lee.

I've read it. It's really good. The book is a hardcover, with a bookmark sticking out about two-thirds of the way through. It's hard to believe someone would callously toss it away. Perhaps even more confusing is the fact the backpack looks like it can't be more than a few months old. So, if the textbook was the problem, why not fling only that into the bushes and keep everything else?

Because the textbook isn't the problem, Liz says.

"Yeah," I whisper. "I know. That's kind of what I was getting at."

I reach into the big pocket where the books are and feel around the bottom, in case there's something there that might ID the owner. The only thing I find is a small key attached to an equally small key ring. The ring is entwined in some loose threads on the backpack's bottom seam. I give it a tug, but it's tangled up pretty well so I just leave it there. In the smaller pocket on the front of the bag, I find some pens and a half full package of gum.

As I stand up, my fingers feel something unexpected along one of the straps, under the material that would have been lying against the person carrying the bag. It's not a big thing but rather a small spot that feels stiffer than the rest of the filler inside the strap. I think it's probably nothing until I feel a slight buckle of cloth along the seam. I take a closer look and discover a secret opening, sealed by Velcro.

I work it open, slip my finger inside, and work it around the hard spot. Out of the opening pops a micro SD card, the kind used in some phones to store data.

That alarm in my head is starting to clang louder.

I examine the ground in the vicinity. For the most part, the rain has transformed the dirt into a blank canvas. But the downpour didn't last long enough to do a complete job, because about eighteen inches from where the bag was is the faint outline of a shoe. It's a big print, at least a size eleven. Statistically, that means the wearer is six feet tall or more.

I move as close as I can to examine the print. Unfortunately, there's not enough of an impression to tell me the style of shoe, but based on my experience, I'm more than willing to bet it was worn by a man.

The question is, does the print have anything to do with the bag? Or was it created before or after the backpack was abandoned? At the moment there's no way to know, but that doesn't stop my mind from working through a couple dozen scenarios of what could have happened. Most have a common theme I don't like, but I can't ignore the possibility.

I step as close to the drop-off as I dare and peer over the edge.

Dammit.

"Hey, you all right over there?"

I twist around and spot a couple of guys on the trail, both thirtysomethings, one holding a leash connected to an excited-looking golden lab.

"Call 911," I say.

They both look surprised.

"What's wrong?" the talker asks. "Are you hurt?"

I look back down the narrow ravine at the bent and battered body of the woman lying at the bottom. "Tell them to send the coroner."

CHAPTER THREE

The police have questions.

"How did you find her?"

"Do you know the deceased?"

"How often do you hike this trail?"

"What made you check the ravine?"

"Did you touch the body?"

I answer all of these truthfully, except for the last.

I was sure she was dead but I needed to confirm it, so while waiting for the police to arrive, I found a less hazardous way to the bottom of the chute. I felt for a pulse on her neck, and from how cold her skin was, I knew she'd been dead for hours.

She is...was younger than my Good Samaritan friends with the phone—early twenties would be my guess—and African American, her skin color on the medium-to-light end of the spectrum. She was wearing jeans and a pullover sweatshirt with the letters CSUN on the front—Cal State University, Northridge.

She couldn't have been more than five foot five, so there was no way the print at the top of the ravine was made by her. I checked her shoes anyway. Sneakers that weren't even close to size eleven. Also, their treads were clean, so she must have fallen before the rain turned the ground to mud.

Because the area she fell into is covered with rocks, I was unable to determine if I was the first to examine her or not.

There is one other question the police ask that I answer with a lie.

"Can I get your name, please?"

"Brian Wright."

Wright is one of my many, many aliases. In this case, it's my current emergency identity, something I keep handy in case of... well, emergency. It's not that telling them my real name would make that much of a difference; other than finding the body, I don't have anything to do with this crime. But I make it a practice to keep my actual identity out of any databases, especially those belonging to law enforcement and other government organizations.

When they ask to see my ID, I'm back to telling the truth. "It's at my bike."

I'm driven down the hill by a rookie cop named Stanhope. When we get to my Yamaha, he takes down my phone number (not my real one, but one that will route to it) and the info off my Brian Wright driver's license, which was in a hidden pocket under the bike's seat. Before he leaves, Stanhope tells me the cops will be in touch if they have any more questions.

If they do call, they will learn that Brian Wright has died due to some...something. I'll have to figure that part out. But he *does* have to die. Because if it turns out someone is responsible for the girl's fall and the police arrest a suspect, I can't risk the possibility of prosecutors calling on me to testify. Even if this is an investigation no one cares about, I wouldn't want my alias appearing in court records.

But people are definitely going to care about this. A young

woman found dead in Griffith Park? Possibly a local college student? It has evening news feature story written all over it.

So, Wright's gotta die.

RIP, fictional buddy.

I ride back to the beach and get home around noon. I may not have been tired when I set out this morning but I'm exhausted now.

I close my blackout curtains, turn on my white-noise machine, and set my phone to DO NOT DISTURB.

Thirty minutes later, I'm still awake.

It's the dead girl.

Don't get me wrong. I see lifeless bodies all the time. It's kind of what I specialize in.

What's keeping me awake is the belated realization that Liz led me to the body. In fact, I have a feeling she's the reason I had the urge to go to Griffith Park in the first place.

How stupid of me to think I found the girl by chance.

When I ask Liz about it, I feel her near but she doesn't respond, which is all the confirmation I need.

She directed me across town on purpose. She took me down that path. She wanted me to see the backpack because she knew I would find the girl.

Liz likes getting me involved in problems that need solving. The Marissa Garza hit-and-run back in September is a good example. As is the Miles Deveaux situation these past few weeks.

The dead girl is the second time in a row Liz has pushed me toward something local. And let me tell you, Griffith Park is a lot closer to Redondo Beach than Newhall is.

Sleep, she whispers in my ear.

"What do you think I'm trying to do?"

Sleep.

I swear, sometimes she doesn't listen to a word I say.

Much to my surprise, I end up sleeping for nearly six hours.

When I check my phone, I see five text messages and seven voicemails. All the texts and four of the calls are from Jar.

The other three voice messages, in chronological order, are as follows:

[2:45 pm]: Mr. Wright, this is Detective Hughes with the LAPD. If you could give me a call at your earliest convenience, I would appreciate it.

[4:02 pm]: Mr. Wright, Detective Hughes again. I really need to speak to you. This is my cell phone so call me anytime.

[5:37 pm]: Mr. Wright, Detective Hughes, LAPD. It is imperative that we speak. Call me as soon as you receive this.

Uh-oh.

Detective Hughes's persistence tells me the dead girl probably didn't slip and fall on her own. And if the police have determined she was murdered, who better to add to their list of suspects than the guy who found her body? I imagine more than a few cops are hoping I did it, so they can wrap up everything before Sunday's over.

I grimace. The calls put me in a bit of a bind.

Before I can kill off Brian Wright, I need to set up a few things, like sneaking news stories onto the internet about his demise and arranging for one of my mortuary contacts to vouch for the body's cremation. This will take me at least a day. And to be honest, it would look better if there's a little more time between Wright finding the girl's body and his imaginary death.

Talk to him, Liz says.

I snort. "I'm *not* talking to the police."

Talk to him.

"You understand the problem, right?"

Talk to him.

"He probably already thinks I killed her."

Talk. To. Him.

I'm not crazy. No one has to convince me it's not wise to argue with a disembodied voice in my head. And probably even dumber to do as it says.

And yet, I find it impossible to ignore her.

It's Liz's voice. The woman I love.

The woman I *loved*.

She's dead, Nate. Don't forget.

And yet, nothing she's said since she started talking to me again last summer has been wrong.

"Crap," I mutter and grab my phone.

Hughes picks up on the first ring, and after I identify myself, he says, "Mr. Wright, thank you for calling back."

"I apologize, Detective. I was trying to get some work done so I silenced my phone."

"Lucky you. I'd get fired if I ever turned off mine. What is it you do, Mr. Wright?"

The question is casual, but I know it's on the list of things he wants to ask me.

"Travel writer." This is what I tell people when they don't know about my real job. Helps explain why I'm away from home so much and don't have a nine-to-five schedule.

"Travel writer? Wow. Go anywhere interesting lately?"

"I've gone to a lot of interesting places. Hard to pick out just one. Is there something I can help you with?" I'm walking a tightrope here. I want to sound innocent and accommodating, but if I willingly start going into details about my fictitious profession, I'll appear to be trying too hard.

"There is," he says. "It would be a big help to us if you could come downtown and fill out a statement, and maybe answer a few questions."

"We can't do any of that over the phone?"

"You'll have to sign the statement, so we find it easier to do everything at the same time."

Liz's lips are at my ear. *It's okay. Go.*

I'm starting to get the feeling she wants to get me arrested. I take a breath, then say, "Okay, sure. I can come in. Would tomorrow morning be—"

"This evening would be better."

"This evening?"

"Are you free now?"

"I'm across town. It would take me a little while to get there."

"Great. When can we expect you?"

I call Jar as I'm racing northeast toward downtown.

"What happened to you?" she asks. "I thought we were going to play some more this afternoon."

"I got sidetracked by a dead body so didn't get to sleep until lunchtime."

"Ha. Ha. Very funny." When I don't respond, she says, "That was not a joke?"

"I wish it was." I tell her about my morning and where I'm now headed.

When I finish, the only response I hear is the tapping of a keyboard.

Several more moments pass before Jar says, "They still do not know her name." Though she hasn't said it, I have no doubt she's using her back door into the LAPD's system, the same back door she'd used to obtain the crime photos I left at Miles's place. "A preliminary check of the body has found bruises near the base of her neck that appear to be caused by fingers."

That would explain why the cops likely think it's murder.

"Is there anything about my alias?" I ask.

"Hold on." After a pause, she says, "There is a transcript of your conversation this morning, and your name appears on a list of people to call in for further questioning." Another pause. "They think you might have done it."

"Yeah. I realize that."

"Maybe you should not be paying them a visit."

"Don't think the idea hasn't crossed my mind," I say. "But if I pull a disappearing act now, they'll only get more suspicious, and would end up wasting time looking for me that they should be using to search for the real killer. The sooner I convince them I'm not involved, the better."

"What if they do not believe you?"

"Don't worry. They'll believe me."

"If you say so."

Her lack of confidence does nothing for my mood. "I gotta go. Keep your phone close. I may need your help later."

"For a jailbreak?" She sounds almost hopeful.

"There's not going to be a jailbreak. I'll be fine."

"If you say so."

"Goodbye, Jar."

I guess I should take some solace from the fact Detective Hughes leads me into a private office instead of an interrogation room, but I'm pretty sure he's doing so in hopes I let my guard down. He even apologizes more than once for the inconvenience of calling me in on a Sunday evening, and makes a vague reference to his bosses not giving him a choice.

"Can I get you something to drink?" he asks after I sit in one of the chairs in front the desk. "Coffee? Water? A soda?"

"Water would be great, thanks."

Hughes is gone for less than a minute, returning with my water and a can of Coke.

Instead of taking the seat behind the desk, he plops down in the one next to me. Once again, he's trying to make me feel like I have nothing to worry about.

If our roles were reversed, I'd be recording our meeting, on a device I've hidden somewhere in the room. I'd probably even put up a camera. I haven't spotted either, but that doesn't mean they're not here somewhere.

That possibility does not please me. Nor does the fact that as we walked through the building on our way here, my image was definitely picked up by over a dozen security cameras. Having footage of me in the LAPD's possession is not something I can tolerate. Thankfully, Jar should be able to remove all traces of me from the system. But as much as I would love for her to perform her digital exorcism the minute I walk out of here, that wouldn't be smart. Better to wait until I'm sure the police are no longer interested in me. For now, I'll ask her to locate everything so that when the time comes to hit the erase button, it will be a simple matter.

"I want you to know how much we appreciate you coming down here tonight," Hughes says. Like with the apologies, this is an echo of an earlier statement.

"No problem, but I'm not sure how much more help I can be."

"Don't sell yourself short, Mr. Wright. You've already done a lot by finding the body. She could have been down there for several days if you didn't. And that would have made our job even more difficult."

Ah, the old butter-up-the-suspect routine. If I was just a normal hiker who stumbled upon the body, I'd be feeling pretty good about myself right now. But I'm not, so while I act that way, my senses are on high alert.

He takes a sip of his soda and then says, "I'm wondering what made you go off the path where you did."

"Like I told one of the officers this morning, I saw the backpack. I thought it was trash so I went to pick it up."

"Do you always pick up litter when you hike?"

"Big stuff, when I notice it." This is true.

"And when you reached the backpack, what happened then?"

"I glanced over the edge and saw the body."

"Why?"

Though I understand the question, my brows slide toward each other. "I'm sorry—why what?"

"Why did you glance over the edge?"

I look surprised. "I...I don't know. I guess because I was right next to it."

"Were you worried you might go over?"

"I don't remember. Maybe."

"And when you looked, you saw the body."

"Yeah." I take in a breath and let my eyes defocus, as if I'm remembering the moment.

"You told the officers you went down to the bottom right after you spotted her."

"No. I said that I asked someone on the trail to call 911, then I went down."

"Right. Sorry. Why did you go down?"

"I was hoping she was still alive," I say this as if my answer is obvious.

"Did you touch her?"

"No."

"Why not?"

"When I got there..." I take a breath. "The way she was lying, I knew she had to be dead."

Hughes gives me a moment to collect myself before saying, "The person who called 911 told the operator to send the coroner. He didn't ask for an ambulance. Do you know why he'd say this?"

Yeah, because I made a mistake but I don't tell Hughes this. I should have been a little less proactive. But in my defense, efficiency is a big part of my job and I was trying to lessen the amount of time the girl's body would be left out in the open.

Oh, well. Best to deal with this head-on. "Because I told him to say that."

"Why?"

"Because she looked dead from above. I went down hoping I was wrong, but I wasn't."

"Don't you think it's unusual for someone to request the coroner?"

"Happens all the time on cop shows."

He wants to cringe. I can see it in his eyes. But, except for a twitch at the corner of one eye, he maintains control. "Which shows do you watch?"

"*Law & Order*, *The Rookie*, reruns of *CSI*. That's my favorite."

This is where I patch over my mistake. *CSI* and its various spinoffs are the stuff of law enforcement officers' nightmares. The real cop world and the fictional *CSI* world are not the same. There's even something called the *CSI* effect, where jurors who are fans of the show expect prosecutors to present evidence in the same way the actors do on TV.

Hughes shifts uncomfortably in his chair, picks up a

notepad from the desk, and flips through it until he finds what he wants. "You live in Long Beach?"

"That's right." It's the address on my Brian Wright driver's license. If they go there, they'll find an empty lot where an apartment building used to be, so I need to convince them not to pay a visit.

"Do you hike Griffith Park often?"

I shrug. "A couple times a month, maybe. Sometimes more, sometimes less."

"That's a long way to come for a hike."

"I suppose. I like the hike, though, so it doesn't seem too far to me."

"Why did you choose to hike this morning?"

"It was a beautiful day, and there was no traffic on the freeways. It was an easy choice." Check me out, getting back to telling the truth again. Well, except for the part about my dead girlfriend probably influencing my decision.

"Ever go there at night? Take in a show at the planetarium?"

"Not since I was a kid."

He glances back at his pad. "Can you tell me where you were early this morning, around one a.m.?"

"One a.m.? Sure, I was home playing video games."

"Alone?"

"There were at least ten other people online with me."

"How long did you play?"

I glance at the ceiling. "Well, we started around midnight and stopped about six thirty. So, a little over six hours."

"You were up all night?"

"I took a nap before we started playing, but otherwise, yeah."

"You do that often?"

"Nap?"

"Stay up all night playing video games."

"Not as often as I'd like."

"Is there anyone who can vouch for you playing all night?"

"Sure. Everyone I played with. PlayStation would probably have records of who they were."

"Correct me if I'm wrong, but anyone could have used your screen name, right?"

"Technically, I guess, yeah. But no one else knows my password."

"You couldn't have given it to someone?"

"I guess, in theory, but I didn't. Besides, we were talking to each other the whole time." I can no longer pretend I don't know where he's taking this, so I frown and say, "Did I do something wrong? Should I not have gone down and looked at the body?"

"Is there anyone who *physically* saw you at home last night?"

"My roommate."

"You have a roommate?"

I didn't until a second ago. "Yeah, Mark. He was in his room most of the time. But he knew I was there and probably heard me playing. I'm not that quiet."

"I'm going to need to speak to him. Does he have a last name?"

"Gibson."

Reminder to self: create a roommate named Mark Gibson and find someone to play him.

"Can you give me his number?"

"Do you think I have something to do with that girl's death?"

He raises an eyebrow. "If you did, it would be a good idea to tell me now."

I look shocked. "I would *never* do something like that." Most people would be tempted to say more but that would be gilding the lily—and likely to make me sound more suspicious—so I leave it at that.

"Your friend's number. Do you have it?"

"Yeah, sure." I pull out my phone but stop before I unlock it. "I'll have to look it up. Is that all right?"

"Go ahead."

I make a show of scrolling through my contacts list, then recite one of the numbers I have memorized. This will send Hughes to a voicemail with a short greeting from a man saying, "Please leave me a message." I have several numbers set up like this, with male and female voices, older and younger. Like my Brian Wright identity, the voicemail boxes are there for emergencies, normally for my job when I need to throw someone off. This is the first time I've ever used one in my personal life, and I don't like it.

After I put my phone away, Hughes says, "Would you be willing to provide us with your PlayStation username and password?"

"Of course. If that'll help."

"It will." He stares at me, waiting for the information.

I let a couple of seconds go by before I say, "Oh, I don't have it on me. I'll have to look it up after I get home. Can I call you back? Or email you?"

He pulls a business card out of his pocket and hands it to me. "Email's fine."

"I'll do it as soon as I get home." Well, as soon as I get home and make sure my account information matches my alias and Jar can change the IP information PlayStation stored so that Hughes can't trace it back to my townhouse. "Do you need to ask anything else? Or is that all?"

"I think we've covered everything for now. Thanks for coming down."

I call Jar as soon as I'm on the road.

"Well?" she asks.

"It could have gone better."

"You were arrested."

"Does it sound like I was arrested?" I gun my motor for a second to hammer home the point.

"They could have released you on bail."

"I wasn't arrested."

"Huh."

I'm not sure I appreciate how surprised she sounds, but I let it go and describe my visit with the detective. When I'm done, I ask her to look into the PlayStation matter, and after she finishes that, to check Hughes's files and see what he says about me. "Also, there's video footage of me at the station. Don't remove it yet, but at least figure out where it is."

"You should not have gone."

"It'll be fine."

"If you say so."

I ride the rest of the way in silence, the whole time thinking Liz will soon make an appearance to reassure me, but she's a no-show.

When I get home, I take a shower and then call Jar back.

The dead girl has a name now. Saundra Moore. This was apparently determined while I was at the station with Hughes.

Saundra was a sophomore at CSUN, but it wasn't her college affiliation that ID'd her. Prior to entering the university, she spent four years in the US Army, where, like all military members, she'd been fingerprinted. That was how the LAPD learned her identity.

So far, that's pretty much all they have on her. The investigation will no doubt hit full steam on Monday morning. But that doesn't mean Jar would wait until then to know more about the girl.

"I read through her army files," she tells me. "She is from Denver, Colorado."

"Was from," I say. "She's dead."

"Okay, was. She joined the military after graduating high school and spent the majority of her enlistment in South Korea. A communications specialist. She was discharged last July, and started university at Cal State Northridge in August. I looked at her school records, too. Classes she took while in the army allowed her to enter as a second-year student. Her major was computer science, with a minor in business administration."

That last piece of information makes me think about the accounting book, which then brings up the memory of the SD card. But according to Jar, the LAPD lists Saundra's possessions as the backpack, the books, the key, the pens, and the gum. No mention of the card.

For a brief moment, I wonder if I should have held on to it, but that's just instinct talking. There was no reason then or now for me to have done that.

"That's all interesting, but I'm just a tangential piece to this thing," I say. "The police are on the case. Neither of us needs to be involved in this any more than we have been already."

"I only thought it would be good for you to know who you found."

Nothing like a little admonishment from Jar to make me feel like crap.

"You're right. Thank you."

Jar changes the subject and asks if I want to play some more *Caverns of Exiles*. I'm really not in the mood, but perhaps it'll take my mind off of things. So, after some gentle prodding on her part, I give in. First, though, she takes care of my PlayStation info, after which I send Hughes an email with my username and password. Hopefully he doesn't try to use it while I'm online.

I expect to play horribly tonight but the opposite is true, and I actually stay alive to the end of almost every round. Jar thinks it's because I'm using the game to work out my aggressions. I can't argue with her there.

After a few hours, I call it quits and head to bed.

In the half-conscious state before falling fully asleep, I find myself kneeling at the bottom of the hill, next to Saundra's body.

"She needs your help," Liz says.

She's beside me. Not apparition Liz, but the fully formed, living version.

"She's dead," I say. "There's nothing I can do."

"Nate, she needs your help."

"She's too far gone."

She puts a hand on my shoulder and locks eyes with me. "Was I too far gone?"

I have no response to this.

"Help her."

"If I need to, I will."

"You will."

As I drift to sleep, I think at least this is only dream Liz, not my ghostly companion. And what she says here doesn't really mean anything.

CHAPTER FOUR

When I turn on the local news in the morning, I'm greeted by an anchor with a graphic behind her reading: DEATH IN GRIFFITH PARK. After a few seconds, the shot changes to show a reporter with Mt. Hollywood in the background.

I turn up the volume in time to hear her say, "...of a woman that was discovered near the summit of Mt. Hollywood by a hiker yesterday morning."

I wince.

I know she hasn't said my name—more accurately, my alias—but even coming this close to public exposure is unnerving. It's happened to me once before, several years ago in New York, when I was on a job. I didn't like it then and I like it even less now. Though I avoided being outed back east, there's a greater chance I would be exposed this time. All it would take is one intrepid reporter working her LAPD contacts and getting all the info the police have on the hiker who found the girl. The reporter would try to pay me a visit and everything would spiral out of control.

Looks like Operation Terminate Brian Wright is back on.

"Police have yet to release the identity of the victim," the reporter goes on, "saying only that she is an African American female in her early twenties. While investigators initially believed her death was an accident, this morning a department spokesperson said that detectives now suspect foul play."

And there it is. The world may not know Saundra's name yet, but it knows her death has officially become a murder investigation.

The reporter starts to give some background on the area, but I've heard enough and turn off the TV.

There's no sugarcoating it. I'm a little agitated.

This is all happening too fast and too close to home. And I don't feel in control of the situation.

Patience, Liz says.

"Patience?!" I shoot back. "Do you understand the kind of trouble I could be in?"

She doesn't answer.

I need to clear my head. A run down the boardwalk might help.

Before I head out, I call an operative friend of mine who lives in Venice Beach, and arrange for him to play the part of my roommate if it becomes necessary.

Outside, it's a cool fifty-eight degrees. Perfect running weather.

This being January, the only people on the boardwalk are locals riding bikes or on foot, no tourists. I nod hellos to several of the other joggers as I pass. Though none of us have ever spoken to one another before, and likely never will, we see one another almost daily. It allows me to feel both anonymous and like I belong here at the same time.

I'm almost to the point where I usually turn back when I feel my phone vibrate against my arm. Whoever it is can wait until I'm done. I'm finally feeling a bit better, and I'd like to stay that way as long as I can. I hit the halfway mark and head for home.

My townhouse is a block off the beach. Nice, right? It would be even nicer if the house between me and the water wasn't a monument to the greatness of concrete. The monstrosity is three stories tall, which means when I sit on the deck off my living room, I have a view through a window into their guest bedroom. It's not all bad, though. I can see a sliver of the ocean if I hang far enough over the railing at the edge of the deck.

The entrance to my place is at the back of the carport, underneath my deck. Everything seems fine until I reach the door and realize it's unlocked.

I never leave my door unlocked.

I quietly back away and move over to the storage cabinets behind my car. They're raised off the ground, so if I want to, I can pull up the front end of a vehicle underneath them. There's plenty of room for my Audi A3 and my Yamaha without having to do that, though.

On the wall below the cabinets are what look like two fuse boxes. One of them actually has fuses inside, but they don't control anything. I'm not a big fan of the idea that anyone could walk up and cut my power.

As for the second box, if anyone tries to open it, they wouldn't be able to, because the cover is welded shut. What no one would notice is the spot along the back of the box, just large enough to slip a finger into. My left index finger to be exact, which I now insert. Inside, a biometrics reader registers my fingerprint, and releases a latch that allows me to tip the entire box downward as a single piece.

Cradled inside are a Glock 9mm pistol, three full magazines, and a sound suppressor. I shove two of the magazines into my pocket, snap the third into the gun, and, as I sneak back to the door, attach the suppressor to the barrel.

Standing off to the side, I twist the door handle and push it inward. When no one opens fire, I use my phone's camera and screen to peek around the corner. On the right is a doorway to the hall that leads to my two guest bedrooms and a bathroom—the only rooms on this level—while straight ahead are the stairs to the second floor. There's no one in view, nor do I hear anyone in the lower bedroom area.

I slip inside and head down the hallway to check the guest rooms. After I see they're empty, I mount the stairs.

I have no idea who might have broken in. My partners and I deal with a lot of bad people, so it could be someone we put out of business. How they could have tracked me down is beyond me. I'm not some newbie who thinks he's covered his tracks by taking a different route home every day. No one should ever be able to find me. No one should even know who I am.

I creep up the steps, careful to avoid the three treads that squeak. The stairs end at the back of my living room, a few feet from the kitchen entrance. I pause just below floor level and listen.

Is that...*music*?

It's low and tinny, but definitely rhythmic. The way something sounds when it bleeds from a pair of headphones or earbuds.

I crane my neck to see above the floor line. My eyes have barely cleared the hardwood when something soft strikes me in the middle of my forehead. I duck back down as it tumbles and lands at my feet.

I must be seeing things. I lean down and pick the thing up. Nope, not seeing things at all. It is indeed a dart from a Nerf gun.

"That was a head shot," Jar says from my living room. "You are dead. I win."

I march up the stairs, jaw clenched. She's kneeling on one of my living room chairs, the Nerf gun propped over the back. The music I heard is coming from her headphones, which are attached to a phone sitting on my dining table, no doubt placed there to distract me.

"I could have killed you," I say.

Another dart flies across the room, this time smacking me in the chest.

"I killed you first. Twice now."

I want to feel more annoyed, but I can't.

When I first met Jar, she would have never joked around like this. She was all business, all the time. Joking is not something that comes naturally to her, and I doubt anyone ever tried to help her learn how to do it, until she met our team. It's good to see her changing.

It's good just to see her.

"What are you doing here?" I asked.

"I thought if you were going to go to jail, it would be good to have someone close who could get you out."

"I told you last night I wasn't arrested."

"That did not mean they would not be coming for you later."

"No one's coming for me."

"You are correct. No one is."

She says this with such confidence that I cock my head. "What does that mean?"

"This morning, Detective Hughes uploaded his notes from your interview. He does not think you are involved."

Going from stalking an intruder in my house to learning I'm no longer a murder suspect in less than sixty seconds gives me mental whiplash. "Too bad you didn't find out before you left," I say. "It would have saved you the trip."

"I did find out before I left. But I had already purchased my ticket. *And* you keep wanting me to come down to visit so here I am."

I snort and shake my head. "How long are you staying?"

Her expression shifts to one of concern. "Oh, I have made a mistake. I should have checked with you first. You do not want me here." She climbs off the chair and heads toward her suitcase, which is tucked against my couch. "I can return to San Francisco right away. I am sure there is another flight."

"Whoa, slow down." I walk over as she extends the handle on her bag. "When did I say I didn't want you here? I'm only wondering if this is a quick trip, or if you'll be able to hang around for a while.

She looks at me, skeptical. "I am not sure what to believe."

"You were the one who got it in your head that I didn't want you here. Those words never came out of my mouth. Hear these, though. You are welcome here anytime and can stay for as long as you want."

"I do not want to be a burden."

"Reverse that. Can you think of any way that *I* would ever be a burden to you?"

She gives the question serious thought. "Perhaps a few ways, but none are likely."

"Well, I can't think of any about you."

She takes this in. Though she's getting better at personal relationships, she still struggles sometimes.

To make things perfectly clear, I say, "I'm glad you're here."

Finally, she says, "Okay. I will stay."

"Good." I smile and hold out my arms. "Come here. You haven't hugged me hello yet."

She hesitates, then tentatively puts her arms around me.

The touchy-feely subset of human interactions ranks high on her list of things she's awkward with. For a few seconds, her body is so stiff it feels like I'm holding an inanimate object, but she eventually relaxes.

"Thanks for coming," I say.

She whispers into my shoulder, "I had nothing better to do."

I laugh in surprise, and after a moment she joins in. This is the joke I say to her every time I go up to San Francisco to visit.

There's a reluctance when we both let go. I only mention this because Liz would if I didn't. I don't want to think about what it means. I'm not ready to go there yet. I'm not sure I'll ever be ready. But I *am* glad Jar is here.

I carry her suitcase downstairs and tell her she can choose whichever room she wants, then I go back up to shower, promising to take her out to lunch when I'm done.

After I clean up, I enter the living room and find her on the couch, engrossed in something on her laptop.

"Hungry?" I ask.

It's as if she doesn't know I'm here.

"Jar?"

"A moment," she says.

One of Jar's strongest points is her ability to focus. When she's like this, I know it's best to let her finish whatever it is she's doing.

I grab two bottles of water from the kitchen, set one next to her laptop, and begin sipping the other.

And sipping.

Annnnnnd sipping until there's nothing left.

She looks no more ready to leave now than she did when I first entered the room.

We may be here a while.

I pick up the book I've been reading, *Hollow Kingdom* by Kira Jane Buxton, and head out onto the deck.

It feels like it's warmed up to the low sixties, but there's no breeze, and sitting in direct sunlight makes it feel ten degrees hotter. I read for nearly an hour before I hear the door behind me slide open.

"Sorry," Jar says.

I lower the book and look back. It's often hard to read Jar's emotions. She wears what I think of as a resting-neutral-observer expression most of the time. She doesn't look that way now, though. The change might be insignificant to someone who doesn't know her well, but to me she looks distressed.

"What's wrong?"

"The girl you found. Saundra Moore is not her original name."

"Not original?"

"She changed it several years ago."

For a second, her composure starts to crack and it looks like she's going to cry. But the moment passes quickly, and her face tenses as she regains control.

"Are you all right?"

"I am fine."

I'm not so sure about that, but I don't want to press.

"Her real name is Naomi Bellows," Jar says. "Have you heard it before?"

I blink.

I have. I just can't remember when or where or why.

"Perhaps this will help," Jar says, as if reading my mind. "Foster, Oregon."

A newspaper headline flashes in my head.

THE GIRL THAT GOT AWAY

Those words, or ones like it, were found on websites and newspapers throughout the country, after a twelve-year-old girl who'd been held captive for over a year escaped her kidnappers. Details leaked out later, telling how she had been able to get away because one of her captors had passed out within reach of the cable that tethered her to the room. As he lay drunk and unconscious, she took his keys, unlocked her restraints, and ran.

That girl was Naomi Bellows.

As I recall, it took her a while to hike through the wilderness before she reached another house and law enforcement could be called in. By the time sheriff's deputies found where she'd been held, the man was gone. Either he'd woken and fled on his own, or the other kidnappers the girl said she'd seen had come and helped him get away.

A manhunt was undertaken, but her abductors were never found.

That's all I remember. Probably all I ever knew. I don't think I ever heard about the girl again.

"She and Saundra are the same person?" I say.

Jar starts to speak, but instead only nods. Her controlled demeanor cracks again, but doesn't break.

I don't know what to do. Do I ignore it? Do I ask her if she's okay again?

Yes, the Bellows kidnapping was a horrible event, but Jar would have been only around eleven or twelve back then, and more to the point, she would have been in Thailand. If the story was mentioned by Thai news at all, I have to believe it would have been only a few lines on the back page of a paper.

As I stand there, frozen in my indecision, she takes several deep breaths and then says, "Before I left San Francisco, I created several bots to find out as much information on Saundra Moore as possible. I was checking their progress while you were taking a shower. What first caught my attention was that the bots could find nothing about her prior to her freshman year of high school."

"In Denver," I say.

"Correct. Her school records said she had attended middle

and elementary schools in another part of town. But she did not."

"Maybe the records were lost."

"They were not lost. There *were* records at the schools about a Saundra Moore, but they were obviously faked."

I don't ask how Jar knows this, but I believe her without needing proof. "I admit, that *is* strange."

"So is the fact that her social security number was issued two weeks before she started high school."

Indeed, that is even stranger. Social security numbers are usually assigned at birth. It is possible to get a new one later, but you have to apply for it.

"Maybe she was hiding from something," I say. "But how does all this mean she's Naomi Bellows?"

"That is what I was trying to figure out when you came out of your bedroom. I mean, I did not know she was Naomi then. I was only digging around for who she really was. I found it in the database for the US Marshals' office."

"Witness protection." Of course. That would explain everything.

She nods. "I checked their records for girls in the right age range. I thought perhaps Saundra might be the daughter of someone who had to go into hiding."

"Not a bad theory."

"Thank you," she says, with little enthusiasm. "But I was wrong. The person I found who matched closest to her was not a dependent of someone else in the program, but rather the focus of the protection."

"Naomi Bellows."

Another nod. "Here, there's a picture."

She brings the image up on her screen and turns it so I can see. The girl pictured can't be much more than fourteen, but she's definitely the woman I found on my hike.

"Does LAPD know this yet?"

She shakes her head. "They may never know. She is no longer under active protection." Jar frowns, then adds, "I mean, *was* no longer."

"Her mother will tell them."

"Her mother died two years ago. Cancer."

"No other family members?"

Jar shakes her head. "There is no record of who her father is, and she had no brothers or sisters. According to the marshals' files, she and her mother successfully cut all ties to anyone from their previous life. Apparently, they both lived in fear that Naomi's kidnappers would return."

Is that what happened? Could her abductors have finally caught up to her and pushed her off the edge? It's as good a theory as any right now.

"We need to let the police know about this," I say. While I still see no need to get actively involved in the case, there's no reason we shouldn't give the cops a nudge. Anonymously, of course. "Who was the last marshal handling her case?"

Jar hesitates, as if she wants to say something, but then dives back into her computer. "Renee Faust."

"She still with the department?"

"Yes.

"What's her phone number?"

Before calling Marshal Faust, I fire up my number-spoofing/voice-altering app. From the menu, I select one of the female voice options, and move the age bar toward the older end.

As the line rings for a third time, I'm hoping all I'll need to do is leave a message. But then the call is picked up.

"Faust." The marshal sounds like I've caught her in the middle of something.

"There has been a murder in Los Angles you need to know about."

"Who is this?"

"The body was discovered Sunday morning in Griffith Park. Look it up."

"If you have a tip, I would—"

I hang up.

I've given her all she needs. After she checks the press reports and finds out the victim's name hasn't been released yet, she'll use her law enforcement connections to get the information. And when she realizes who really died, she'll let the LAPD know.

Our job here is done. That's the last we have to worry about Saundra Moore/Naomi Bellows.

CHAPTER FIVE

M eals with Jar are never flush with conversation. Though she is more social now than when we first met, she is most comfortable in silence.

But something is different about the quiet that envelops us at lunch.

I thought by setting the wheels in motion for the police to learn the dead girl's true identity, I would be removing whatever burden Jar seems to be holding on to. But instead of returning to her normal self, she seems to be spiraling further down a hole.

"Hey," I say between bites of my sandwich. "If there's something bothering you, you can tell me. You know that, right?"

"Nothing is bothering me," she says in a rush, not looking at me.

Jar's a horrible liar. "I'm glad to hear that. But if something ever does, I'm here for you. Just so you know."

She glances at me for the first time since we sat down. "I am fine. Thank you."

I let it drop, hoping eventually she'll open up to me.

After lunch, we catch a South Korean horror film at the

Nuart Theatre in Santa Monica. There's nothing like a good scare to lighten the mood, and by the time we walk out, Jar's almost normal Jar again.

To keep things going in the right direction, I take her to Button Mash in Echo Park, where we play on the retro video games and pinball machines for nearly two hours before we split one of their famous *banh mi* sandwiches. By the time we return to my townhouse, it's going on ten p.m.

Thinking we can watch something on Netflix, I turn on my TV and head into the kitchen to make some popcorn. By the time I return, Jar is sitting on the couch, her computer open, and her expression serious again.

Crap.

I drop down beside her and pick up the remote. "What are you in the mood for? There's a new sci-fi movie that just came out. Some big alien conspiracy thing, I think. It looks good."

From the way she doesn't even twitch at the sound of my voice, it appears she's in ignore-the-world-mode again.

I give in to the inevitable. "What are you looking at?"

It's as if a soundproof wall has dropped between us.

"Jar, what are you looking at?"

A few more seconds pass before she turns to me. "I was checking to see if the marshal made the connection."

"And?"

"She has, and she has let the police know."

"That's good. That's what we were hoping."

"Yes. I guess so."

I study her. "I'm not trying to pry, but I can see something about this is bothering you."

"I told you, I am fine. It is just..." She closes her eyes and takes a deep breath. "I think I will go to bed now. You do not mind, do you?"

I have never once, in the entire time I've known Jar, seen her go to sleep before one a.m. I keep the shock off my face, though, as I say, "Of course not."

She smiles weakly as we stand, and after a quick hug good night, she heads downstairs.

That sense of helplessness I had earlier returns. Maybe I should go down and make sure she's okay. Maybe, if I ask the right questions, I can get her to open up.

I take a step toward the stairs.

Don't, Liz says. *Not now. Let her be.*

I hesitate.

She needs time.

I let out a breath, turn away from the stairs, and whisper, "Okay."

———

"Can I join you?"

Hearing Jar's voice from the sliding door behind me nearly causes me to jump out of my seat.

I look back and smile. "You never have to ask that. Come. Sit."

She lowers herself onto my patio couch, leaving a gap between us.

"I like the fire," she says.

After she went to bed, I grabbed a few beers and came out onto my deck. It's still cold out, but I'm bundled up and have a fire going in my portable firepit so it's not that bad. Last I checked, it was already well after midnight.

"Nice, isn't it?" I say.

I like it out here at this time of night. The only sounds I usually hear are crashing waves and the occasional riff of muted music, floating down from the bars near the pier. If that isn't enough to lull someone into a state of relaxation, I don't know what is.

I hold out my bottle to her. "Want some?" I'm on my third but I've spaced them out so I'm barely feeling any buzz.

She grabs my bottle and takes a long pull.

At the risk of repeating myself too much, this is not typical Jar behavior. The only times I've seen her drink are a few sips here and there.

After she lowers the bottle, she says, "Thank you."

She tries to give it back to me but I say, "Keep it," and pick up an unopened bottle off the ground.

I pop off the top and we clink beers.

"*Chon kaew*," I say, using a Thai version of cheers.

This earns me a half smile.

Though she's wearing a stocking cap and a San Francisco 49ers hoodie, I can see she's cold.

"We can go inside," I suggest.

"No. I like it here."

We sit silently, looking at the stars and listening to the waves pound the unseen beach.

"I need you to promise me something," she says, her voice so soft that if this was any other time of day, I wouldn't be able to hear it.

I grin and say, "Depends on what it is."

"Never mind. Forget I said anything."

I am an idiot. I played that completely wrong.

"Jar, I'll promise you whatever you want. You know that."

She looks at me, then away, and says nothing.

Yep. I screwed it up all right, and I fear her desire to share whatever it was is gone.

But then—

"You cannot ask me any questions about what I will tell you. Not now. Not tomorrow. Not ever."

"Of course. Whatever you want."

"Promise me."

"I promise."

When we fall back into silence, it takes every ounce of my will to keep from saying something encouraging, afraid she might misinterpret it.

The fire pops as one of the pieces of wood drops into the coals, and still Jar says nothing.

Her shivering has not stopped. Should I put my arm around her? Should I leave her be?

To hell with it.

I stretch an arm over her shoulders. She flinches at my touch, but then relaxes and leans into me. I rub my hand up and down her arm, hoping it helps warm her, but I realize now it's not the cold making her shake.

After a breath so deep her shoulder pushes into me, she says, "I was like her."

I'm afraid to move. Jar does not talk about her past. Ever.

"Not exactly like her. I was not kidnapped. I was sold. By my uncle."

Oh, my God.

"He was what you would call my guardian. When I was four, my mother was killed when she was hit by a truck. My father I never knew. She never told me who he was. I do not think she ever told anyone. Naomi and I had that in common, too. After my mother was gone, I lived with my uncle and aunt and five cousins. They did not need or want another mouth to feed, but I had nowhere else to go."

She pauses, lost in some memory I wish she never had.

"They were poor. It was difficult for my uncle to find

enough work to keep his family fed. Having me there did not help. But work is not the only way someone in the countryside can get money. Some resort to selling their daughters...or nieces. They are told the girls will work in factories, but the truth is a large percentage of those sold end up in the sex trade. I mean the business for Thai men, where women and girls are held prisoner in brothels, sometimes tied to beds. The captives will work until they pay off the debt of their purchase, plus the cost of keeping them alive. It can take years to earn one's freedom."

She takes another sip of her beer.

"I was...seven when my uncle sold me to one of these men, earning him some cash and getting rid of me in a single transaction. Lucky for me, my new masters considered me too young to take on customers yet, so I cleaned the rooms after clients left.

"Because I did not talk much, they would usually leave me alone. Most of the time I was a piece of furniture to them, and they would discuss all sorts of things in front of me. When I was eight and a half..." She drifts off for a moment, lost in a past she should have never had to live through. She closes her eyes for a second before continuing. "When I was eight and a half, I overheard a conversation that...terrified me. I mean, everything there terrified me, every day, but this, this was worse. They did not use my name, but I knew they were talking about me. One of them said I was old enough to start *working the beds*. That's what they called it." She clenches her jaw. "After the others agreed, they talked about holding a...I guess you would call it an auction. The highest bidder would be my first customer."

Outwardly, I maintain my composure, but inside I'm boiling with anger. If I am ever within a thousand kilometers of these people, I will kill them. And just so I'm clear, that is not an idle threat.

Jar takes another sip and goes on. "Two weeks. That is how

long the auction would last. And then I would be presented to the winner. I should not have understood what this person would be taking from me. Not at my age. But my eighteen months of working around the other women had taught me exactly what the prize was, and there was no way I was going to let anyone have it. I had fourteen days to plan and execute my escape."

Can you even imagine what she must have been feeling then? I know whatever I'm thinking is only scratching the surface. She was *eight and a half* years old. She should have been at home in her village, playing with her friends. She should not have been fighting for her very survival.

"I knew every part of the building where they kept us," she says, her voice intensifying. "I knew the men's patterns, both the customers' and our guards'. I knew which guards liked to take naps when they were on duty, and which ones liked to hit the girls who did not move fast enough to their next appointments. I knew where the guards hid the pills they used to keep the problematic girls high, so that they would be more cooperative. And I knew which of the men carried keys to the only exit.

"I had never been in it, but I had seen glimpses of the bar on the other side of the locked door, where customers would wait their turns. I had never seen what was beyond that, because the day I had been brought in I had been blindfolded. But I did remember the flight of stairs we walked up—twenty-two steps—and the smell of exhaust coming through open windows, and the echo of my steps as I was led down a long, narrow hallway. So I knew the building was large."

Jar raises the beer and takes in just enough to wet her mouth.

I want to say something. I want to comfort her with words of support. But I worry she would stop talking if I did.

"No one told me how the auction was going, but every time

my captors looked at me, they smiled. It made me feel..." She shivers. "They never smiled like that before, so I knew it was going well. And as the final day drew near, I could feel their anticipation building."

Her breaths have started coming faster, each leaving her mouth with a growing sense of anger.

"Their plan was to throw a party on the night of my... promotion," she says, spitting out the last word. "Of course, they did not inform us what the party was for. They just told the girls and me that they expected us to be on our best behavior. I even acted surprised and excited when I was given special clothes to wear. But the party was not going to happen. I would not let it."

She seems to realize she has become too worked up, as she takes a few deep, calming breaths. It doesn't eliminate her tension completely, but it does help.

"I am sorry," she says.

I shake my head, and then, against my better judgment, say, "Don't be."

I think she tries to smile, but it's hard to tell.

After another moment or two, she starts again. "The quietest time was always in the morning, from sunup until around ten a.m. This was when the girls could sleep uninterrupted. But for me, it was when I was at my busiest, making sure everything was clean and ready for the next round of customers, who usually started showing up before lunch. Because I was the only one active at this time, the number of men guarding us would be reduced to two or three at most.

"I waited until the morning on the day before the party to make my move. The daytime guards relieved those who had been there all night, not long before the last customer left. There were three that morning, including one of the men who had been present when my uncle sold me."

Her eyes shut for a second, at what I'm guessing is the thought of what her uncle's actions had cost her.

"I went about my business and started cleaning the customer rooms, while the guards made themselves comfortable in the TV room near where the girls slept. Like I knew would happen, it was not long before one of them yelled for me to bring them some beers.

"On the way to the kitchen, I stopped in one of the customer bedrooms, where I slipped my fingers into an open seam on the mattress that only I knew about, and removed a folded piece of paper I had placed there days before.

"In the kitchen, I opened three bottles of beer, unfolded one end of the paper, and poured equal parts of the powder contained inside into the drinks. The powder was from pills I had stolen and crushed, the ones that made the girls docile. They never gave anyone more than two pills, but I wanted to make sure they worked. I don't remember exactly how many pills I used to make the powder. Twenty, maybe. Twenty-five? Whatever it was, I remember still worrying it wouldn't be enough."

If two pills were enough to make someone docile, six and a half to eight pills each would do a hell of a lot more than that.

"Most of the substance dissolved right away," she said, "but I remember some sticking near the lip of one of the bottles and I had to wipe it clean. I was so scared I was taking too much time, but the guards barely acknowledged me when I finally walked into the television room and handed them their drinks.

"After I left the room, all I could do then was wait, so I started cleaning again, just in case my concoction did not work. I gave it thirty minutes, and when I returned, the guards were all leaning back on the couches, their eyes closed.

"I checked the nearest man. He had a pulse but it was so slight I almost did not feel it. The other two were the same. I found the keys on the man who had helped bring me there, and I started to walk out of the room but stopped in the doorway. I knew I should leave, but all I could think about was how these men had been part of the group that had kept me there, about what I had seen them do to the other girls, about what they were joyfully planning to let happen to me."

She stares silently across the deck, and I know she is back in that room, reliving that moment. In a half whispered voice, she says, "I could not stop the men who weren't in the building from doing any of those things to others, but I could stop these three. So I grabbed a pillow from the nearest bedroom and used it to smother them, one by one."

Holy crap.

I mean, *holy crap*.

I want to think I would have done the same thing, but I'm not sure I could have. Not at eight and a half years old.

For the next several seconds, I can't hear her breathe. If I didn't feel her under my arm, I would almost think I was alone.

She takes another drink, and then says, "I went straight to the exit, taking nothing with me. I did not want anything that would remind me of that place. If I could have left the clothes I was wearing, I would have.

"I was sure there would be a guard stationed in the waiting area beyond the door, but the room was empty. I did see a camera, though, and it reminded me of the other cameras hidden in the back rooms. Without proof of what had happened, no one would ever think I was involved. I was a small kid who did not know anything, and they would assume I had either been kidnapped by whoever had raided the place or had escaped during the chaos. But if my actions had been recorded, the others would search for me until they found me. I could not leave until I was sure I had removed any recordings of what I had done. I did not know much about electronics at that time, but I am very smart, as you know."

I should point out what she just said is not a brag. She's merely stating a fact. She *is* smart. Like genius-level smart.

"My thought was if I followed the wires, I could find where the recordings went," she says. "I was lucky. Back then, wireless cameras were not as popular as they are today, so I was able to trace the feeds to a cabinet behind the bar. Inside were three plastic boxes where the cables were attached, so I assumed they were the storage devices."

"Computer towers." The words slip out of my mouth before I even realize it.

Instead of penalizing me, she nods. "I spent several minutes looking for where tapes would be inserted. There were no tapes, of course. Everything was stored on hard drives, but I had no concept of what one of those was. I just knew these boxes somehow contained the video that would reveal what I had done. I disconnected the wires, dragged the boxes onto the floor, and shoved them onto their sides, hoping that would break them. When it didn't, I looked around for something to help me and found a club hanging from a hook below the bar. I smashed the plastic into pieces and then broke everything inside that I could. I am positive I destroyed the hard drives, but that was purely by accident.

"I think it was right after I finished when I heard footsteps coming from the back of the building. I hid behind the bar. I was sure that the guards were somehow still alive and were now coming after me. But it was two of the girls." She squints, concentrating. "Pon and...Da, I think. No, not Da. Sai. They stopped in the doorway between the bar and the back area and scanned the room. I can still see their eyes. They were full of surprise and fear. Pon started to step into the lounge but Sai grabbed her arm and whispered something to her I could not hear. She probably believed they would get in trouble and was trying to stop her friend. But Pon shook free and hurried through the lounge and out the exit. She never looked back. I thought Sai would return to the rooms, but maybe seeing that nothing had happened to Pon gave her the confidence she needed because after a moment, she left, too."

She frowns. "I knew I should have gone back to wake the other girls so they could also leave, but...but I was scared and needed to get out of there. So I did."

I have no doubt it's a decision that has weighed on her. But no one could fault her for leaving when she did.

"I'm glad you got away," I say.

"Just because I escaped the brothel does not mean I got away."

"What do you—" I stop myself. No questions. Dammit.

She takes a deep breath. "I knew I would not truly be safe and free until the remaining men who had held me were dealt with. For the first few months, though, my only focus was finding places to sleep and food to eat. It turned out the building we were held in was on the outskirts of Bangkok. I worked my way deeper into the city and spent the next few months hiding in parks and alleys, and stealing food wherever I could. When I found a hidden basement room in an abandoned building, I was finally able to think about more than just survival.

"I knew I was intelligent, but I also knew my lack of education made me ignorant of so many things. My best chance at defeating my kidnappers would only come if I did something about that." A slight smile graces her lips. "I started by stealing textbooks from elementary schools. The lessons were ridiculously easy, and within a few weeks I had already moved on to the high school courses. This took longer, only because there was a larger variety of things to learn. I had no idea there was so much. I wanted to know it all, so I studied night and day, reading and working through problems, and hunting down answers to things that didn't make sense. The only breaks I would take would be to hunt for food and more books.

"Four months later, I started my college education. I thought the high school classes were diverse, but choices in college were at a whole other level. There were so many different specializations that I realized if I didn't prioritize, I would be in my basement for years. I decided to focus on electronics in general and computers specifically. These seemed to be very important parts of society, and if I could master them, I could master whatever I needed to help me defeat the men who ran the brothel.

"An electrician's training textbook taught me how to wire power into my room. I stole several computers and set them up on a table I made from bricks and wood planks. Another book showed me how to disconnect the computers' speakers so they could not be heard by anyone nearby. I used headphones when there was something I needed to listen to. It turned out there was a lot. I realized there was only so much I could learn about computers without knowing English so I taught myself that, mostly by watching YouTube."

Jar would have been what? Nine at this point? I'm feeling incredibly inadequate.

"On the anniversary of my escape, I decided I was ready to deal with those I had left alive. I had this fantasy of smashing in everyone's heads with the club I had taken from their bar, but I knew I could not do it for real. Maybe two or three of them, but not all of them. And I wanted *all* of them. I needed someone else to do it for me.

"I must have spent an entire week trying to come up with different ideas of how to make it happen. Right from the start, I knew I could not go to the police. I had seen officers in the brothel using the girls, so I knew my captors had at least some police protection. I decided the only way to guarantee success was to expose my captors to the public by involving foreign media. I knew more about computers now so I was confident I could steal footage from inside the brothel, and then leak it to international news outlets and relief organizations. I believed pressure from them would make it impossible for Thai authorities to do nothing. The best part was, I could achieve it all without leaving my room."

"It was a sound plan," I say.

"Thank you."

There's something in her voice that tells me things didn't go exactly the way she wanted them to, and I carefully phrase my next words as a statement. "It didn't work."

"Until I knew what I was going to do, I avoided everything about the brothel. Not only did I stay away from that part of town, I also did not conduct any internet searches that might bring up information about the men and their business. I thought it unlikely they could track me down because of a search, but I did not want to risk it. Now that I was ready to make my move, it was time to find out everything I could.

"I started by finding the address of the building, and then used that to search online. I hoped this might tell me who owned the building, at the very least. What I did not expect was that the first three pages would be full of articles about the brothel itself, detailing how it had been raided by a rival gang.

"At first, I thought they were writing about what *I* had done, but as I read further I realized this had happened two months after my escape. Eight members of the group that ran the brothel had been found dead inside, and the women who had worked there were gone. There was no mention of who the rival gang had been, only speculation that the raid had been the result of what you would call a turf war. Eight was the exact number of my captors who I had not killed. If the stories were correct, my job had been done for me."

She lifts the bottle to her lips and drinks the last of her beer.

"Another?" I ask. It's a question, but I'm hoping not one she'll see as a violation.

She shakes her head.

The silence that follows stretches for nearly half a minute before I say, "You were truly free then," thinking her story has come to an end.

A humorless snort. "I was, but I did not realize it then. I hunted for more articles about the raid and read everything I could, but everything I found told the same story. I tried to hack into the Bangkok police computer system to see what they knew, but I was not yet skilled enough to get past their firewall.

"I had no choice but to return to the area near the brothel to see if anyone there knew the truth. I went pretending to be the sister of a missing girl who had been held there. Not everyone was willing to talk to a kid about what had happened, but I found a few who did, and what they told me was essentially the same things that were in the newspaper stories, except for two people, who also mentioned that they had heard the rival gang was run by a woman named Christine." Jar glances at me. "You know her."

I do.

Christine is an American who lives in Bangkok and operates a business that straddles the line between legitimate and not so much. She's also the person Jar had been working for when my partners and I enlisted Christine's help on a personal matter a year ago. So, she's who we have to thank for Jar joining our team.

"You went to see her," I say.

"I knocked on her door and *demanded* to see her. I think her people let me in because they were amused. When I told Christine that I wanted to know exactly what had happened at the brothel, she asked me why, and I said, 'Because I am the one who killed three of them and escaped two months before you destroyed the place.'

"I remember several men in the room laughing. They did not believe me. But Christine did not laugh. She asked me to describe how I did it. But I was not going to do that until she responded to my question first. So she did, and that was when I learned for sure that everyone I had been hiding from was dead. I then asked her, 'What about the girls? Did you kill them, too?' and she said, 'Of course, not.' So I said, 'You put them to work somewhere else.' She smiled at me. 'No. I let them go.'

"I did not believe her. She smiled again when I told her that, and said that she would not believe her, either, but it was the truth. She told one of the men to bring me a list of all the girls and where they could be found. When he went off to get this, she said to me, 'Now it is your turn.'

"There was no reason to keep what I had done from her so I told her everything. I guess I impressed her, because she offered me a place to stay as soon as I finished my story. I was not in the right frame of mind to take her up on that then, so I left with the list of names. It took me a month to confirm that Christine had let all the girls go without any strings."

I can see a young Jar riding the buses through the country on money she probably made from selling stuff she stole, and stopping at villages to verify her former co-captives were indeed free.

"When I came back, I returned to Christine's and apologized for not believing her. She offered me a room again. This time I did not say no."

Jar falls silent.

Am I shocked by what she's told me? You bet I am.

And yes, I have questions. Tons and tons of them. Like did

Jar ever see her uncle and aunt again? Does she know what happened to the two girls who left when she did? And is she ever haunted by the men she killed? But I keep my promise and accept that I may never know the answers.

I'm still reeling from her story when I notice her breathing has become deep and even. Sharing her secret has exhausted her. Other than Christine and whoever else had been there when Jar told her everything, I have little doubt I'm the only person she has ever confided in. How she's kept this all wrapped up inside her without going crazy, I don't know. She is a far stronger human being than anyone I have ever met. Or ever will, for that matter.

I sip my beer as she sleeps against my shoulder, and watch a satellite cross the sky between the stars. Jar is short and slight, and even as her body moves with each breath, it's as if she's barely even touching me. This only makes me want to pull in her tighter, to protect her from the world. But if I didn't already know it, after what she's told me, it's clear she doesn't need my protection. She's doing very well on her own, thank you very much. The best thing I can do is be here for her. Support her when she requests it.

Be her friend.

I consider letting her sleep all night like this, but the fire is dying and soon we're both going to freeze.

"Hey," I whisper and give her a nudge.

She moans but doesn't wake up.

Instead of trying again, I put my arms under her and rise to my feet, holding her against my chest.

She stirs, her eyes fluttering halfway open, and mutters something in Thai.

"Shhh," I say, and her eyes close again.

I move her inside, but pause in the middle of my living room. I'm fairly confident I can carry her downstairs without dropping her, but there's no reason to tempt fate. I take her into my bedroom, set her down, and pull the covers over her.

"Nate?" she says as I head for the door.

I look back and see she has pushed herself up on an elbow.

"Go back to sleep," I say.

"This is your room. I am not taking your bed."

"It's fine. I have plenty of beds, and I'm not tired yet."

She, on the other hand, can barely keep her eyes open. "Are...are you sure?"

"I'm sure."

I turn to leave.

"Wait a minute."

I look back again.

"There is something I need you to understand first."

I return to the bed. "If it's about what you told me before, you don't need to say anything more."

"Please." She touches the mattress beside her, so I sit. Though she gives me a tired smile, her eyes are alert now. "After I moved in with Christine, I searched for stories about other girls taken from their homes, especially one about girls who were able to get away. I wanted to know how the experience affected them, and if they felt the same anger I felt.

"Naomi Bellows' kidnapping happened a couple years after I escaped. I read everything I could about her and her ordeal, and felt so happy after she freed herself. When I learned the body you found was her, I..." Her gaze drops to the mattress, and she takes a couple of deep breaths before looking at me again. "It is like I have lost a part of myself. But more than that. I am sorry."

"I told you, there's nothing to be sorry about. Your reaction was exactly what it should have been."

I can tell she doesn't necessarily agree with me, but she

doesn't argue. What she does say is, "I need to know who did that to her. I need to make sure they are found."

"The police are on it. And because of you, they know about her past. They'll find the killer."

What I hear next is a kind of Greek chorus. Two voices—Jar's spoken, and Liz's in my head—both saying the same thing, at the same time. "What if they fail?"

There's only one answer I can give. "Then we will find who did it."

CHAPTER SIX

In the morning, I follow Jar's lead and make no mention of last night's conversation. Instead, we spend most of the day playing *Exiles*, then head to the area near Redondo Beach Pier, where we grab dinner and take a walk down the boardwalk.

Jar seems to be back to her old straight-to-the-point, no-BS self. But I'm sure she won't be completely normal again until Naomi's killer is caught. Before I go to sleep, I check the local news on my laptop, and see that Naomi's true identity has been released by the police. There's an entire story recapping her kidnapping from before. As far as new developments in the investigation of her murder, however, there doesn't appear to be any.

(On a side note, I also find an article about Miles Deveaux being identified by several of his victims as the man who assaulted them. The district attorney won't say anything, but I get the impression his office believes it will be an open-and-shut case. At least there's some good news, right?)

The next day is basically a repeat of the last—videogames and walks and food and no breakthroughs in the murder investigation. Naomi's identity is still making headlines—mostly local, with a few national mentions—but it's fighting with stories about the presidential primaries, an upcoming debate, and the flare-up of a virus in China, so I have a feeling it won't hold its front-page status for long.

Early Thursday morning, Jar has to return to San Francisco for a doctor's appointment.

We've seldom been able to spend so much downtime together. Having her here these past few days has been great.

Who am I kidding?

It's been more than great, and I'm sad she's leaving. I almost suggest going with her, but as much as I'm sure she's also enjoyed our visit, she needs her alone time. It's part of who she is. And the last thing I want is for her to get sick of being around me.

After dropping her off at LAX, I run a few errands, then spend the rest of the day on my deck, reading about a crow and his bloodhound buddy navigating the apocalypse.

Today the sky is big and blue and free of clouds. It's warm, too, mid-seventies. What we really need is some rain, though. That shower the night Naomi died was only the second recordable rain we've had this month, and we're in the heart of what's supposed to be our wet season. If it stays this dry through March, the fall fires will start a lot earlier and burn a lot more.

When Jar calls, the sun is hanging just above the horizon and I've been contemplating what to do about dinner.

"How'd the appointment go?" I ask.

There's a brief pause, then a dismissive, "Fine," followed immediately by, "I take it you have not seen the news."

"Not since this morning. Should I have?"

"Yes."

She hangs up.

She's not being rude or angry at me for not being up to date.

She was merely finished with what she had to say, so from her point of view, there was no need to continue the conversation.

I head inside and turn on the living room TV. The first local channel I try has a report about a string of robberies in Whittier. The second shows footage from an accident on the 710 freeway, in which a big rig has spilled a load of hand sanitizer, killing whatever bacteria might have been living in the asphalt. And a third station has gone to commercial.

I should have grabbed my laptop from the start. I do so now and bring up the website for KTLA. Right at the top is the headline:

Griffith Park Murder Suspect Dead

Liz is instantly at my side.

I click on a video, and the story begins with a male reporter standing at the side of a road, near what looks like a freeway overpass. Not too far behind him, on a sidewalk in the shaded area under the bridge, are several makeshift tents of a robust homeless encampment. Parked on the street beside them are over a dozen police cars, emergency lights flashing, sirens off.

"At just after two p.m. this afternoon, LAPD detectives came to this downtown L.A. underpass, looking for a person of interest in the Griffith Park murder of Naomi Bellows. But what they found instead was another body."

The image cuts to footage shot around the encampment—police taping off the area; homeless men and women sitting on the curb in a line, watched over by several cops; and other officers moving into and around the tents.

Over this the reporter says basically the same thing again, with different words. Next comes a shot of an officer with the aura of being in charge. He stands in front of several reporters, their microphones pointed at him.

"At approximately 2:10 p.m. this afternoon, detectives from the Robbery-Homicide Division attempted to contact a man named Carl Harrison. When they looked inside the tent that they were informed he would be in, they found the body of a man approximately fifty-five years old. Cause of death has not yet been determined, but at this point, there's no reason to suspect foul play."

The shot cuts back to the reporter standing near the bridge. "Earlier today an LAPD spokesman identified Carl Harrison as a person of interest in their investigation into Naomi Bellows's murder. While the police have yet to confirm anything, a source has told us that the body found in the tent is Harrison's. At the same briefing, the spokesman said that they now believe Naomi had been in Griffith Park to attend a special showing at the planetarium, but that she never made it inside. This is Raul Staggs reporting from Downtown Los Angeles. Back to you in the studio."

The video stops.

I lean back on the couch, wondering if Harrison was one of the people who'd kidnapped Naomi in Oregon. But whether he was or not, if the police have solid evidence linking him to her murder, then it seems the case is closed.

I sense Liz's skepticism, and then she disappears.

I call Jar.

"They found her killer," I say.

"They found a body."

She, like Liz, is apparently not yet sold on this Harrison guy's guilt. I swear it's like they've formed an alliance.

"I'll rephrase," I say. "The body of the man they think killed her."

"They did not say that. Only that he was a person of interest."

"That's usually what person of interest means."

"Not necessarily."

I roll my eyes. "I assume you've checked the police files."

"Yes."

"And?"

"They received a call last night, an unknown tip."

"Anonymous."

"Right, an anonymous tip. Thank you. The caller said he overheard a homeless man near Union Station claim he pushed a girl off a mountain in Griffith Park."

"So, the informant was a man?"

"An unnecessary question. That is why I used 'he.'"

Jar, serving up logic for twenty-one years.

"Did he give the police the guy's name?"

"He did not. But he did tell them what the man looked like. A couple of officers went to the area around the station and asked if anyone had seen the man. It turned out that someone matching the description had left two bags at a temporary luggage storage place nearby. When the police showed up, one of the employees found the bags in their storage room, and in the process, felt the shape of a gun inside one of them. The police used that to get a search warrant."

"The bags belonged to Carl Harrison."

"Yes."

"But Naomi wasn't shot, so...?"

"In the bag, the police found two dozen pictures of her, and notes that indicated he had been stalking her for some time."

"That makes more sense. So they tracked him to the underpass?"

"After they released his name and picture to the public, someone called in a tip and said he had seen him at the encampment and told them which tent he had been inside."

"Another anonymous tip?"

"It was."

It all sounds pretty straightforward, but I have to admit, also a little too convenient. "You said two bags, right?"

"Yes."

"Were there pictures and notes in both?"

"No. According to the police file, the items concerning Naomi were all in the satchel."

"What was the other bag?"

"A suitcase."

"And what was inside it?"

"Only clothes."

My natural skepticism has yet to fade. "Are they doing a handwriting analysis on the notes?"

"They have nothing they can compare it to yet."

"Is there mention of how they think he died?" I ask.

"There was a needle in his arm, so the current assumption is that he overdosed."

I *really* want this guy to be the killer. I want the closure it would bring for Naomi and for Jar. But the details aren't making it easy. "Let me see if I've got this right. One, the police discovered their only suspect from an anonymous tip. I'm not saying that's impossible, but things like that happen on TV a lot more than real life."

"Correct."

"Two, cops then find incriminating evidence at a luggage storage facility. Evidence that any sane criminal would have destroyed by now."

"Yes, and I agree. It does not make much sense."

"Three, the evidence was found exclusively in one bag. There was nothing in the other."

Jar makes no comment about this. It is admittedly my weakest point, as it is not that unusual to separate things by type into different bags, but it does leave room for doubt.

"And four, they receive another tip that points them to the

exact tent where they later find Carl Harrison already conveniently dead from an overdose."

"Correct."

"Doesn't sound suspicious at all," I say.

"Please tell me you are joking."

"I am."

"Good," she says, sounding relieved. "Because it sounds very suspicious to me, too."

"It also doesn't mean they haven't found their man," I say. "Or at least one of them. Could be the tipster was Harrison's partner, and thought his best way not to get caught was to set up his colleague."

"I have thought of this also. We need to find the man who called."

"Hold on. *We* don't need to do anything. This is still an active police investigation, and the LAPD isn't some rinky-dink, two-man outpost. They have resources, and I'm sure they're already trying to find the caller. Just because everything isn't adding up yet doesn't mean we should jump in. They already figured out why she was at the park, and have a witness who says this Harrison guy claims to have been there, too."

"An anonymous witness."

"You're right, but that doesn't change the fact that they're making progress. We need to let the cops do their job."

"I disagree. I think we do need to be involved."

I understand Naomi's death is personal for Jar, and that the idea of letting it go doesn't sit well with her. But I really don't think there is anything for us to do. Not at this point, anyway. My side gig of helping the helpless does not apply. Naomi *is* being helped, by one of the largest police departments in the country. And I have no doubt the detectives handling the investigation are good cops. Us meddling in the case could muck things up.

But I can also sense Jar's pain, and her desire to make sure Naomi is avenged. So, despite what I've already said to her, I can't tell her to drop it and move on.

"How about this," I say. "We keep an eye on things, see where the investigation goes. If it looks like they have things wrong, we can talk about doing something then. Fair enough?"

She says nothing.

"Jar?"

"All right. I will send you updates on their progress whenever something changes."

I want to say one update every other day is enough, but I know that won't go down well. "Sounds good. Hey, why don't you come back down, and you can give me the reports in person?"

"I will think about it. But I am not happy with you right now." She hangs up.

At least with Jar, you always know where you stand.

CHAPTER SEVEN

J ar stays mad at me for exactly twenty-four hours before flying back to L.A. We spend the next two weeks playing video games, hiking, going to movies, and eating way too much of everything before we both receive calls from my work partners.

We have a new job. This one in Cancun, Mexico.

By the time we fly south, I have forgotten all about Naomi Bellows.

The Cancun job takes eleven days and involves three body removals, two late night disposals in the dark waters off the coast, and a near run-in with the Mexican coast guard. There's also a lot of downtime that we fill with seafood and tacos and beers and margaritas and laughter. I really do work with a pretty cool group of people. And I'm glad the riff I had with my main partner (and former mentor) has healed over for the most part.

He's Liz's brother, and her death hit both of us hard. In my case, harder than anything I've ever dealt with before. I suspect the same goes for him, though we haven't explicitly talked about that. Our falling out stemmed from the fact we had different ideas about how to deal with those responsible for killing her. I've said it before, and I'm sure I'll keep saying it until I die, his was the more rational, appropriate way to handle things. But I was in the darkest of dark places at the time, and wanted nothing more than to rip Liz's murderers apart limb by limb.

My partner's plan prevailed, which drove a giant wedge between us for a while. I know now his was the right course to take, but that doesn't mean I still don't lie in bed some nights, fantasizing about sneaking into the secret prison where Liz's killer is being held and choking the life out of her.

Perhaps I haven't completely left the darkness behind yet. I'll never act on those black thoughts, though. Liz won't let me do that. She's much more of the forgive-and-move-on kind of ghost, and a better person than me, even in death.

Liz.

Sometimes I wish she'd leave me alone and let me live my life.

Sometimes I fear that's exactly what's going to happen.

Two days after my return from Cancun, someone knocks on my door.

This is not something that happens often, and when it does it's usually someone wanting to preach to me or ask me for money. Or both.

When I open the door, I find Jar standing there, with her backpack over her shoulders and her suitcase in her hand.

"Hi," I say, not masking my confusion. After the job, she returned to San Francisco for one last appointment and is due to leave from there for Thailand tomorrow.

"May I come in?"

"Of course."

I take her suitcase and she follows me upstairs.

"Thirsty?" I ask.

"Not right now."

I go into the kitchen anyway and grab a bottle of water for myself and another for her, just in case. Back in the living room, I say, "Aren't you about to head home?"

"I changed my flight to one out of LAX."

"When are you leaving?"

She looks at her watch. "In two hours and forty-three minutes."

Now I'm really confused. "Don't you think you should go back to the airport?"

"As soon as you are packed."

"As soon as *I'm* packed?"

She taps her phone a few times, then says, "I have sent you your boarding pass. Now hurry, like you said, we need to leave."

"Boarding pass? I can't just go to Thailand on a whim."

"It is not a whim. And I never said we are going to Thailand."

"Excuse me?"

"We are going to Arizona."

"And why are we going to Arizona?"

The look she gives me makes me think I should already know. "To find Naomi Bellows's killer."

I have to admit, the murdered girl has not been on my mind for a while. The updates Jar had been giving me, up until we left on the Cancun job, amounted to not much more than the cops being convinced Harrison was their man. Once we were in Mexico, the updates stopped, which I took to mean Jar had let it go. Apparently, I was wrong.

"Last I heard, the police believe Harrison acted alone," I say. "And isn't he from San Diego?" If I recall correctly, it was the picture from Harrison's California ID that police released to the public when the man had been a person of interest. They hadn't said anything about where he was from, but Jar found that information and shared it.

"Do you not remember? I told you they went to his address and it was an abandoned building no one lived in."

That's right. She told me that just prior to leaving for Mexico. I remember something else, something that made me dismiss the address at the time as unimportant. "Didn't you also say that the police thought he used the address for convenience?"

"The police were wrong. About that, and many other things."

"What makes you think that?"

"We are wasting time. Our driver will be here in three minutes. Get your things. I will tell you at the airport." When I don't move right away, she says, "I thought you trusted me."

"I do."

Then why aren't you getting your bag? Liz whispers.

"Then why are you not getting your bag?" Jar asks.

I swear, if they do that one more time, I'm taking a long sabbatical on a deserted island.

I turn toward my bedroom.

"It will be cold," Jar calls after me. "Pack accordingly."

Our Southwest Airlines flight from LAX deposits us in Phoenix at a little after one p.m.

Jar has arranged, from one of our day-job contacts, for a nondescript Honda Accord to be waiting for us. While the Accord's exterior is unlikely to garner a second look, it is not your standard, off-the-lot import. Under the hood, the normal four-cylinder engine has been replaced by an aftermarket, supercharged V6. And beneath the carpet in the trunk are half a dozen hidden compartments, each containing weapons and other not-exactly-legal devices.

As Jar makes sure everything she ordered is there, I give her a side-eye glance. If she notices, she doesn't acknowledge it. I'm not sure what she thinks we might be heading into, but from the inventory, I'd say a small-scale civil war wouldn't be out of the question.

I'm still in the dark as to why she thought we should come here. We couldn't discuss it in the car because of the driver, and at the airport, there were people everywhere. Even when we did find a spot that felt private enough, she wouldn't talk.

After Jar finishes her inspection, we put our bags in the trunk and she hands me the keys. "Interstate 10 east. I will tell you when to exit." She heads to the front passenger door.

I stare after her, an eyebrow raised, and whisper, "Oookay."

When I climb in, she's already belted up and sitting pensively, staring out the window. I start the engine but don't put the car into gear.

She looks over. "What's wrong?"

"What's wrong is I still don't know why we're here."

She frowns. "Naomi's time of death was between twelve thirty a.m. and two a.m. Carl Harrison could not have been in Griffith Park at that time."

"How do you know that?"

Jar's backpack is sitting between her legs in the footwell. She unzips one of the compartments and removes her computer. After a few moments, she shows me an image of a train platform.

"This is the Amtrak station in Tucson, Arizona, at 7:36 p.m., five hours before the window for Naomi's murder opened." She hits Play, and we watch as passengers board the train. About thirty seconds in, she pauses the footage. Centered in the screen is a husky man, around five-foot ten and middle-aged. "Carl Harrison."

I stare at the screen. The person in the video looks like the pictures of the man I've seen on the news, but the image is not particularly high res so it could be any number of people. Plus, the man in the video doesn't strike me as someone who's homeless. Then again, homeless people don't all look the same. "I'm assuming you have a better shot than this."

She clicks on another file, and a photo pops up of the man sitting in the train's restaurant car. The resolution is much better.

"That certainly looks like him," I say. "Where was the train headed?"

"Los Angeles."

"That would put him in the right city. And close to downtown, which isn't that far from Griffith Park."

"Yes, but the train did not arrive until 4:27 a.m. Naomi was dead at least two and a half hours by then."

I look at the photo again. He definitely looks like the guy the police were hunting. "How sure are you that it's Harrison?"

"Enough that I thought we should come here to prove it one way or the other."

"We could have just passed this on to the police."

"They believe the investigation is complete. Do you really think they would take the time to check this out?"

Actually, I do, but the determined expression on her face stops me from saying this. And it hits me, probably later than it should have, that this trip isn't about whether the police would get it right or not. It's about Jar doing something to solve Naomi's murder.

The two women may have never met, but Naomi is important to Jar. Sisters of separate yet shared traumas. Jar needs to do this.

"One more thing," she says. "Take another look at this." She brings up the picture of the train platform and points at the bag in his hand. "This matches the photograph in the police files of the suitcase they found at the luggage storage facility."

That definitely helps bolster her claim that the man is Harrison.

"What else do you notice?" she asks.

I look at the photo again, and given what we've just discussed, I see what she's talking about right away. "Where's the satchel with the photos of Naomi?"

"Where, indeed?"

The man is carrying only the suitcase.

Take her where she wants to go, Liz whispers in my ear.

"Do you see now why we need to go check?" Jar asks.

Take her.

I shift the car into Drive. "To Tucson, then."

"To Tucson," Jar replies.

To Tucson, Liz echoes.

Tucson lies in a surprisingly lush desert valley, about an hour and a half south of Phoenix. In the summer, when daytime temperatures barely dip below a hundred degrees, the area is regularly battered by afternoon monsoons. The storms can get so bad that parts of the city flood in a matter of minutes.

Winters are a different animal. They're drier, with temperatures ranging from cool to downright cold.

Lucky for us, an arctic front has just passed through, and daytime highs are hovering around the forty-degree mark. I don't hate the cold as much as some people do, but I prefer mine to come with snow and slopes and hot tubs and a beverage or two. A cold desert feels like an oxymoron.

At a truck stop outside of town, I change into a white collared shirt and a pair of slacks. I didn't bring a tie, but it's not like this is New York so the business casual look should be fine.

"You are sure you know what to say?" Jar asks as we drive toward the Amtrak terminal.

"I *have* done things like this once or twice before."

"Right. I am sorry. It is just..."

I give her my best roguish sneer and say, "I've got this, Chewie."

"Han Solo you are not," she says, not in a Yoda voice but it's implied.

We arrive ten minutes later, and I park in the closest open spot to the terminal. Jar hands me the final piece of my wardrobe after I climb out of the car. It's an FBI windbreaker, the kind with the big yellow letters on the back. I didn't bring it. It's one of the items Jar had included with the car. What I did bring is an FBI ID in the name of another alias, John Springett. It's one of several official-looking IDs I own. Among my collection are badges for the ATF, the NTSB, and a few other alphabet agencies. My FBI one lives in my go bag. In my life, I never know what situation I might run into where it might come in handy.

The train station is a block-long, two-story, Spanish-style structure fronting the tracks. I stride inside and approach the ticketing window. There's a line of four people, but my jacket gives me a fast pass to the front, where I say to the customer being served, "Pardon me for a moment, ma'am," and then lean over and ask the clerk on the other side, "Where can I find the station manager?" I flash him my badge in case he hasn't noticed my jacket.

Yeah, it's kind of an asshole move. But it would be more suspicious for an FBI agent to wait in line until his turn comes.

After the man points me in the correct direction, I apologize to the customer I interrupted and to the others waiting in line. There's being an asshole and then there's being an *asshole*, if you know what I mean.

I take a hallway to an office at the end. From behind the partially closed door, I hear a man talking on the phone. Things like "I'm not sure that's a good idea," and "No, you can't do that," and "Fine, but promise me you'll get your math done first" slip through the gap. Sounds like a personal call.

I tap on the jamb and push the door open enough to stick my head inside.

A man in his late forties looks over, his brow creasing when he realizes he doesn't know me.

"Hold on." He puts his hand over the receiver and says, "Can I help you?"

"William Shelby?"

"Yes. And you are?"

He can't see the letters on my jacket, so I show him my badge. "Special Agent Springett."

"FBI?" His confusion turns into the subtle form of fear I often see in people when I show a badge.

"Yes, sir. Sorry to bother you, but if you have a moment, I'd like to ask you a few questions."

"Of-of course." He takes his hand off the phone and says, "Laura, do what I said, and we can talk about the rest when I get home. I've got to go...yes...love you...bye-bye." He hangs up and waves at the chairs in front of his desk. "Please, have a seat."

As I do so, I say, "I'm sorry to drop in on you unannounced, but sometimes it can't be avoided."

He forces a smile that I assume is meant to assure me it's not a problem. "What can I help you with?"

"Nothing too major. We're trying to track down someone we think came through here a few weeks ago."

Boy, would I love to play poker against this guy. He seems

incapable of keeping his feelings from showing on his face. Right now, his sudden grin and bright eyes are telegraphing relief in a big way. So much so that I'd think he was up to something he shouldn't be, if I didn't already believe he wouldn't be able to keep it a secret. At most, I figure he's sneaking home a few rolls of government-issued toilet paper and feeling guilty about it.

He turns to his computer, his fingers poised over his keyboard. "If you give me a name, I can see if your suspect bought a ticket here."

"I never said the person was a suspect."

"Oh. I just...I thought..."

"Last name Harrison, first name Carl. This would have been for a trip leaving in the evening on January eighteenth."

He types in the information. "Okay. Do you know the destination?"

"Los Angeles."

"That would be the Sunset Limited."

He busies himself on his keyboard for a few more moments, then hits ENTER and sits back. I can see part of the screen from where I am, so I know the moment the results pop up. From the frown on Shelby's face, I'm betting the news isn't promising.

"I'm sorry," he says. "No one with that last name purchased a ticket for the Sunset Limited on the eighteenth. Are you sure he boarded here?"

"We are reasonably confident."

"I'm not sure what more I can do."

"It's possible he traveled under a different name," I say. "Unfortunately, we don't know what that might have been." When Shelby opens his mouth, he looks like he's going to tell me how sorry he is that my trip has been a waste, so before he can, I speak again. "I noticed cameras in the main lobby. Do you have the entire station covered?"

"Almost everything, yes."

"How long do you hold on to the footage?"

"Four months, I believe."

"Then you should still have footage from January eighteenth."

"We should. Would you like to see it?"

"Yes, please."

He takes me through a door marked AUTHORIZED PERSONNEL ONLY, then leads me down a hallway to a room with two television monitors and an old desktop computer.

"I need to find Devon," he says. "He knows how this stuff works. Wait here. I'll be right back."

He leaves.

I text Jar to see how she's doing. Her answer is FINE, which doesn't tell me anything. She's supposed to be checking the businesses near the station for other security cameras, in hopes one of them picked up Harrison's arrival at the station.

Shelby returns a couple of minutes later, with a shaggy-haired college-age kid sporting a well-trimmed goatee.

"This is Devon," Shelby said. "He can help you. Unless there's something else you need from me, I really have to get back to my office."

"No, I don't think so," I say. "Thank you for your assistance."

Shelby is out the door as quick as he can.

"So, we're looking for what, exactly?" Devon asks as he drops into the room's only chair.

I give him the particulars.

"Got it." He turns to the computer.

I'm not really here to watch their footage. Jar showed it to me before I changed clothes at the truck stop. What I want is for the Amtrak people to see it, so they can pinpoint the exact moment Harrison purchased his ticket. With that information, it should be a breeze for them to determine what name the accused killer traveled under.

In short order, we're looking at video from the night in question. When Harrison enters the frame, I point at the monitor. "That's him."

The time stamp on the footage indicates Harrison walked into the Amtrak lobby at 6:12 p.m. Again, I can't help but think he doesn't look like someone who lived on the streets. Nor does he act like he only cleaned up so he could ride the train. I'm not saying he's dressed to the nines. He just seems...normal. So how did he end up dead from an overdose in a Los Angeles homeless camp a few days later?

"Can we see where he goes?" I ask.

"Sure."

We watch Harrison walk directly to the ticket desk, where he gets in line and buys his ticket for the train. I note the purchase time is 6:21 p.m.

Devon definitely knows how this stuff works, because he is able to keep tabs on Harrison all the way until the man climbs on board the Sunset Limited, without missing a moment. In the hour or so before the train arrives, Harrison appears to be killing time by reading posters on the walls, staring at the floor, and purchasing a few items from the snack shop.

Everything after he bought his ticket, except for when he boards the Sunset Limited, is footage I have not seen before, though Jar has. She told me what to expect, but now that I've watched it, I'm wondering if she purposely left some things out of her description to see if I'd notice, because I can't believe she would have missed them. Details do not escape her. Of course, the only reason I noticed is because Devon sped up the footage to get through it faster than real time, making the odd moments easier for me to pick up.

Huh. I guess I *am* here to watch the video.

The missing details are all similar. On five separate occasions, Harrison glances at something offscreen. Whatever he's looking at holds his gaze for several seconds. Two of the times end with him looking away suddenly, as if not wanting to get caught by whoever he was staring at. The other three times wrap up with Harrison giving an almost imperceptible nod. Whoever or whatever was holding his interest was not in any of the shots.

I'm sure Devon could find reverse angles that would show us, but there's no need to let him know I'm interested. Jar can check the footage later—if, that is, she hasn't already done so and just hasn't mentioned it to me.

What Harrison's looks do tell me is that he's pretending to be there alone but he's not. In the two incidents when he looks away quickly without nodding, there's something in his body language that implies caution or maybe even distrust.

Again, a supposition: the person he is there with is not a friend.

And how about one more: perhaps this not-friend forced Harrison to be there.

It's a leap, I admit, but one backed by years of experience.

"Can you match up the time he purchased the ticket with sales records, so we can get the name he used?" I ask.

"Piece of cake," Devon says, smirking.

Within half a minute, he has the info, but before he gives it to me, he says, "Aren't you supposed to have a search warrant for this kind of thing?"

Smart kid.

"We're trying to find this man before something bad

happens, so we need to keep it on the QT. Consider it more of a polite request. In the spirit of interagency cooperation."

Devon mulls this over.

"Or we could ask Mr. Shelby," I suggest. "See what he says."

Devon snorts. "He already told me to give you whatever you wanted. I guess if there are any problems, I could put the blame on him."

I pat him on the back. "If this tech stuff doesn't work out for you, you might want to consider a career as a middle manager."

He looks confused by my attempt at humor.

To get him back on track, I say, "I believe you were going to tell me something."

"Oh, yeah." He looks at the screen again. "The ticket was purchased by David Weeks."

"Did he happen to give a home address or a phone number?"

He looks at his screen. "Nope. Sorry."

"How did he pay?"

"Credit card. I could print everything out for you, if you'd like."

"That would be great."

CHAPTER EIGHT

J ar and I get a pair of hotel rooms with an adjoining door, at a Marriot near the I-10 freeway.

I was hoping David Weeks/Carl Harrison's credit card would give us the man's home address, but that prospect evaporates as soon as Jar runs it through the system. It's one of those gift credit cards with a prepaid balance on it, in this case five hundred dollars.

This at least tells us where and when the card was purchased, and what it was used to buy. The train ticket was the first item, the snacks at the station the second. After that, Weeks/Harrison used the card to purchase dinner on the train and pay for a taxi ride once he reached L.A. There have been no additional purchases, even though over two hundred dollars are still left on the card.

Jar's search for alternate security footage near the station turns up only a distant shot that appears to show Weeks/Harrison approaching the station on foot. Unfortunately, it doesn't tell us anything new. She tries to find a camera showing where he came from but is unsuccessful. Turns out there are a whole lot of camera-less dead zones near the station.

"What about the people he was traveling with?" I ask.

She looks at me, brow furrowed. "What?"

"The people he looked at?"

When her confusion doesn't go away, I tell her what I saw.

She turns to her computer and starts looking for those incidents. When she finds the first one, her face tenses, but she says nothing until she's watched all five. "I did not see this. I should have seen this."

"It's okay. I did. That's why it's better if we work together."

"I should have seen this," she repeats, still staring at the screen.

"Jar...Jar!"

She lets out a breath and looks over at me.

"Do you think you can find who he was looking at?" I ask

The strain in her expression eases a bit. "Yes. Of course." She turns back to her computer.

While she works on that, I walk over to the window. Though I didn't show it earlier, I'm as surprised as Jar is that she didn't catch Weeks/Harrison's looks. I wasn't lying when I said details are her thing. But this is the first time we've worked on something that she has such a strong emotional connection to, and I wonder if it's interfering with her abilities. I hope not.

"Take a look at this," she says.

I return to the table and sit back down. On her screen is a still shot from inside the station.

"This is incident number one."

She lets the footage play. Three people are standing close but not next to one another, near a wall inside the station. Let's call them Men A, B, and C. A and C are Caucasian, while B appears to be Hispanic. Everyone else in the shot is on the way to somewhere else.

"That bag," I say, my gaze on the satchel hanging from the shoulder of Man C. "Does it match the one the police found?"

Jar brings forward an image that was already open. It's of the bag that held the pictures of Naomi that the police found at the luggage storage place.

"What do *you* think?" she says.

It's a rare month when Jar asks a rhetorical question, but that's precisely what she just did. The bag the police now have is an exact match for the one Man C is carrying.

She switches back to video and brings up a new window. "Incident number two."

It's the same area, same camera angle, but now only Man B and Man C remain. Again, they give off the appearance of not being together.

Pause. New window.

"Incident number three."

A different area of the lobby. Several people moving around in this one, but the only familiar person is Man A. For a brief second, he appears to look directly at Naomi's accused killer, which, if I'm correct, coincides with one of the times Weeks/Harrisons nods. (We really need to figure out what this guy's name is. Until I know better, I'll refer to him as Weeks, since that's the name he traveled under. Or maybe I should call him Harrison, since that's what the cops know him by. Crap. Weeks/Harrison it is.)

Jar pauses the video and brings up another window.

"Incident number four."

The platform now. Plenty of passengers milling about, including Men A and C. This time it's the latter who seems to catch Weeks/Harrison's eye.

Pause. Another window.

"And incident number five."

The platform again. B has joined A and C, and by *joined* I mean they are clearly standing together. I can't tell which one shares a glance with Weeks, because at one point or another, they all seem to.

"He definitely wasn't there alone," I say.

"No, he was not."

"And they're carrying his bag."

"They are carrying *a* bag," she says. "How hard would it have been for them to give it to him in L.A. and tell him to store it and his suitcase together at the luggage facility?"

A second rhetorical question in as many minutes, because the only answer is not hard at all. Where's the Jar I used to know?

"Do you believe me now that something is not right?"

"It's not a matter of believing," I say. "It's clear Harrison or Weeks or whoever he was couldn't have killed Naomi because he wasn't in town yet."

"But he did take the fall."

"And he shouldn't have," I say. "I'm surprised the police didn't discover the train issue already."

"They did check Amtrak records. But they were looking for the name Carl Harrison."

"And they didn't find anything."

"Incorrect. According to their notes, someone arrived the day before the murder, on the Surfliner from San Diego, traveling under that name."

"The police would love that," I say. San Diego is where Harrison was supposed to be from. Though it sounds preposterous even as the question comes into my mind, I have to ask, "Did he take that train then fly to Phoenix and take this one? I assume you've looked at the footage, right?"

"There is no footage."

"What?"

"The stations in San Diego and Los Angeles and the cars on the Surfliner experienced intermittent camera failures that day.

It was reported as a code error and was working by the next day. Though Union Station in Los Angeles did have one additional outage."

"Let me guess. When the Sunset Limited arrived from Tucson with the real Weeks/Harrison?"

"Yes," she said. "The outages on the San Diego train prompted me to take a closer look. When I saw that there was a similar outage the next day at the station in L.A., I checked what trains had arrived at that time. There was only the Sunset Limited. I was curious as to why."

"But the cameras on the Sunset Limited and at the station in Tucson work."

"We would not have been able to watch video from them if they had not," she says, like I'm an elementary kid who's having problems understanding two plus two equals four.

"What I mean is, why weren't they blacked out, too?" I ask.

I'm pretty sure I know the answer, but Jar says it for me. "Because they did not need to be."

The police believe Weeks/Harrison is the murderer based on what they found in the bag they think was his. They believe he came from San Diego because a ticket on the Surfliner was purchased in their suspect's name, and it would have put him in town in plenty of time to kill Naomi. There was no reason for the cops to look at anyone else.

If this were my operation, though—not that I would ever do anything like this—I would still have wiped the cameras on the Sunset Limited Weeks/Harrison rode, just in case. The fact that this did not happen tells us something about the person or persons who actually killed Naomi and the man they framed.

A third party is responsible for the camera outages. Possibly someone the killer knew who was asked to do it, but more likely someone who was paid to perform the task. Monitoring the cameras to make sure no one could get them working again before their mission was accomplished would have been part of the job. Which meant this person could've seen things that weren't recorded. Things like who was on the train. This wouldn't have been a problem on the Surfliner. But if his job included dealing with the Sunset Limited, too, he might've seen Weeks/Harrison. Then, if a few days later he saw a picture of the man on the news, he might've made the connection, and realized he'd just covered up a whole different kind of crime than he probably thought he was dealing with.

It's a tale of the lesser of two evils, or I guess a tale of the less likely. Better to let Harrison be recorded traveling on a train no one would check than having someone you paid to disable the cameras see him and turn you in to the police.

"You didn't think about sharing all of this with me before we flew out here?" I say. "You realize that would have gotten me on board with all this a lot sooner, don't you?"

Jar's eyes narrow. "Are you saying you did *not* believe me earlier?"

"That's not what I'm saying."

"You just implied you were not 'on board with all this,' which would mean you did not think I was right."

I'm the one who's supposed to be upset here. How did I suddenly become the bad guy?

"I got on the plane, didn't I?" I say. "You hadn't even told me *anything* at that point, but I came with you because I trust you. And when you did tell me, I believed you."

She silently studies me and then nods and looks back at her computer. I take this as a decision to de-escalate. Though what I say next may inflame things all over again.

"I think we should send what we've found to the police."

She freezes, her body suddenly rigid, and when she speaks, her words come out slow and precise. "So they can bury it?"

"They won't do that."

I'm treated to a withering, don't-be-so-naïve gaze. It's impressive, and I hope she never has cause to look at me this way again. "Police bury things all the time."

All the time might be a stretch, but I do know it happens on occasion. "I have faith that Detective Hughes and his partners will look into it," I say. "We can even threaten them with public exposure of what we've found, to make sure they do."

She looks at her screen again. On it is the image of Men A, B, and C on the platform. "I would like to find one of these three first."

"Jar, that's not—"

Help her find them, Liz whispers in my ear.

And the evil alliance of Jar and Liz is complete. Or am I the evil one in this scenario?

Crap, crap, crap, crap, crap.

Jar looks at me, waiting for me to finish what I was starting to say. When it's clear I'm not going to, she says, "By the time the police start tracking these men down, *if* they do, these three could be long gone."

"They're probably already long gone."

"And if they are, it will be easier for us to find them than it will be for the police."

Her point is valid. We're not bound by the same rules of evidence gathering that the police are. Getting search warrants to view footage from various agencies or to obtain copies of records will take them time.

Help her find them.

Dammit, Liz. You could at least do me the favor of talking to me when no one else is around so I have the ability to argue.

"How about this?" I say. "We'll give it a day, see what we can find out, then we send everything to the police and move on."

"Two days."

"Jar..."

"Two days," she repeats. "Starting at eight a.m. tomorrow."

Help her.

I rub my eyes. I'm not going to get my way here. Hell, if the main two women in my life continue to work together, I may never get my way again.

I sigh and climb to my feet. "Two days, starting at eight a.m., and you buy me dinner. Final offer."

I'm awakened in what feels like the middle of the night by someone shaking my shoulder. Which is weird, because I could have sworn I was alone.

"You are wasting the day," Jar says.

I peel my eyes open just enough to see her standing next to the bed, backlit by light coming through the doorway between our rooms. She's dressed and raring to go.

"What time is it?" I ask, though I think it comes out more like *wa tie mezit?* We stayed up pretty late last night, watching back-to-back episodes of *Dexter* on Netflix. Well, I did most of the watching. I was hoping it would be a fun distraction for Jar, but I don't think she really paid attention.

"Come on, get up." In typical Jar fashion, she's showing no effects from minimal sleep.

I slap a hand on the nightstand, find the power cord to my phone, and pull it until I can grab the device. I click the button and look at the screen.

Five-oh-two a.m.

"I thought we agreed on eight a.m.," I say.

"We agreed the forty-eight-hour period begins at eight a.m., not that we would start then. I have been working for two hours already."

"The sun isn't even up yet."

"Which means there will be less traffic on the road. Here."

She holds something out to me. In the semidarkness, it takes a moment for me to realize it's clothes.

"I'd, um, at least like to take a shower first."

She considers this for a moment, then pulls the clothes back. "Ten minutes." She walks back toward the door, dropping off the clothes on the dresser as she walks by.

"Are you going to time me?"

"I will meet you in the lobby," she says and disappears into her room.

I get washed and dressed in what has to be a new world record. Still, Jar scowls at me when I reach the hotel lobby, so I know I have exceeded my allotted time limit.

"Where are we going?" I ask as we walk to the car.

"Phoenix."

Before I drive us onto the interstate, Jar finds it in her heart to allow me to pick up some coffee. Mainly I think it's because she wants some, too. Apparently even those who operate efficiently on almost no sleep can use a caffeine boost now and then.

The sunrise over the desert is spectacular. A few scattered clouds near the eastern horizon reflect the coming day in an everchanging light show of purples and reds and oranges and yellows. We've traveled for over an hour in silence by the time the sun starts to paint the sky. In the darkness, it was easy to concentrate on the coffee and the road and staying awake. But now, with the sky turning blue above us, it doesn't seem as if words will feel as intrusive.

"What's in Phoenix?" I ask.

"That is a broad question."

"You know what I mean."

A beat. "One of the men from the video is associated with an address there."

"How did you find that out?"

"By analyzing all the tickets purchased by passengers boarding in Tucson that night, then eliminating those that I could prove weren't bought by one of the watchers until I had only three left."

A logical approach, but I doubt it was quite as straightforward as that.

We reach the outskirts of Phoenix just in time to enjoy some early morning traffic, and end up slogging along at a mind-numbing eighteen miles an hour. When the I-10 turns west toward California, we take the 51 freeway north, exit near Town Heights, and work our way to East Morten Avenue and the address Jar obtained.

I'm not sure what I was expecting, but a two-story, Spanish-style office complex is not it. It's easiest to describe it as the kind of place that's popular with dentists and insurance agents and mortgage brokers. Easy to find, with a big parking lot all the way around it.

After I pull off the road, Jar directs me to a spot on the east side of the building.

"This is supposed to be where one of the watchers lives?" I ask.

"I never said it was."

That's true. The phrase she used was something like *an associated address*. I made the obvious, but apparently wrong, leap that it was where his home would be.

"So, what is this? His workplace?"

"No." She climbs out of the car.

I feel like we're playing a game of Twenty Questions that I am never going to win. I climb out and follow her down the sidewalk to one of the building's entrances. There, she stops in front of a directory and scans it, column by column.

"I'd really like to know what we're doing here," I say.

"Just a moment."

She continues searching the list until her gaze stops on something in the third column. Her lips move slightly as she reads the entry, and then she looks at me. "This way."

My assumption is she's going to lead me inside. But nope, she takes me across the street to a restaurant called Rico's Bar and Grill, which, despite its name, appears to be open for breakfast.

I haven't even thought about food yet, but when the smell of grilling sausage hits me as we walk in, my stomach growls.

The hostess starts to take us to a table in the back, but Jar stops her and points at a booth by the window.

"That table is free. We would like to use it."

"Oh. Um, let me check." The woman returns to the hostess podium and talks with one of her colleagues. When she comes back, she says, "No problem. Right this way."

After we take our seats, the hostess hands us menus and departs with a promise that our server will be along shortly.

Jar leaves her menu sitting on the table and looks around, making sure no one is near us. In a low voice, she says, "There is an office on the ground floor of that building, number one-eighteen. It is used by a company called NCSG Info Services."

"Sounds like a computer company."

Sneering, she says, "According to their website, their focus is data management."

"I take it that's not what goes on there."

"They are a forgery service."

As my dozens of faux IDs can attest, I have more than a passing knowledge of these kinds of businesses. Here's a quick tutorial:

All forgers are not created equal. Those I deal with sit at the very top of their profession and can churn out fakes that pass official inspection every time. The expertise (and quality of work) dips gradually but steadily every level you descend from there. The most talented group the public at large has access to —if they have the means *and* the right contacts—is perfectly serviceable. Below this, skill levels become hit or miss, with prices still high but often negotiable. Most of the time, the product will serve the customer's needs without issues. Sometimes not.

My guess is that NCSG Info Services falls somewhere between perfectly serviceable and hit or miss.

"Let me guess," I say. "They sold the watcher something."

"The credit card he used to buy his ticket. Probably a fake ID, too."

Working out of a storefront is convenient for clients, but also comes with a greater risk of getting caught. Which is why places like NCSG prefer knowing as much as they can about their clients. This means there is an excellent chance they'll have a record of the watcher's real name and even an address.

"Is it a solo operation, or are they connected?" I ask.

"As far as I can tell, they are solo."

That's good. There are a few regional forger rings out there, plus one that spans the entire country. It's best not to tangle with any of them, as word might get around you're causing problems. Not that Jar has said we'll be causing any problems, but I'm pretty sure we're not here to just stop in and say hi.

A waiter approaches our table and introduces himself as Randy. Randy is a happy guy for eight a.m. Too happy, if you ask me.

He's happy to get us coffee. And happy to take our order. He's also happy to help us with anything else we may need. I'm doubtful of this last. I mean, if we ask him to come with us after we're done and help us bounce a few heads around, would he be up for it? I think not.

"Coffee, oatmeal, and a side of fruit," I say.

"Pears, pineapple, and plums. Is that okay?"

"Do you have anything that doesn't start with a *p*?"

He looks confused for a moment, then laughs. "That didn't even dawn on me. I'd be happy to check with the kitchen to see if there's something different."

"No, those will be fine."

"And you, ma'am?"

Jar hands him her menu. "A side of bacon, two pieces of sourdough toast, and also coffee."

"Is that all?"

"Yes."

He reads back what we told him and says, "I'll be happy to put your order in. And I'll be back in a few with that coffee."

After he walks away, Jar says, "I think there is something wrong with him."

"I'd be happy to talk with you about it, if you want," I say, smiling sickly sweet.

She stares at me. Then laughs. Twice. "Ha. Ha." Okay, not real laughs, but she got my joke so I'll take it.

After Randy brings us our coffee—"Let me know if you need anything and I'll be happy to get it for you"—we get back to discussing the felonious activity across the street.

"How many people work there?" I ask.

"I believe four."

"Do you know the name of the forger?"

"Thomas O'Sullivan."

"*That* doesn't sound made up."

A narrowing of Jar's eyes is followed by, "You are being facetious."

"I am."

"Good. Because it is made up. I do not know his real name. I did not feel it necessary to spend time on that."

"So, the other three people are..."

"A receptionist to turn people away who might wander in. An assistant who does everything Mr. O'Sullivan does not. And a bodyguard."

"I take it you've tried to get the information out of their computer system."

"We would not be here if I was successful. Their system appears to only be used for the internet by the girl at the front desk. She watches a lot of YouTube."

"Wi-Fi?"

"No. Hardwired."

"So, you're saying any records they're keeping are either done by hand or on secure devices."

"That is the logical assumption."

"And you want us to walk in there and find something that tells us who the watcher is."

"You are stating the obvious."

"Oh, I'm not done. You want this to happen preferably without them realizing what we're doing."

"That would be the least problematic solution, yes."

I see Randy heading toward our table, holding a tray with our food on it.

After he sets everything down and leaves with a "Happy dining," I say to Jar, "What's your plan?"

She breaks off a piece of her toast but says nothing.

"You do have a plan, don't you?"

Keeping her gaze off me, she grabs the pat of butter off her plate.

"Jar?"

As she spreads the butter, her toast crunches almost loudly enough to cover up her mumbled "I do not have one yet."

"Well, I guess we could just walk in and ask."

Apparently I haven't put enough sarcasm into my voice, because Jar says, "I do not think that will work."

"Really?"

Her glare tells me I've finally hit my mark. "Oh, I see. Very funny." No courtesy laugh this time. You can't win them all. "I am sure you can come up with a better idea than that."

I stare at her, then very deliberately put a spoonful of oatmeal into my mouth.

"What?" she says. "You are good at this kind of thing."

I swallow, set down my spoon, and take a sip of my coffee. Finally I say, "All right. I'll come up with a plan. But we need to set a few ground rules first."

"For what?"

"For this. Whatever it is we're doing."

"You know what we are doing. It is your hobby."

A few months ago, I made the mistake of saying something like, "Thanks for being a charter member of my hobby club," after she'd yet again provided assistance on one of my side projects. It feels weird hearing the word out of her mouth.

"It's only my hobby if I'm driving the bus," I say. "Right now, I'm barely even a passenger."

The bewildered look on Jar's face tells me I used a metaphor she hasn't heard before. There are a handful of metaphors she understands now, but each new one requires explanation.

"What I mean is, if we're going to do this, you can't keep me in the dark. You need to tell me what you're looking into and why, and then we'll figure out what we're going to do —together."

"Have I not been doing this?"

"No, you haven't."

She's quiet for several seconds as her mind mulls this over. "You are right," she eventually says. "I am sorry. I...I just—"

"You're just a little stressed. That's all. And I get it. This is personal."

"It is."

"I'm here to help you, but I can only do that if you keep me in the loop."

Nodding, she says, "I understand, and I will," then picks up her toast. "So, what are we going to do?"

CHAPTER NINE

My plan starts with a phone call, followed by a half-hour drive to the parking lot of a Walmart in Scottsdale. There, I pull up next to a Ford F-150 crew cab truck with tinted windows.

"Wait here," I tell Jar.

The front passenger door of the pickup opens as I exit the Accord, and a bull of a man rolls out. His droopy, salt-and-pepper mustache and matching ponytail make him look like a fifty-year-old version of Danny Trejo. (You may not think you know who that is, but you probably do. Google him and you'll see what I mean.)

Not-Danny-Trejo's name is Victor Ramos.

"Nate," he says as he wraps his arms around me. "Good to see you, my friend."

Victor has perfected the art of the bear hug. He squeezes just strong enough to let me know he could hurt me if he wanted to, but gently enough so that I don't actually feel any pain.

"Good to see you, too."

When he lets go, his smile morphs into an exaggerated frown. "Why didn't you tell me you were coming to town?"

"Thought we were just passing through and wouldn't need your help."

He laughs. "You know better than this. You *always* need my help." He thumps me on the back. "Is there something going down I need to know about?"

"Not really. This is a small gig." I nod toward my car where Jar waits. "Only me and my friend."

"You branching out on your own?"

"Nothing like that. Don't need the whole team on this one, that's all."

Remember those suppliers I mentioned? The ones you can find in almost any city in the world? Most big cities have more than one. Here in Phoenix, I can name five off the top of my head. Whenever possible, I go with people I have a preexisting relationship with, such as Victor. I wouldn't be surprised, since this is Jar's first time in Arizona, that when she chose who we got the car and original supplies from, she did so by going alphabetically.

"You have what I requested?" I ask.

His head bobs back and forth as he winces. "Not quite yet. Some of what you need I don't usually stock."

"You said it wouldn't be problem."

"And it isn't. I've got someone taking care of it right now. But come on, turning that stuff around in thirty minutes? Anyone would need longer than that."

I get his point, but the delay is not exactly making me happy. "How *much* longer?"

"Not to worry, my friend. There's a good chance that by the time we get to my office, it'll already be there."

"You could have led with that."

He shrugs. "Sorry?"

I roll my eyes and say, "I assume I need to ride with you."

"If it wouldn't be too much trouble."

"Mind if my friend tags along?"

He looks over at the car. "If you vouch for her, fine by me."

I wave for Jar to join us. When she does, I make introductions, then we all climb into the pickup, with Jar and me in the crew cab's backseat.

Victor hands me two black cloth sacks. "You know what to do."

I give one to Jar. "Over your head."

She looks at me, an eyebrow raised.

"It's all right," I say.

After we put them on, Victor says, "If you can both lean down below window level, I would appreciate it. People get a little anxious when they see someone with a bag over their heads." After we comply, the driver drops the truck into drive and takes off. (He's the same wiry guy who's always with Victor but whose name I've never learned.)

The trip lasts around fifteen minutes, and involves a lot of turns meant to ensure we don't figure out where we're being taken.

After we come to a final stop and the driver kills the engine, Victor says, "You can take the hoods off and hop out."

The truck's parked inside the same large, shabby-looking building I've been brought to several times before.

With a "Wait here," Victor leaves us at the truck and disappears through a doorway along the right side of the room.

"I do not like wearing a sack over my head," Jar whispers. "Besides, it was unnecessary. I know exactly where we are."

This does not surprise me.

When I don't respond, she says, "Were you not tracking our route, too? It was easy to follow. The driver did not try very hard."

"I didn't have to," I whisper.

She stares at me, then her eyes widen a bit. "You knew already."

"Do you think I would have agreed to go with him otherwise?"

There are plenty of spur-of-the-moment, underinformed decisions one has to make in my world. Being taken to a supplier's secret lair needs not be one of them. I've known Victor's place is located in an old printing facility since before I first met him in person. Figuring that out had been a task given to me by my mentor many years ago.

When Victor returns, he says, "Good news. Your items have been located."

"That doesn't sound like they are here yet."

"A little patience. My associate's on his way with them as we speak. He should be here within thirty minutes. I trust that's okay."

If I'm being honest, I half expected to wait a whole day. So, another half hour is fine, but I'm not going to let him off the hook that easily. Frowning, I say, "I guess we'll have to make do."

"The other things on your list we do have on hand. Shall we grab them while we wait?"

He leads us to a large storage room loaded with lab equipment and electronics. Trafficking in these kinds of items makes up the bulk of his income. The stuff we're interested in, however, is located beyond a secret door at the back of the room.

On the other side, a set of stairs takes us down to a basement that is not on the building's blueprints. Victor unlocks the door at the bottom via a fingerprint scanner, enters the room, and flicks on the lights.

The space is about half the size of the storage room above us and has only the one entrance. Shelves line each wall, with an additional three rows of them running down the middle.

He leads us to a shelf filled with cardboard boxes. On the side of each box, someone has written a series of letters and numbers, no two boxes sharing the exact same sequence.

"Help me with this, will you?" Victor says.

He works the top box off a stack, and hands it to me so I can set it on the ground. When I stand back up, he gives me another one and I place it on top of the first.

Victor pulls out a pocketknife and slices the tape sealing the box still on the shelf. He folds the flaps back, removes some stuffing from inside, and steps out of the way. "These work for you?"

I look inside and whistle appreciatively. "These look next gen."

A grin. "Released last month. Got two boxes of them."

Sitting on a layer of shredded cardboard stuffing are six, surprisingly slender dart guns. I pick one up and admire it for a moment before holding it out and checking the sights. It's not loaded, so it's lighter than it will be, but even with the darts in, I figure it'll be about half a pound less than the older version.

"Capacity?" I ask.

"Five in the magazine, one in the chamber."

My plan does not call for the use of any weapons, but that doesn't mean we won't end up needing some. And if we do, I would like to avoid anything lethal. "You have the prefilled darts?"

"I've got four mags' worth. I assume that's enough."

"It is."

We take two of the dart guns and all four magazines, then Victor leads us down the center aisle, back toward the door. Before we get there, he stops and opens another box. "And you wanted a few of these, too, I believe."

He pulls out an aluminum drink can. It's black with yellow letters on the side that read SIDEWINDER ENERGY DRINK. Next to the name is a snake, looking ready to strike.

He tosses me the can. The weight is about right for what it's pretending to be, the illusion created by weights inside. The remainder of the space is filled with something not nearly as heavy.

"Remote trigger?" I ask.

He shook his head. "Sorry. All out."

"Does it at least have a delay?"

"Would I leave you hanging like that?" He points at the top of the can. "Turn the opener a full three-sixty before you pop it. That will give you three minutes. Work for you?"

Not optimal, but better than nothing. "Yeah. That'll work."

We take four, add them to a workout bag Victor gives us to carry everything, and head back upstairs, where we have to wait only a few minutes before Victor's courier shows up with the rest of our order. We put the three large duffel bags he brought into the back of the truck. After I settle up our debt, Victor's nameless driver takes us back to Walmart.

"In position," Jar says over the comm. Normally, this would be preceded by "Jar for Nate," but since it's just the two of us, the formality is unnecessary.

"Copy." From the front seat of our car, I scan the front of the building that houses NCSG. "All clear. Green light."

"Copy."

I exit the car and walk quickly around the building to a fenced-in pen, where several dumpsters are stored. Because of the unseemliness of the trash area, no windows look upon it. It's also positioned so that it can't be seen from the street. The only people who would have a view of it would be those coming from or going to cars parked nearby. No one is around as I duck through the gap between the cinder-block wall and the sliding gate. Normally it is locked, but I took care of that earlier.

I check my watch.

A minute has passed since I gave the go signal. Which means two minutes before the show begins, and another one or two beyond that before I can make my appearance.

I zip open the two duffel bags that I placed next to one of the dumpsters, remove the gear from inside, and start pulling it on. When I check my watch again, the initial three minutes are almost up.

I pull on the air mask but leave it propped on my forehead, then crouch down and wait.

The three-minute mark passes without any fanfare, exactly as expected.

Thirty seconds later, Jar says in my ear, "Activating phase two."

"Copy."

After another few minutes pass, the late morning calm is shattered by the *whooooop-whoooop-whooooop* of a fire alarm blaring from inside the building. When people step out of their offices to see what's going on, they will immediately smell the smoke billowing out of the four Sidewinder Energy Drink cans Jar hid in a pair of utility closets and the two public restrooms. This should cause everyone to rush for the exit, including those working at NCSG Info Services.

Right on cue, the backdoor flies open and several people hurry out.

"What's going on with our friends?" I ask.

"The receptionist just ran out the door. No one else has left yet, though."

"Copy. Hold tight."

As the alarm keeps wailing, people continue leaving through the back door. I'm confident the same is true for the front door on the other side.

I wait a little longer, then check my watch again. It's been ninety seconds since Jar pulled the alarm. I want to go, but I can't do anything until I hear—

There it is. The not-so-distant sound of emergency sirens heading this way.

I make one last check of the official Phoenix Fire Department outfit I'm wearing—that gear Victor obtained for me—adjust the straps holding the oxygen tank on my back, then pull down the face mask, and slip out of the enclosure.

No one sees me running toward the back door. Most are running away from the building, while the few that aren't are staring at the smoke now wafting out the door they just used.

"Back! Back!" I yell.

They finally notice me.

Waving an arm at them, I shout, "Get as far away as you can!"

This is the kick in the ass the stragglers have been waiting for, and they all hurry after their smarter colleagues.

"Entering the building now," I say into the comm.

"Copy," Jar replies. "On my way."

Smoke is thick in the hallway as I rush in. Victor's smoke bomb canisters are the high-density kind. Setting off all four ensured smoke finds its way into every inch of the place.

I reach the door to NCSG a moment before Jar arrives. She, too, is wearing a mask and oxygen tank. No fireman gear for her, though. There's not a department in the country that would have an easily obtainable outfit for someone of her diminutive stature. She is carrying a bag, inside of which would be the four now depleted cans. We don't want to leave those lying around for the real firefighters to find.

"Are they all gone?" I ask.

She shakes her head. "I only saw the receptionist and the assistant."

"All right. Stand back where you won't be seen."

After she's moved a few meters down the hallway and melded into the smoke, I open the door to NCSG's office and rush in.

The reception area is smoky, though not nearly as bad as the hallway. It's also deserted. "Everyone out!" I yell. "Everyone out!"

I head through a doorway that leads to the back offices and find Thomas O'Sullivan and his bodyguard in one of the rooms, trying to stuff files into a box. Both men are coughing but seem determined to finish their task.

"You've got to get out of here!" I yell.

They jump at the sound of my voice. Then O'Sullivan says, "Give us a minute."

"No! Now!"

The bodyguard turns toward me and tries to puff up his chest, but his bravado is undercut by a series of coughs. He manages to squeeze out, "He said just a minute," before another coughing fit hits him.

"You're putting your lives in danger!" I say. "You need to leave now!"

"We just need to grab a few things."

"There is no time to grab anything." I take a beat then say, "Look, if you get out of here, we should have enough time to put the fire out and none of your stuff will be damaged. But that might not happen if I need to stay here to make sure you leave."

What the hell is wrong with these people? As far as they're concerned, there's a real fire heading their way.

The effects of the smoke seem to have gotten through to the bodyguard. He looks at his boss and says, "We need to go."

"This first," O'Sullivan says.

"Not worth it. I'm out of here." The bodyguard rushes past me toward the door.

O'Sullivan looks undecided about what he should do.

Giving him a nudge, I say, "The fire is at the other end of the building. Your stuff will be fine."

"Are you sure?"

"The only thing I'm sure about is that the smoke will kill you if you don't leave now."

This finally seems to get through to him. He starts to pick up the box to take with him.

"You might drop that and trip over it," I say. "Leave it!"

He jumps at my bark and drops the box onto the desk, then runs after the man who was supposed to be protecting him.

As soon as I'm sure he's left, I say, "We're clear. Come on in."

Once Jar joins me, I set the timer on my watch for three minutes. It doesn't sound like a lot of time to conduct our search, but hopefully it will be enough. I'd rather us not still be here when the real firemen come through.

While Jar searches for computers that aren't hooked up to the network, I rifle through the files, starting with those O'Sullivan was putting into the box.

As expected, everything is in code. What I'm looking for are records created in the last month and a half. That's not to say the dates aren't falsified, but I can tell, for the most part, which files are newer and which have been around for a while. I take photos of everything that falls into the proper category.

When my alarm goes off, I've shot somewhere north of seventy-five pictures and made it through almost everything. I go looking for Jar and find her in another office, sitting behind a desk. In front of her is an open laptop, and beside it the device she's using to clone the drive.

"I need twenty seconds," she says.

"Twenty, then we go."

She's still a few seconds away from finishing when I hear the main door to the NCSG offices open. I rush out of the room, down the hallway and into the reception area, arriving a few seconds after two similarly clothed firemen entered from the main corridor.

They stop short when they see me.

I shout, "This area's clear," and hurry past them into the corridor, hoping they will follow.

They do.

I lose them in the smoke and slip into another office until they run by.

"On my way back," I say into the comm. "We need to go now."

"I am ready," Jar says.

She's waiting for me in NCSG's lobby when I get back. As we planned, I pick her up and carry her like she's someone I rescued, then head into the corridor. For appearance's sake, we probably should ditch her mask and oxygen, but there's still enough smoke hanging around that I'd rather risk questions as to why she has them than damage her lungs.

When we reach the main building lobby, I see at least two fire engines in the parking lot out front. I take a hard right and exit through the back door. There's another truck in the rear area, but most of its crew must be inside because only two men are at the vehicle.

When one of them looks over and sees me, I yell, "EMTs?"

He points to the right, and I rush off in that direction.

The moment the two firemen can no longer see us, and before we come into view of those out front, I put Jar back on her feet and act like I'm making sure she's all right, in case any civilians are watching us. I then point in a direction that will take her "out of harm's way."

As she runs off, I backtrack the way I came, jogging as if I'm fulfilling someone's orders. When I pass the two firemen again, they're so busy pulling equipment out, they don't even look my way.

Soon after, I'm in the dumpster area, my fireman gear removed and stored back in the bags. I dump the duffels into one of the bins and push a few trash bags of shredded paper over them. I don't particularly like leaving the equipment here, but I worry the duffels would draw too much attention if I walk away with them. One of Victor's guys will have to pick them up when the area is clear.

———

Thirty-five minutes later, we're in a Starbucks and have set up shop in a corner that's marginally more private than the rest of the place.

Sitting on the table, on one side of Jar's laptop, is the device she used to clone the hard drive, and on the other my phone with the photos I took.

There's really nothing I can do to help, so as soon as Jar finishes importing my pictures, I grab my phone and tell her I'm going for a walk. I take the ever-so-slight movement of her head as a sign she heard me.

The Starbucks is located in a strip mall that includes a burger place, a Chinese takeout restaurant, an H&R Block office, and a comic book store.

Back in high school and most of my time in college, I was a fairly dedicated comic book reader. In those days, I could tell you the good and the bad about the latest X-Men plotline, which characters DC was underserving, and how Marvel's

Annihilation series was freaking awesome. I'm not as clued in as I used to be, but I've picked up the habit of reading a graphic novel series now and then. *The Walking Dead*, of course, is excellent. And *Y: The Last Man*, also amazing.

The guy behind the counter greets me with a nod and says, "Help you find anything?"

I'm tempted to say I'm just browsing. I like to explore places like this. But there is something I'm looking for. "*Paper Girls*, volume 5?"

He nods toward the back. "Right side. About three-quarters of the way down. Should have a couple in the Image Comics section."

"Thanks."

It's not a huge store but it's packed to the gills, and I have to step around a few boxes marked DISCOUNTED before I reach the area I'm looking for. Sure enough, there are three copies of volume five, and four of volume six, which is the last in the series, as I understand. I pick up one of each. Depending on how long Jar will be, I might be able to get through both of them before we move on.

The counter guy hands me the receipt, and as he puts my books in a bag, Jar calls.

"Thanks," I say as I take the books, then hit ACCEPT on my screen and head for the door. "Hey."

"Where are you?"

"I told you I was going for a walk."

"You did?"

I guess the head movement I saw was just random.

"I did. But I'm only a few stores away. What's going on?"

"I am ready to leave."

So much for having time to read.

She's waiting at the car when I get there. After we climb in, I say, "So...?"

She looks at me. "What?"

"Did you find anything that will help us?"

"Why did you not ask that? Why did you only say 'so'?"

"The question was implied."

"It is one of several questions you could have been asking. In situations like this, it would be better if you were clear."

I'm hard-pressed to think of another question that would have been as likely, but what I say is, "Fair enough. So, did you find anything that will help us?"

"More than one thing."

"That's great. From the pictures or the hard drive?"

"The pictures you took, but I would not have been able to decode them without a program I cloned from their drive. So I guess the answer is both."

"And...?"

"Once more you are implying a question, but this time it is clear because of context. Before we did not have context."

"I'd argue the context was actually there before."

"Of course you would. You are the one who did not speak clearly, so you would like to pretend it did not happen."

"I'm not trying to—"

"I only point this out so that you see the difference."

I have to learn when to stop myself before falling into one of her linguistic traps. "Point taken. Thank you for teaching me English."

"You are welcome."

"I repeat the question. And...?"

"The watcher's name is Juan Sanchez. He has an address in Goodyear. According to the map, it is approximately forty-two kilometers away."

(For the metric system-challenged, that's twenty-six miles. Despite the fact that my education was steeped in the imperial measuring system until I was recruited into the secret world, I tend to use the metric system for most things now, in case you couldn't tell already. It's cleaner, it's easier, and about ninety-eight percent of the world uses it. I'm just saying, the States are doing our kids an injustice by not making it the standard they learn by. But, hey, that's only my opinion. Don't hate me for it. End of unplanned rant.)

"Excellent," I say. "You said there was more than one thing?"

"One of the documents you photographed was a list of the services they provided Mr. Sanchez. We already knew about the credit card, and suspected they made an ID for him, which they did. But there was one other item. Another ID, but considerably more expensive. Five thousand dollars."

"Whoa. That's a lot of cash for a fake ID."

"Because it is not fake. He requested something that would hold up if checked by authorities."

That put the price into perspective. What she means is he wanted an official ID that police or anyone else could look up and find in their system. Bribes would have had to be handed out to a government official who had access to the appropriate database.

"I don't suppose there was anything in their notes about what he needed it for?" I ask.

"The inventory included the ID's number. I had an idea which of your states it came from, and I was right."

She opens her laptop and clicks on a jpeg file. On the screen is a California ID, the kind provided for people who don't want a driver's license. The name on the card is Carl Harrison, with an address in San Diego. And the picture is of Weeks/Harrison. It's the same ID we saw in the police file of Naomi's case.

I say, "I think this means we can officially declare that Carl Harrison is not the guy's real name."

"I agree with that."

"But is it David Weeks?"

"I do not know yet. I am planning on working on that while you drive."

"Is that a hint?"

"Unless you require me to be more direct?"

"Nope, I got it," I say and start the engine.

CHAPTER TEN

Thanks to afternoon traffic, it's forty-five minutes before we're off the freeway again, and another ten until we reach the address in Goodyear that Jar gave me.

The place is down a street lined with rectangular brick houses that look like they were built back in the 1960s. In other words, older Goodyear, not newer.

No one would call any of the homes flashy, but most are nice and neat. It's a working-class neighborhood, populated by people who seem to take pride in where they live. People who undoubtedly watch out for one another. That could be a problem.

The house we have come to see fits in well with the others. The only deviation is that its bricks are painted a faded mint green, whereas most of the other houses are tan or gray or white.

The front yard is done in a simple but attractive low-maintenance style, with rocks and dirt and plants that don't need a lot of water. The curtains are closed on all three of the windows facing the street, but this seems to be a theme with a lot of the homes. As do the bars those windows sit behind.

Two cars are parked in the driveway. One is a twenty-year-old Dodge pickup, the other a sedan of some kind hidden under an off-white car cover. No way to tell if their presence means somebody's home or not.

As I drive down the block, two men who've been talking in front of another home stop their conversation long enough to watch us pass, reinforcing my neighborhood-watch concerns.

I turn left when I reach the end of the block and am pleasantly surprised to discover an alley running behind the houses. Since Sanchez is clearly part of whatever operation set up and killed David Weeks, and is at least tangentially involved in Naomi's death, I'm hesitant about making a direct approach and knocking on his front door. Given the likely tightknit makeup of the area, even the thought of a clandestine approach on the street side of the house makes me uncomfortable.

Coming at it from the alley, though? Now that's something I can get behind.

There are still two issues, however. The first, and probably the most important, is that we don't know for sure if this is indeed Sanchez's house. Could be, the address O'Sullivan obtained is as fake as the documents the forger created for the guy. (Well, except for the Harrison ID, which is real though the name is fake.)

The second issue is one I expect a little pushback on from Jar. Though the alley does give us a more appealing path to the home, it would be a mistake to do anything before dark.

I tell Jar as much after I park at a Sonic Burger a block away.

As I predicted, her response is not positive. "You have limited our time already, and now you want to waste more waiting?"

"It's too risky right now. We wait until everyone's settled in for the night, then we go in."

"That will be even later."

"You know it's the right thing to do."

She stews for a moment, looking frustrated. "Maybe," she says. "But this will reduce the time we will have to do anything about what we might learn there. Nate, I *need* to solve this."

An image of eight-year-old Jar racing from the brothel flashes in my mind. There are still over thirty-six hours left until our Sunday morning cutoff time, but I say, "How about I extend the deadline twenty-four hours, to Monday morning? That will more than make up for any wasted time."

She cocks her head. "Monday eight a.m.?"

"Yes."

Her hand shoots toward me. "Deal."

I shake it. "Let's find a home base. I don't know about you, but I'm pretty sure I'll want to sleep for a while after we pay Sanchez a visit."

Jar is looking at her laptop. I can see a map on the screen and assume she's looking up hotels.

But when she speaks, she says, "Since we have a little time, there is something else we can check first."

"Something else?"

"Yes. Please return to the I-10 and go west."

My eyes narrow. "Did you just trick me into giving you more time for no reason?"

"I never asked for more time. You offered it."

She closes her computer, sits back against the seat, and looks out the windshield. My gaze remains on my sneaky friend.

"Technically, perhaps. But that's not quite accurate."

She turns to me. "Why are we not moving?"

The sun is about twenty minutes from setting when we reach our destination.

When Jar said go west, I didn't realize she meant into the middle of nowhere, because that's where it feels like we are.

Okay, not exactly *nowhere*. A sign a little way back declared this area as Crestville. It's more a wide spot in the road than a town, though. The one business I've seen is a rundown café that I'm not even sure is open anymore. Around this is a smattering of houses—a dozen, maybe—spread over a mile or two of desert.

We're stopped in the middle of a road that I doubt sees more traffic than ten cars a week. To my left is a dirt driveway leading to a mobile home. To be more accurate, the remains of a mobile home.

I pull onto the dirt road and park about ten meters from the trailer before we get out and walk over.

The metal frame is scarred black from a fire, as are the few remaining bits and pieces of the exterior walls extending from it. The rest is pretty much all ash or rubble.

I walk all the way around the house, stopping on occasion for a closer inspection of things that catch my eye.

When I return to where Jar is waiting, I say, "Couldn't have happened more than two months ago. Probably less."

I have experience with fires. I know what to look for. I know how to tell, within reason, the general time frame of when a blaze took place. I also know how to tell the difference between an accident and arson, even if the clues are subtle and easily missed by most, like they are here.

"Whoever did this started it in the kitchen," I say, pointing at an area on the other side of the trailer, where some blackened pipes poke out of the floor.

Jar nods but says nothing.

The home in front of us belonged to David Weeks, which is indeed his real name. Jar was able to confirm that during our drive between Starbucks and Sanchez's house. What she didn't run across was any news of a fire. But, really, why would she have? Few, if anyone, would be interested in the destruction of a mobile home way out here in Crestville. It's probably noted in county fire department records somewhere, but there was no reason for Jar to check those.

"Come on," I say. "Let's see if someone knows what happened."

Weeks's closest neighbor is a quarter-mile away, but there are no lights in the windows and no vehicle parked outside, so we drive on.

Now that it's starting to get dark, the sign on top of the café is lit. Apparently, I was wrong about the place.

We park out front and go in. Out of the seven tables in the dining area, only one is occupied. The old guy sitting there has a plate of something brown in front him, but he stops eating when we enter and his eyes follow us all the way up to the counter.

I see a cook in the kitchen, but no one else around. "Excuse me," I say.

The cook looks up from what he's doing, gives me a nod, and heads over. As he approaches the counter, he pulls two menus off a very short stack and holds them out to us. "Sit anywhere and call out when you're ready to order."

"Actually, I just have a question."

His congenial expression fades. "Oh." He points north. "The interstate's that way."

"No. We're not lost," I say.

His brow furrows. "Then what do you need?"

I contemplate showing him my FBI badge but decide against it, thinking it might make him clam up even more.

"We're looking for someone."

This does not improve his demeanor. "Who?"

"A man named David Weeks. We drove by his trailer but it was—"

"Burned down?"

"That's right. Do you know what happened?"

"Uh-huh. His trailer burned down."

Helpful answers are really not this guy's strong suit. "Do you know when it happened?"

He shrugs.

"Please, I'm just asking for a little information."

"And why would that be?"

"We're private investigators. We were hired to find—"

"She looks a little young to be an investigator."

"She's older than you think."

"He is training me," Jar says.

I can't tell if he believes us or not, but instead of making another comment about her, he says, "What are you investigating?"

"We were hired by his aunt's estate," I say.

"Estate?" He sneers. "She leave him some money?"

"A little, but mostly some family heirlooms. She lost touch with him several years ago, so that's why the estate came to us."

"Is that right?"

I can tell he's starting to believe me.

"But if you can't help us, we'll try to find someone else. We appreciate your time."

I start to turn away.

"Hold on now," he says. He looks past us toward the old man at the table. "Hey, Jerry, when did David burn himself up?"

"Let me see," the guy says. "Last month, for sure. Maybe the second to last week, something like that. I had a doctor's appointment on the twenty-third, and I know it wasn't too much before that."

"You said he burned himself up?" I say. "He died in the fire?"

"Yeah, not a great way to go," the cook says.

"Someone found a body?"

"That's how it usually happens."

"And it was positively ID'd as Mr. Weeks?"

"From what I understand, he was all charred up and..." He curls the fingers on both his hands as if he's going to grab something, and tenses the muscles all the way up to his shoulders. What he's describing is the pugilistic stance seen in bodies burned in fires, when muscles stiffen and contract. I've seen it many times. It's not a pleasant sight.

I nod, letting him know I understand what he means.

"Cora Vance was the one who found him," he says. "The way she described it, I'm not sure anyone could have made a one hundred percent positive ID. But he certainly hasn't come in here since then, so who else could it be?"

"I had to ask," I say. "This is not what we expected to find, and I'm sure our client will have questions. Need to make sure I can answer them as best as I can. About the fire, did you mean he set it himself?"

"That's what they said. Not on purpose. His place was old, and I don't think he kept it up very well. If he had, it probably wouldn't have burned down."

"They? Fire investigators?"

He snorted. "We're not in the city here, buddy. At most, the sheriffs gave his trailer a quick look around. But I can't imagine he'd set it deliberately. You ask me, it was probably faulty wiring."

"So, who's going to get his inheritance now that he's dead?" Jerry asks.

I look over at him. "No clue. I'm just supposed to find Mr. Weeks. I don't know anything else."

"Probably them lawyers will keep it. That's the kind of thing those people do."

"I really have no idea." I turn back to the cook. "Did you know him well?"

"As well as anyone could, I guess. He'd come in here once or twice a week."

"How long did he live out here?"

"I'm not sure. At least ten years. Jerry?"

"That's about right, I think," Jerry says. "He used to live in the city. If I remember right, he said he was a truck driver."

Beside me, Jar starts fiddling with her phone.

"Did he say why he stopped and moved out here?" I ask.

"Nope. Never did."

"I have a question," Jar says. She holds her phone out, the screen facing the cook. "Did you ever see Mr. Weeks with one of these men?"

He looks at the display. I lean forward a bit so that I can see it, too. The image is from the Tucson train station, of Men A, B, and C standing together on the platform, not long before the Sunset Limited left. She has cropped it as close as she can without losing too much detail.

His eyes widen. "Actually, I have." He points at Man B. "Him." Though we don't know for sure, Jar and I both suspect B is Juan Sanchez. "They ate here one night. David said he was someone he used to work with. I thought he was joking because the kid couldn't have been much more than thirty. But when I called him on it, David said they'd known each other since the kid was a teen. I don't know. Maybe he was yanking my chain."

"Can I see that?" Jerry asks.

Jar walks over and shows it to him.

"I've never seen any of these people. Sorry."

"It is all right," she says. "Thank you."

I pull a twenty out of my pocket and set it on the counter. "We appreciate your time." I walk over and give another twenty to Jerry to forestall any complaining, then Jar and I head outside.

"Good call on the picture," I say.

"Thank you."

"At least now we know how Weeks was recruited."

"We do."

"I doubt anyone mentioned the job he was offered involved dying, though."

"That is something we can ask Sanchez about tonight."

"It is indeed."

We find a seedy motel called The Desert Lantern, about a mile away from Sanchez's house. It's single story and U-shaped, with a parking lot and a fenced-in swimming pool (empty) in the middle. It's the kind of place Norman Bates would have felt at home managing. I snag the two rooms at the opposite end of the U from the office and use mine to take a nap.

When I wake, Jar shows me county records she found that confirm the house in Goodyear is owned by a man named Juan Sanchez. Whether he's our Juan Sanchez or not, we will find out soon enough.

We grab dinner down the street, then take another drive through Sanchez's neighborhood. Most of the houses have lights blazing. Several have opened their curtains, allowing us to see families moving around inside. I imagine if this was summer, a good portion of the residents would be sitting on chairs in their front yards, shooting the breeze. The area has that kind of vibe. But it's too cold for that right now.

Unlike elsewhere, no lights shine from Sanchez's house, not inside or out, and yet the two vehicles from earlier are still in the driveway. If Sanchez is away, he either has a third car or someone picked him up.

I turn again at the end of the block and drive slowly by the opening to the alley. The passageway is wonderfully dim, the only illumination coming from a handful of backyards' floodlights. In a few hours, the alley would be even darker.

Back at the hotel we change into black clothing and pack our gear into a single backpack. We don't need to take too much —lockpicks, the hard-drive cloner, collapsible batons, rope, duct tape, a pair of loaded dart guns, and a few other items that might come in handy.

By ten p.m., Jar is getting so antsy that I decide we might as well leave. Ideally I don't want to climb over Sanchez's back fence until after eleven, so I drive us around Goodyear, mapping out potential escape routes I'm sure we'll never use.

When the top of the hour finally comes, I turn back toward our target.

On our previous trips, we turned down Sanchez's street from a wide thoroughfare dotted with businesses, such as the Sonic Burger Jar and I stopped at earlier. The alley empties onto the same main drag. Though the road is busier than those in the neighborhood, we'll draw much less attention parking here than we would on one where the houses are. There's an open spot right next to the alley entrance. Hopefully it's a sign things will go smoothly tonight. (No, I don't actually believe in signs, but then again, I do talk to a ghost sometimes, so...)

We don our gloves while we wait for a lull in traffic. When it comes, we exit the car and slip into the alley. Cinder block is the building material of choice for the fences that line the passageway, essentially creating a single long wall, broken only by gates behind each property. From a couple of the houses we pass, I hear the low rumble of TVs, but otherwise most places are quiet and dark.

Both Jar and I count the homes until we reach number nine, Sanchez's place. Like his neighbors', a wooden gate is built into his back wall. It's tall and solid and looks as if it hasn't been opened in years. I try to peek into the backyard through the space between the gate and the wall, but the opening is narrow and all I see is darkness.

Jar uses a special app on her phone to scan for any nearby security devices.

"There is an alarm on the house, but it's not activated. The backyard appears to be clean."

"No cameras?"

"None connected to the alarm system, and nothing else showing up on his Wi-Fi."

I scoop up some pebbles from the road and toss them into the backyard. They hit the ground in a muted rain of plops that should be loud enough to rouse any dog sleeping outside, but there's no response.

I give it a few more seconds in case someone inside did hear the noise and is coming out to check. But the backyard remains quiet.

"Comms on," I say.

We both turn on our earpieces.

"Ready?"

She nods.

I interlock my fingers, creating a cradle into which Jar puts her foot. I lift her until she's leaning over the top. She stays tucked against the wall to cut down on her shadow, raises her legs until her whole body lies across the top of the block, and then slips down the other side.

"On the ground," she says. "Scanning." A few seconds pass, then, "No motion detector lights, and the curtains are closed."

"Copy. Coming over."

I pull myself up the wall, curl over the top, and land with

barely a sound, like I've done this a thousand times. (Which, give or take, is about right.)

Sanchez's backyard boasts arid landscaping similar to what's in the front. It has a few extras, like an outdoor kitchen with a built-in barbecue off to the left, and a storage shed tucked into the back corner on the right. Off the house, covering a concrete slab that butts up against a sliding glass door, is a cloth awning, and sitting on the slab is an old redwood-style picnic table. The sliding door isn't the only way into the house, however. There's also a regular door near the right corner.

I give Jar a nod, and we move to the house. Though sliding doors are usually simple to unlock, they tend to make a very distinctive sound when opening, and I've been trained to use alternatives whenever possible. We creep to the other door.

Jar checks her app again to make sure the alarm is still off. Once she gives me the okay, I pick the lock and turn the knob. When I push inward, one of the hinges starts to squeak. I stop and retrieve a small can of WD-40, slip one end of the attached red straw through the gap between the door and the jamb, and spray the lower hinge. I repeat the process with the upper one.

This time when I push, the door glides open without a peep.

The house breathes stillness in a way that makes it feel like no one's been home in days. If that's the case, then I hope Sanchez left something behind that will be useful to us. I step inside and Jar follows.

We've entered a laundry room. The washer and dryer are avocado green and look nearly as old as the house. An open box of powdered detergent sits on a shelf above the appliances, two big bottles of bleach beside it. In the corner leans a broom, with a dustpan resting against it on the floor.

The other thing I notice is that it's as cold inside as it was out, which means it's been awhile since the heater was run. This reinforces my feeling Sanchez isn't simply out for the evening, but has been gone for at least twenty-four hours, probably longer.

That's unfortunate. I was really hoping we could talk.

There's a door between the laundry room and the rest of the house. It's not shut all the way, but almost. I test it first for squeaks, then pull it open.

That's when I get the first whiff.

Behind me, Jar lets out a gasp.

Our evening has just taken a hard left turn.

From the small front pocket of the backpack, I pull out a container of menthol scented gel. It's one of those things I need on the day job, so I always keep some in my go kit. I scoop out a dollop, hand the canister to Jar, and spread the gel above my upper lip, right below my nose.

It's great at masking nasty odors, like garbage cans baking in the sun, teenaged boys' unwashed laundry, and decomposing bodies. The first two don't apply in this case.

I'm all but certain no one else is in the house now, not alive anyway, but I proceed with caution all the same.

The smell leads us into the master bedroom, where the body of a man lies facedown on the floor near the foot of the bed. I can't see his features from where I am, but I have a sinking feeling we've found Juan Sanchez.

"No visible blood stain," Jar whispers.

I nod. If there is a stain, it's hidden under the corpse.

I move around until I'm between the body and the bed, turn on my flashlight, and shine it into the side of the dead man's head.

Even with his discolored skin and slack face, I can tell it's Man B from the train station video. Dead bodies are a specialty of mine. Not creating them, but getting rid of them. Don't judge me. It's a living.

Since the body is lying in the master bedroom of Juan

Sanchez's house, I think we can operate under the assumption that Sanchez and Man B are one and the same.

The corpse's condition makes it seem Sanchez hasn't been dead more than three days. But the house is cold. Freezing, really. Temperatures like this will slow decomposition, so it's possible he's been this way for at least a week. Maybe even as much as ten days.

I check the nearby furniture, wondering if he tripped and hit his head against anything. But I find no evidence of that.

There's nothing else to do but check the body itself. I lift Sanchez's head, looking for abrasions, but stop when my flash-light's beam reflects off something partially tucked under his torso. It appears to be translucent plastic.

"Help me roll him on his side," I say. "But we've got to be careful. We don't want him to fall apart."

"That would be inadvisable."

She kneels on the other side of the body.

"Hold on to him here and here." I point first at Sanchez's right shoulder, and then at his hip. When she's ready, I say, "We'll only move him enough so I can get a look underneath him. Slowly on three. One. Two. Three."

She pulls while I push. "That's enough," I say.

Not only can I now see the plastic item, I also have a view of the man's left arm, which is tucked under his body.

"Can you hold him by yourself?" I say.

"Yes."

I open my phone's camera and take several pictures.

"Okay, let's set him back down."

After we return Sanchez to his resting position, I examine the points we touched and am happy to see we've left no visible marks.

"What did you find?" Jar asks.

I show her the first picture I took. On the floor below

Sanchez's body is a syringe. What initially caught my attention was the end of the plastic plunger. Also featured in the image is a band of rubber tubing, tied around the body's left arm.

When Jar's eyes narrow, I know she's thinking the same thing I am.

While this looks like an unintentional overdose, the tableau is eerily similar to that of Weeks's death in L.A. So much so that the color and placement of the rubber tourniquet on Sanchez's arm is an exact match to the one we saw in photographs of Weeks's body from the police file.

It's as if someone thought, It worked well the first time, why not do it again?

And why not? It's not like whoever did this would have any reason to believe the police would—or even could—link Sanchez's death to Weeks's.

"They are covering everything up," Jar says. "What is it they say in American movies? Throwing away loose ends?"

"Tying up."

"I am sorry. Tying up loose ends. Thank you."

No argument there. Weeks and now Sanchez. Makes me wonder if the other two watchers have "killed" themselves, too.

Chances are whoever did this to Sanchez has taken anything of interest, but we search the house anyway. If he owned a computer, it's gone now. We also can't find his mobile phone. Everyone has a mobile phone. I look for hidey-holes where he may have stashed something, while Jar checks the furniture for hidden compartments.

When I hunt through the closet near the front door, I find a jacket that looks like the one Sanchez was wearing at the train station. In the inside pocket, I find four pieces of crumpled paper. Three are wrappers for Halls cough drops. The last is a receipt, dated the Sunday I found Naomi's body. It's from a CVS store in Hollywood, California. If we needed any more proof that Sanchez was in L.A. not long after the murder, here it is.

Jar comes up from behind me and asks, "Find something?"

I hand her the receipt and shine my flashlight on it.

She studies it, nods, and puts it in her pocket. "I will check security footage. Maybe he was not alone."

A glance at my watch tells me we've been inside nearly twenty minutes. Though I'm confident we could stay all night without being discovered, my natural instinct is to get out of here as soon as possible.

And let's not forget the smell. That hasn't gone away. If we stay too long, we're going to have to take all-night showers just to get the stink out of our hair. I'm pretty sure it's already too late for our clothes.

Before we go, though, there's something I need to do.

When I walk back into the master bedroom, I'm hit with a new wave of stink from the body. Technically it's not new; the gel under my nose is just losing its strength. And while I can tolerate the smell of the dead more than most people can, it's still not something I actively search out.

I move to the bedroom window that looks out at Sanchez's neighbor to the north, and pull the curtain back to peek outside. The other house is about three meters away, just enough room for a fence and two narrow walkways down the middle. The other home also has a window. It's not directly across from the one where I am, but not far off. It's shut and no lights are on behind the shade.

I undo the latch holding Sanchez's window closed and push up on it, as gently as possible. It creaks a bit, but not loudly enough to be heard by anyone. When the sill clears the frame by about five centimeters, I stop.

The gap should be wide enough for the body's odor to drift

through. And in a day or so, maybe even less, someone will notice and call the police.

———

Jar goes over the fence into the alley first. Before I can pull myself up the wall, she whispers over the comm, "Hold."

I press against the fence, thinking she must have spotted someone in the alley. A few moments later, she says, "All right. It's clear."

I climb over and crouch down next to her. "What happened?"

"There was someone down at that end." She's looking in the direction we need to go. "But I think they were just walking by."

I scan the area. Everything looks quiet. "Did they see you?"

"I don't think so."

We remain there for a full minute, our attention focused on where the shadow was. But whoever, or whatever, she saw appears to have gone.

CHAPTER ELEVEN

———————————

Did you know there are exactly forty-seven water spots on the ceiling of my motel room? Some of them are small and hard to see, but they're there. I've counted them. Three times already.

I wonder how they got up there. Did a previous guest take a shower and then do a hair flip without drying off first?

Is it even water?

I hope it's water.

God, why am I still awake?

Because you know.

Liz may not be the reason I can't sleep at three a.m., but she seems content to keep me company.

And she's right. I do know why my brain refuses to switch off.

When Jar and I arrived in Arizona, I figured we'd anonymously pass on any leads we found to the cops and that would be that.

Now I'm not so sure that's a good idea.

It's not that I don't trust the LAPD, but there's a lot more going on here than I expected. And if we did leave it in their hands, the time it would take them to get up to speed and unravel everything could very well mean Naomi's killer or killers would get away.

Or worse, Liz whispers.

Thanks. I was trying not to acknowledge that possibility, but yeah. The potential of more deaths is something I'd like to prevent, too.

I'm not going to be able to let this one go, am I?

Of course you're not.

Dammit.

You need to see this through.

"Yeah, I know."

My acceptance appears to quiet her. Good. Maybe I'll be able to sleep now.

Don't say it.

I already know.

Sleep might be a smart idea, but what I really need is a good therapist.

I guess I must have drifted off, because the next thing I know sunlight is bleeding through the curtains and someone is knocking on my door.

It has to be Jar. I mean, who else would it be?

"Hold on," I yell.

I pull myself out of bed and stumble across the room.

As I open the door, I say, "What time is—"

I don't finish because standing on the other side is not Jar but a police officer. In the parking lot, a second cop is leaning against a squad car idling behind our Accord.

"Can I help you?" I ask.

"Sorry to wake you, sir," the man says, "but are you the owner of that car?" He points at the Honda.

The first thought that races through my mind is that Sanchez's body has been found and someone *did* see us at his house. But I can't tell from the cop's behavior if he suspects me of murder or is doing some kind of random room check.

"It's a friend's car but I'm using it."

He glances past me. "Is your friend here?"

"No. I borrowed it from him."

Anytime we get a vehicle from a supplier, we're given contact information for the name on the registration. In this case, the Honda's owner is listed as a guy named Peter Hall. The registration will hold up. That's part of the deal with suppliers like the one we used, and why it costs us a lot more than Hertz would. If anyone calls the phone number I have for Hall, someone purporting to be him would answer and confirm he loaned the car to us.

"Is there something wrong?" I ask.

"I'm sorry to tell you this, but it looks like someone broke into your friend's car last night."

Any relief I might have felt at not being questioned about Sanchez's murder is undercut by the thought of someone finding the secret compartments in the Accord's trunk—and taking the pistols hidden there.

"What? When?"

"About forty-five minutes ago."

"Did they break anything? Is there—" I stop myself. "Give me a moment to put something on. I'll be right out."

I exchange the gym shorts and T-shirt I slept in for jeans and a hoodie and pull on my sneakers without any socks.

When I open the door, I see the cop who came to the door has joined his colleague in the parking lot. What I don't see is any obvious damage to our car.

I hurry to the vehicle and look through the driver's-side window. Nothing seems to be out of place. When the officers see me, they head my way.

I'm about to ask why they think someone broke in when I notice the trunk is not completely shut.

A chill runs through me. Granted, it would be extremely difficult for anyone who didn't know about the hidden compartments to find and open them. But that doesn't mean it's impossible.

I walk around, intending to open the trunk, but the cop who knocked on my door says, "Sir, please don't do that."

"I just want to see if anything's missing."

"It hasn't been checked for fingerprints yet. A tech is on the way from the station."

There's absolutely nothing about what he said that makes me happy. Both Jar and I have touched the trunk, but that's not my biggest worry. Our prints aren't on file anywhere, so they won't set off any alarms. My concern centers around the supplier Jar got the car from, and the people who work for him. If any of their prints are in the system and one of them touched the car, things could get ugly very quickly.

But I can't appear uncooperative. Jar will have to work her magic to make any prints the police find disappear from their system.

"Oh, okay," I say. "How did you know someone broke in?"

The officer nodded toward the motel's office. "The night manager saw a guy looking inside your trunk. When he called out to him, the guy ran off. The manager lowered the lid then called us."

"Were any other cars broken into?"

"We had a look around. Nothing else appeared disturbed. I think it was just yours."

"Lucky me." I glance at the back of the Accord. "The

trunk's unlatched. Can't we at least push it up with something? I want to make sure everything's okay."

The cops exchange a glance, then the talkative one nods and pulls his baton from his belt. "Sure."

The trunk is completely empty, which is exactly how Jar and I left it. But I can't let my new cop buddies know that.

"Dammit," I say, frowning.

"Something missing?"

"There was a present for a friend. A vase. It wasn't that expensive, but..." My face is tense with the indignation of the made-up theft. "Can we check to make sure he didn't take the tire?"

The cop looks skeptical. "I'm sure the manager would have seen that."

"Please."

The cop peers inside the trunk, sticks the end of his baton into the handhold along the edge of the carpet, and awkwardly levers up the floor.

The tire looks untouched, and more importantly, so do the areas around the hidden compartments. I won't be entirely relaxed until I can open them and look inside, but that will have to wait until the police are gone.

"Thank you," I say.

The officer lowers the cover and says, "If you don't mind, we'd like to get some information."

"Uh, yeah, sure."

After giving him the alias I'm traveling under, my faux contact information, and that of fictitious car owner Peter Hall, I give them a description of the "missing vase," and then am allowed to go back to my room. The moment I shut my door, my phone rings.

"What was that all about?" Jar asks.

As I suspected, she's been watching from her window.

I gave her a quick rundown.

"Just our car?" she says.

"Yes."

A pause. "I do not like that."

"Neither do I," I say. "Stay in your room until they leave. I don't want you pulled into this."

After we hang up, I peel a curtain back to peek at what's going on.

The two police officers have been joined by a woman wearing dark pants and a blue jacket. She's taking a close look at the Accord's trunk, which I take to mean she's the fingerprint tech.

I glance toward the motel office. The view is partially blocked by other cars in the lot, but I can still see three people standing outside the office door, watching the police from afar. One is the guy who checked us in the day before. Another is a woman I saw pushing around a housekeeping cart when we carried our bags to our rooms. The last is a guy I haven't seen before, but he's wearing an identical red polo shirt to the other guy, right down to the gold splotch on his breast. I'm too far away to read it from here, but I remember from yesterday that the splotch is the name of the motel, with the not exactly original tagline underneath: HAVE A NICE STAY.

Is he the night manager? If so, his shift is either over or close to it, and it's unlikely he'll be hanging around for much longer.

I step back outside, which draws the attention of the cops again.

"Any idea how much longer you're going to be?" I ask.

"We'll let you know."

The tech glances up and says, "This is your car?"

"Yeah."

"Shouldn't take me more than fifteen minutes." She glances

at the officers. "I don't know if there's anything else you guys have to do."

"When you're done, we're done," the officer says.

"Fifteen minutes, then," the tech says to me. "But I'll need to get a sample of your prints before I leave so we can eliminate those you made."

She has no idea how cold my skin just turned. "Sure. No problem. I'll be back in a few minutes."

I take the walkway around the U and to the office, the trio of motel employees watching me the whole time.

As I near them, the manager who checked me in says, "Your car, right?"

I nod. "I hear one of you saw what happened."

He points his chin at his red-shirt twin and says, "Adrian did."

"Can you tell me what he looked like?" I ask the night manager.

Adrian shrugs. "Normal, I guess. He was wearing a nice coat—you know, puffy, for the cold."

"You saw him from inside the office?"

He shakes his head. "Thought I heard something, so I stepped outside and there he was, with your trunk open. I assumed it was his car and he was getting an early start on the day, but when I started to walk over to let him know we had coffee in the office, he ran."

"Did you get a look at his face?"

"Not really. He had one of those knit beanies on his head, wore it pretty low. And he never looked in my direction."

"Bummer. I do appreciate you scaring him off, though. Thanks."

A little laugh. "I didn't mean to, but...you're welcome."

"Did he take anything?" This question comes from the woman.

"Only a present for a friend," I say.

"He didn't look like he had anything with him when he took off," Adrian says.

"It wasn't that big. Probably had it under his coat."

We all silently watch the cops for a minute or so, before the day manager glances at me uneasily and says, "Just so you know, we're not liable. But...I, um, guess I can give you a discount on your rooms."

After the tech takes my fingerprints and she and the two officers leave, I wait for thirty minutes before I carry my suitcase and our gear bags out to the Accord. Before stowing them, I check the secret compartments. Everything is there, thank God. After I close the trunk, I open the back driver's-side door and lean inside.

I check the seat backs first, making sure they're locked in place. The one on this side doesn't budge. But when I grab the one on the other, it pulls free with only a nudge.

Not good.

I knock on the door to Jar's room. When it opens, she's standing there with her bag in her hand.

"Anything?" she whispers.

I tell her about the backseat and then we head to the Accord.

Neither of us says a thing during our fifteen-minute drive to a parking garage serving St. Joseph's Hospital. There, I find an empty spot on the third level and kill the engine.

Jar plugs a pencil-shaped sensor into her phone and begins scanning the car for electronic bugs. While she does this, I slide my chair backward and run a hand under the dash and around the steering wheel.

When I feel nothing unusual, I move on to examining the center console, then search the space between it and my seat. Once more, everything seems normal.

I get out, open the back door, and glance under the driver's seat. A couple of coins, a golf tee, and the cap to a plastic water bottle, but that's it.

I'm starting to think the break-in was random when Jar reaches back, taps me on the arm, and shows me her screen. Her app has detected a signal.

She points at the backseat and hands me her phone.

I sweep the wand over the cushions, and when I'm almost to the other side, the signal spikes.

I back out of the car and grab a pair of durable thin rubber gloves from my suitcase in the trunk. After donning them, I return to the backseat, slip my fingers into the crease between the upright and bottom cushions—where the signal is strongest —and work them down until they hit a solid object that I'm sure shouldn't be there. The edge I've touched is straight and about as long as my little finger.

I glance at Jar, letting her know I found something, then tentatively push against the object to see if it will move.

It does.

Carefully, I work a finger under the bottom cushion and push the obstruction upward.

A few seconds later, an iPhone pops onto the backseat. I touch the power button and the screen lights up. It's not one of the newer models. I'd guess it's at least three generations old. And though it's getting a strong, four-bar signal, it doesn't appear to be in active call mode.

I check the battery strength. One hundred percent. Even in standby mode, if the phone has been tucked between the cushions for more than a few hours, the battery would be down at least a few percentage points by now. The same would be true if it had an app running in the background, for example one that would record everything within range of the microphone. So, I'm fairly sure it's currently not being used as a listening device.

What I think it's actually being used for is something we refer to in the business as a lazy man's tracker.

Used smartphones can be found on the cheap pretty much anywhere. Turn on its share-location function, hide it in someone else's vehicle, and boom, instant tracking bug.

I can't help but look out the window to see if anyone is watching us, but our parking level is as deserted as it was when we arrived. Of course, there's no reason for whoever put this here to be within visual range. In fact, I'd be willing to bet he or she (or they) will keep a few blocks away from us for a while.

Jar and I exit the vehicle, leaving the iPhone on the seat, and walk a dozen cars away. Again, I don't think the phone is recording us, but as I say ad nauseam, it's best to be cautious.

"Someone *did* see us last night," Jar says, "and followed us back to the hotel."

I nod. It's the only possibility that makes sense.

She frowns. "But why wait until the night is almost over to put the bug in the car?"

"Maybe they had to talk to someone first. It also could have taken them a while to round up a phone they could use."

She gives me a look I can't completely read.

"What?" I ask.

She hesitates. "Nothing. It is just...nothing."

"Jar. We don't hide things from each other, remember?"

Another pause. "You sound angry."

I am angry. Angry that someone followed us last night and put a makeshift tracking bug in our car. Angry that the police now have my fingerprints. Angry that Naomi's young life ended at the bottom of a hill in Griffith Park. Angry that David Weeks has been framed for something he couldn't have done and was killed to keep the truth a secret. Angry that Juan Sanchez was murdered before we could talk to him.

Oh. I get what Jar means now.

It's not my anger per se she's reacting to. It's that my anger speaks to how this case is starting to take ahold of me and become personal. Like all my hobby missions eventually do.

"No more deadline, okay?" I say. "We see this through to the end. But what I said before about telling me everything still applies. Don't hold anything back."

"I won't." Her eyes lock onto mine. "Thank you."

I don't feel as if I'm doing any favors here, so I don't want her thanks. If anything, I'm feeling guilty that I put limits on our involvement in the first place.

I say, "You think you can crack the phone and track down who's trying to follow us?"

She smiles. "That is a stupid question."

We stop at a place called Jody's Coffee and Pancakes and choose a table that allows me to keep an eye on our car and the area around it. Jar sits across the booth from me, her laptop in front of her. Beside it are the two pieces of toast, side of bacon, and cup of coffee she ordered. I've come to realize it's her standard breakfast when Thai food is not available.

We left the iPhone in the car but it's within Bluetooth range, allowing Jar to access it from here. If we brought it inside with us, those tracking it would see its location move into the building and realize we've found it.

As for me, I'm diving into a plate of Jody's Famous Pancakes, doused liberally with Jody's Real Maple Syrup, and thinking about Naomi's past.

About her kidnapping and confinement.

Yes, her murderer could have come from some other part of her life, and I know we can't rule out that possibility, but none seem as likely. Okay, sure, maybe when she was in the army, she came across information she shouldn't have and no one realized it until recently. Perhaps she was going to pass it on to someone in the press. Or maybe she wasn't as good a person as Jar seems to think she was, and was using the information to blackmail someone. Possible? Yes. Likely? My gut says no. And the other segments of her life seem even less likely.

That's why I keep circling back to those horrible eighteen months of her youth and her heroic escape.

According to the FBI files, Naomi told the police and federal agents there were two kidnappers she saw almost every day, and a third who came in maybe once a month and never said a word in her presence. They all wore masks and gloves anytime they were around her so she never saw their faces. The best she could do was describe their body types and the voices of the two main ones. Unfortunately, there were few distinctive details that could be used to identify the perpetrators, other than they were either lightly tanned Caucasians or light-skinned Hispanics or Asians or maybe Native Americans. This was based on their necks, which were seldom covered, and on times when a shirtsleeve was pulled back and she saw a wrist or forearm.

She'd been held in the basement of a remote building, miles from anything else. And calling it a building is a generous term, because the pictures in the file show only parts of a single wall still standing, and the concrete floor covering the basement, most of which was buried under dirt. After she escaped, the kidnappers set fire to the room, destroying any evidence that might have been left behind.

In the first few years after Naomi saved herself, about a half dozen people were questioned and cleared. Then the leads dried up and the case went cold.

If I have to name anyone as my top suspects in her murder, it would be her trio of kidnappers, perhaps worried someday she would expose them, or simply angry she got away. Maybe it had taken them so long to come after her because they had only recently learned of the alias she was using.

As right as this feels, there is a part of me that says, Why come after her now at all? They'd gotten away with what they had done—why tempt fate?

"Nate?" Jar says.

I look up from my breakfast.

Her head is tilted to the side, her expression concerned. "Did you hear me?"

"You mean when you just said my name?"

"No. Before that."

Oops. Talk about lost in thought. "Sorry. What did you say?"

"That I am in."

It takes me a moment to understand she's hacked into the iPhone. If law enforcement organizations knew she could do that so quickly, they'd keep her constantly busy. If, that is, she'd actually work for them. "And?"

"The call logs have been cleared and all messages and emails deleted."

"*Deleted* deleted? Or...?"

She doesn't exactly grin, but she does have that look she gets when she's about to demonstrate exactly how smart she is. "Not deleted deleted. It should take no more than an hour for everything to be recovered."

That's the thing most people forget. Deleting something from your phone or computer usually doesn't erase it. To do that, you need to write over it or wipe the drive.

"And the people tracking us?" I ask.

"The next time someone checks the phone's location, I will have them."

"Good work."

She gives me a quick smile, then begins tapping on her keyboard again.

My mind drifts back to what I was thinking about, and a new question pops into my mind. But it's one we could probably answer without much effort.

"Do you know what happened to Naomi's stuff?"

Jar glances up at me. "You mean from her apartment?"

"Yeah. The LAPD wouldn't have taken it. And it's been over a month now. I can't image it's still sitting in her old apartment. The owners would want to rent the place out as soon as they got the all-clear from the police."

"In Thailand, if family didn't claim it within a week or two, the owner would probably sell what he could and throw the rest away. Is it the same here?"

"More of an effort would be made to find family first. There are also laws about leases and how long things need to be held after someone dies, I think."

"So, what would they do with everything if they were still looking for family but wanted to rent the room?"

"I'm not sure."

"You are wondering if there is something in her things that might help us."

"I am."

I can see in her eyes she likes this idea. "Do you want me to find a phone number for the apartment manager?"

The manager's name is Andon Kasparian. I wait until we're

back in the car before I call him. In case you're wondering, Jar has tweaked the stowaway iPhone's software so that its microphone can't pick up anything.

After four rings, I'm sent to voicemail. No personalized greeting, only a digitized voice repeating the number I called, followed by a beep.

"Mr. Kasparian, this is Robert Bender from Franklin-Wells Insurance," I say in my most official-sounding voice. "I'm calling in regards to a former tenant of yours named Saundra Moore. I would appreciate it if you could call at your earliest convenience." I recite one of the numbers that would forward his call to my phone, and then I hang up. I glance at Jar's computer. "Anyone ping the phone yet?"

"Not yet."

"Let's see if we can wake them up."

Four minutes later, we're on the freeway, heading toward downtown Phoenix.

When we near the interchange with I-10, Jar says, "Contact."

Her fingers fly over her keys as she works out who just checked on the iPhone's location.

Seconds later, she says, "I have their number."

We transition onto the I-10 eastbound and travel for another minute in silence.

"Got them," she says. "They are following us. Two kilometers back."

We continue east for several miles. Right after the freeway takes a turn to the south, I exit onto Jefferson Street and head east until it transitions into Washington. We are near Sky Harbor Airport, in an area of supply businesses, brewery tap rooms, industrial bakeries, and long-term parking garages.

The Parking Spot is one of the latter. It's a chain you'll find close to airports around the country, where people leave their vehicles while they go on trips. There are two locations in Phoenix, both of which I have been to several times. One is right ahead of us.

When we reach the entrance, I pull up to the attendant booth and roll down my window.

The woman inside smiles and says, "Good morning. Do you have a reservation?"

"No, sorry. Last-minute trip."

"No problem, sir. How long do you plan on being gone?"

"Three days."

"Credit card?"

I hand her a card that's not in my name. (In case you're concerned I'm some kind of deadbeat, I'm not in the business of stiffing people and always pay off my cards, no matter which alias is stamped onto them. I am in the business of stiff people, though. You know, dead, stiff. Never mind. It was funnier in my head.)

When the woman hands me back the card, there's a ticket with it. "Use that when you leave. You'll be charged then. Have a nice trip."

The Parking Spot near Los Angeles International Airport is a multilevel garage, tucked among the hotels off Century Blvd. The one we've entered here in Phoenix is a vast, single-story lot, with a giant roof covering everything from the relentless desert sun.

I find a spot near the middle, between two oversized SUVs.

"They're getting close," Jar says.

"Go. I'll meet you at the shuttle."

She closes her laptop and jumps out of the car with the computer under her arm. After grabbing her backpack, she runs toward the front of the facility.

I exit the car, too, but I'm not going anywhere yet. From the trunk, I grab a dirty T-shirt from my bag and use it to wipe down all surfaces we may have touched, inside and out. I then remove our two suitcases, my backpack, and our gear bags. I stow anything that might cause a problem in the trunk's secret compartments. This completely depletes one of the gear bags and a good portion of the other. I toss the empty bag in the trunk and close everything up.

The last thing I do is make sure the stowaway iPhone is in the same spot I found it, between the cushions of the backseat. If our new friend (or friends) decides to retrieve it, I want to make sure nothing will give the impression we discovered what they did.

With my backpack hanging on the handle of Jar's suitcase, and the remaining duffel over the handle on mine, I wheel the bags toward the shuttle area.

Jar is waiting for me.

"Dark blue Dodge Durango," she said. "Two people in front, one in back."

"Where are they now?"

"Pulled into a parking lot next door."

I'm sure they're wondering if we're leaving town, which is exactly the impression I want to give them.

A Parking Spot shuttle enters the lot a few minutes later and stops near us. When the doors open, the riders coming from the airport pile out, then we and the other waiting passengers climb aboard.

Jar and I take seats that will make it easy for those in the SUV to see us.

I spot the Durango before we come abreast of the parking lot it pulled into. It's right up front, as close to the street as it can get. The moment they see we're in the bus, a guy hops out of the backseat and heads toward the Parking Spot, likely to retrieve the iPhone. The vehicle then heads quickly toward the exit.

Half a block later, the Durango is two car lengths behind us.

The shuttle bus takes us into the airport and to the Terminal 4 departure area, where Jar and I get out. We stop on the sidewalk and I pretend to check something on my phone.

"They are pulling to the curb," she says.

She's positioned to see what's going on behind me without drawing attention.

"The guy in the front passenger seat is getting out. Five centimeters shorter than you. A few years older. Dark hair, almost black, cut short. Looks like he lifts weights a little too much. Gray sweater and dark slacks."

"Got it," I say.

I put my phone away and we head inside, where we stop in front of monitors displaying upcoming flights.

The man enters the terminal a few seconds later. This time, I'm the one better placed to see him. He's decent enough at the tailing game. While he does look in our direction, his gaze moves past us like we're not here. If I wasn't a trained operative, I wouldn't have noticed him.

After a moment, he strolls in our general direction.

"The Houston flight at one thirty-five," I whisper to Jar.

She scans the monitors and nods.

When the man is within hearing distance, I say, "We should get something to eat here."

"I am not that hungry," Jar says.

"The connection in Houston is tight, so it's either now or never."

"Fine. Just, something healthy, okay?"

By now the man has moved far enough beyond us that we can curtail the act. We grab our suitcases and wheel them over to the escalator that will take us up to the security checkpoint.

As we ascend, Jar buys two refundable tickets on the Houston flight. We have to pause right outside the entrance to the security line while she finishes the transaction, but that's fine, because our shadow has not come upstairs yet. By the time he does, the purchase is complete, and Jar has sent me my digital boarding pass.

We show the passes and our IDs to the guard waiting at the entrance, then get in line. We snake our way through, Jar and I talking about nothing in particular as I snap a few clandestine photos of our tail.

The guy is persistent, I'll give him that. Most people would have been satisfied when the guard let us enter the security line. Our shadow stays until we've both cleared the bag and body scanners.

To give him a little time to return to his SUV, we grab a table at a restaurant in the terminal. Not that we plan to eat much. After all, breakfast wasn't that long ago. A cup of coffee each and a sandwich split between us, and it cost only twenty-five dollars. What a deal.

As I'm about to take another bite, my phone rings, the name onscreen ANDON KASPARIAN. I show it to Jar, then swipe ACCEPT. "Robert Bender. How can I help you?"

"Yes, eh, I'm returning your call. This is Andon Kasparian." He has a slight Armenian accent.

"I'm sorry, this is in regards to...?"

"Your message said you wanted to talk to me about one of my former tenants, Saundra Moore."

"Ah, right. Thank you for getting back to me. Can you hold one moment?"

"Yeah, sure."

I put the call on mute, nod at the sandwich, and tell Jar, "Feel free to finish my half if you want."

A little ways down the terminal, I find a gate that has only a few people sitting in its waiting area. It's not perfect, but it will be quieter here than where I was. I put on my earbuds and take the man off mute.

"Thank you for holding. I'm traveling today so I apologize for odd noises. Just waiting for my plane."

"We can talk some other time, if that would be better."

"No, now is actually perfect. I believe I mentioned I work for Franklin-Wells Insurance. I'm calling because I'm trying to close out Naomi's file and—" I pause. "You do know her real name was Naomi, right?"

"I heard that on the news. They talked about what had happened to her as a kid. And now this? What a tragedy. That poor girl."

"She did not get many breaks, that's for sure. As I was saying, I'm closing the file and there's an item I think you can help clear up for me."

"I didn't know her that well, but she was a good tenant. Quiet. Respectful. She never caused any problems."

"You're not the first to say nice things about her." I give it a beat, then say, "Our records indicate she lived in apartment seventeen?"

"That's correct."

"What we're interested in finding out is the whereabouts of the possessions. The ones that were left in her apartment after she died, I mean. Do you know what happened to them?"

"Yes, I do. We moved them to a storage locker."

"They're at your apartment building?" I ask.

"No. Store-U-All, down the street."

"Who's paying for that?"

"We are. I mean, the building's owner. The police told us they were looking for her family. Hopefully, they will find them soon. If not, we'll have to pay for another month, and that money comes out of her security deposit. It would be a shame to waste it like that. She had a policy with you?"

"That's right. Life insurance."

"Then you must be in contact with her family."

"She didn't have any close relatives, so we're in the process of locating someone in her extended family. I could make a note in the file that if we do find someone to have them call you."

"That would be great. Thanks."

"Happy to do it. Now, for our records, could you give me the address of the Store-U-All facility and the unit's number?"

"Yeah. Give me a second. I've got it here somewhere."

After I receive the information and we say our goodbyes, I make one more call.

"Victor? It's Nate."

"Hey, man. What's going on? I take it the Sidewinder cans worked well."

"They did, thank you. Were you able to retrieve the gear?"

"Picked it up last night. Everything looked good. You just checking in, or is there something else I can help you with?"

CHAPTER TWELVE

Victor sends his wiry driver to deliver us a gray Subaru Crosstrek at the airport. On the way, the guy did us the favor of stopping by the Parking Spot garage and collecting the gear we'd left in the Accord.

Once Jar and I take possession of the vehicle, we start tracking those who were tracking us, and find the Durango parked at a Mexican restaurant called Vallarte's in Tempe.

Jar runs its plate and finds the owner is listed as Mateo Yanez. A subsequent search identifies him as a local businessman who owns an interstate trucking company and several properties spread throughout the city, including the building housing Vallarte's.

"You got a picture?" I ask.

Jar turns her screen and shows me the photo from Yanez's driver's license.

Though the only guy from the Durango I had a good look at is the guy who followed us into the airport, I saw enough of the other two to know Yanez isn't one of them.

I check the time. It's 3:40 p.m. "We've got to get you back to the airport."

Jar scowls out the front window, then sighs and says, "All right."

I know she's been hoping the men would come out of Vallarte's before we have to leave, but we haven't had even one glimpse of them.

I pull from the curb and make a U-turn, so that we don't pass directly in front of the restaurant, and head back to the freeway.

There are so many things to follow up on, the only way we'll speed up our progress is if we split up tasks. That's why Jar is flying back to L.A. this afternoon. While I figure out who these assholes in the Durango are, she'll search the storage unit holding Naomi's things.

We reach the departing passenger unloading zone at five minutes after four.

"Be careful," I say.

"You do not need to tell me that."

"I know. But I am."

She hesitates, then says, "I will be."

What follows is an awkward moment when neither of us seems to know what to do. Finally, we move at the same time. Me, reaching over to give her a hug. Jar, reaching for the door.

"Oh," she says. "Um..."

She twists back around and returns my embrace, stiffly at first like always, but not for long.

"If you think you're going to need help," I say, "let me know and I'll get you someone."

"I will not need help."

"I know, but humor me."

"You want me to tell you a joke?"

"That's not what that means. Just... say you'll let me know if you need help."

"I will let you know if I need help."

"Thank you."

When I release her, our eyes lock for a moment before she looks away, embarrassed.

"You be careful, too," she says as she grabs the door handle.

"I will be."

Since she won't be gone that long, she takes only her backpack. When she reaches the terminal entrance, she glances back, gives me a tentative wave, and disappears inside.

She's good for you.

I nearly jump in my seat at the sound of Liz's voice.

Don't ever hurt her.

"Why would I hurt her?"

But Liz has already vanished.

I pull back into traffic, trying desperately to pretend I don't understand what she was implying. After all, what could be more unsettling than the thought of my dead girlfriend playing the role of my matchmaker?

———

I'm almost back to Vallarte's when the dot on my tracker app begins to move.

It's about damn time.

It appears to be headed to the very freeway I'm already on. What I don't know is which direction it will go. If this were any other time of day, I would exit and wait near the on-ramps until I know the answer. But it's 4:34 p.m. and I'm crawling along, trapped in the early stages of Phoenix rush hour. Staying where I am seems as good an option as waiting on a side street. Potentially better, if the dot ends up going in the same direction, and I don't have to get off and on again.

Unfortunately, the traffic gods look unkindly upon me, because getting off and on again is exactly what I end up having to do. By the time I'm able to head in the correct direction, the dot has passed by me and is now nearly a mile ahead.

That might sound like a lot of ground to make up, but the traffic actually helps. Individual drivers can be unpredictable, but a traffic jam, taken in its totality, tends to follow certain patterns and tendencies. (I call it the Hari Seldon psychohistory rule of traffic. I know, you don't get it, but it's funny to me.) If you understand these tendencies, you can exploit them. I spent an entire month doing just that when I was an apprentice operative and have continued to sharpen those skills ever since.

I move up through the pack, playing a real-life game of Frogger, slowly cutting the distance between me and the dot. After about fifteen minutes and a few angry honks, I see the Durango ahead and soon I'm settled three cars behind it.

It's another forty grueling minutes of moving at the speed of annoyance before we get off the freeway.

Interestingly, we are back in Goodyear, home of the recently departed Juan Sanchez. We do not, however, end up going to the same working-class neighborhood. Instead the Durango leads me south, past all the housing developments and over a ridge. According to my map, I'm still in Goodyear, but there's a hell of a lot of open desert between where I am now and the last buildings I passed.

After coming down the other side of the ridge and turning onto Estrella Parkway, I'm suddenly in what appears to be an entirely new town. But it, too, is technically still part of Goodyear. There's even a manmade lake, with docks and boats and some kind of resort or club at one end.

When the Durango turns again, I keep going straight so its occupants won't get suspicious. I work my way through a couple of the cookie-cutter neighborhoods that seem to have sprouted up like weeds all over Phoenix, and stop only a few streets away from the SUV.

As I close in, I enter a neighborhood decidedly not like the others. Here, large houses sit on giant lots, with wide strips of open land between each dwelling. Nothing cookie-cutter about this area. All the homes are unique.

The Durango's dot stops moving on a road called San Marcos Way. If I want, I could be there in thirty seconds. But since no one is behind me, I stop and zoom in on the glowing dot on the map.

Well, well, well. Whoever's holding on to the phone isn't on the street anymore, but within the boundaries of one of the properties.

I take a left when I reach San Marcos and drive by.

The Durango is parked in front of a sprawling one-story adobe-style house, the car now empty. The home has a multi-tiered roof and a low plaster wall around the front yard, but nothing around the rest of the property. This, I've seen, is not unusual here. Only a few of the houses I've passed have fenced-in yards.

The adobe house's address is 10979. That's a lot of numbers, but maybe that's what you're left with when you build a community this far away from the rest of the city.

I turn at the next street and park in front of a wide spot of open land.

Before leaving, Jar sent me copies of what she'd found out about Yanez. The page listing his properties includes the entry 10979 SAN MARCOS WAY.

This must be where the man himself resides.

I want to go in for a closer look but I can't leave my car here. In a neighborhood like this, I'm sure the streets are patrolled by private security who would be very interested in an empty, unfamiliar vehicle. Though I could drive back to the nearest homogeneous neighborhood, I'm not sure that would solve my problem. From what I saw of the ones I drove through on the way here, it was pretty obvious parking on the street is frowned upon.

That's okay, though. With the sun minutes from setting, I should soon have some options that aren't available during the day.

I switch the map to satellite view and examine the area.

At least a dozen dry creek beds are scattered throughout the undulating land surrounding Yanez's neighborhood. Two or three of the larger ones look like they're flanked by banks high enough to hide a car.

Near one of the other streets in the neighborhood, about three hundred meters from where I'm parked, is the start of a small tributary that leads to one of these hidden waterways. And unless there's been some new construction recently, the area is clear of houses.

I drive over and am pleased to find everything is the same as in the photo. I turn off the car's lights and creep the Subaru up and over the sidewalk into the desert. If I still had the Honda, I wouldn't be able to do this, but the Crosstrek's continuous all-wheel drive gives me the stability I need on the loose sand.

When the tributary connects to the larger creek, I take a hard right and travel down the dry waterway for thirty meters, before turning right again onto another tributary, which will take me closer to Yanez's place.

I creep along until the darkness deepens to the point where I can't see much of anything, then let the Subaru roll to a stop before I shut off the engine.

One of the special features cars from suppliers like Victor usually have is a single switch that disables all interior lighting—dome lights, dash lights, the lights some car doors have, even the light in the glove box. I check to make sure the switch is in the correct position and climb out.

The temperature has plunged with the setting sun, which is

more than enough encouragement for me to grab my dark sweater and hoodie from the back. After I'm layered up, I transfer several items into my backpack and strap the bag over my shoulders. The one thing I didn't shove in the bag are my night vision goggles. Those I prop on my head.

A short hike up a nearby knoll puts me about thirty meters behind Yanez's property. I lie on the dirt and scan the back of the house through my binoculars.

I see the hood of the Durango jutting out a meter or so around the front corner of the house. There are three other cars. These are parked in an area beside the home I wasn't able to see from the street. One is another Durango. It's gray, but otherwise a clone of the one out front. The second is a Lexus ES sedan, and the last an older VW Jetta. There's a garage on the other side of the house, which might contain more cars.

I see no one outside or sitting in the vehicles.

The people I do see are all inside the house, sitting at a long, rectangular table, eating. Seven men, to be precise. The view is courtesy of several floor-to-ceiling windows along the back. Not exactly a standard design for an adobe house, but I get the appeal. The view of the open desert must be beautiful from the weather-protected comfort of the inside.

I train my binoculars on the diners. Two of Jar's and my friends from the Durango are facing my direction and are immediately recognizable. And I'm fairly sure one of those whose backs are to me is the man who followed us into the airport. Three of the others I have never seen before. Technically, I haven't seen the seventh person, either. Not in the flesh, anyway. But I have seen Mateo Yanez's photo so he's instantly recognizable. He sits at the head of the table, nodding while stuffing some kind of meat into his mouth.

There are no women among them, and I'm curious if Yanez has a wife. Jar made no mention of that one way or the other in her notes, but she didn't take too deep a dive into him because neither of us knew I'd soon be looking into his house. If he does have a wife, no place is set for her at the table.

I search through the other windows for anyone else who might be there. I can't see into every room but in those I can, I see no one. I switch my attention to the outside of the house, and scan for security cameras and motion activated lights. On the patio, I see three cameras and a couple of lights that I bet would come on if I pass within sensor range. But there are gaps in the coverage of the lights, which is good. Even better? The cameras are wireless.

Jar isn't the only one who has an app on her phone for hacking into internet and security systems. I move carefully down the hill and toward the house until my app picks up Yanez's network. Turns out he has six cameras, but the other three are in front of the house and I don't need to do anything about them. I turn the back three off, though if he checks his feeds, he'll see the last thirty seconds playing over and over. None of them are perfect loops, but he has no reason to check them now and I'm not worried.

I continue toward the house. When I'm about fifteen meters away, I veer to the left and parallel to Yanez's home, as I arc around the back and check out the side I couldn't see from the hill. The home boasts several expensive details like hand-etched copper rain gutters, those giant rear windows I mentioned before, and a built-in outside barbecue with hand-painted tiles that look imported from somewhere exotic.

I have to give Yanez a *well done* on his choice of windows. They're a top-notch European brand and are almost impossible to open from the outside without breaking the glass. The French doors, on the other hand, might be better than your average set but I've unlocked plenty of their kind without anyone being the wiser.

My phone vibrates twice with a text. I slip back into the desert and find a crease in the land where the phone's light won't be seen.

The message is from Jar.

Arrived. Heading to the Uber pickup area. How is it going?

I raise the phone high enough to take a picture of the house and send it to her with a text:

Yanez's place

She responds with:

Plan?

My answer:

I'm working on it. Does this guy have a wife? Is there anything else I should know?

Jar:

I will check once on the road and get back to you.

I return to my lookout knoll and watch the dinner party through my binoculars.

Four of the men, including the three from the Durango, are of a particular type I like to refer to as thug-lite. They all have the hard, chip-on-the-shoulder look of enforcers, but in medium-sized packages. A fifth man is the only one large enough to be a true enforcer.

Only Yanez and the man sitting to his left don't look like

people who spend their days getting into street fights. Both men are older than the others, Yanez probably approaching sixty, and his friend ten plus years beyond that. The older man looks like a long stick, with a gray goatee and a wispy fringe of Friar Tuck hair. Yanez has a little more meat on him, fat more than muscle. Would I call him obese? No. But if he's not careful, he could be someday.

Turns out there's an eighth person in the house—a woman, no more than thirty, who shows up to remove plates from the table. Did she cook the meal, too? Or is someone else in the kitchen?

I settle into a kind of meditative state as I monitor the party, time itself fading into the background. It's one of the skills you develop in my profession, otherwise the waiting would drive you crazy. About forty-five minutes after I saw the woman from the kitchen for the first time, Yanez and his guests get up from the table.

Laughter and one or two backslaps are followed by Yanez and Gray Goatee shaking hands. The two then walk through the room, with the others following.

Because of the house's semi-open concept, I'm able to see them proceed all the way to the front entrance, where they stop again and share a few more words. When they're done, Yanez opens the door, shakes the man's hand again, and smiles as Gray Goatee steps outside. Leaving with him is the medium-sized thug who wasn't in the Durango.

Yanez waits a respectful number of seconds after his guests leave before he shuts the door. When he turns to those remaining, they huddle around him.

I swing my binoculars to the side of the house where the cars are parked, just in time to witness the arrival of Gray Goatee and his friend. They proceed to the Lexus, climb in, and drive away.

Back in the house, the group conversation continues, while at the dining table, the woman is clearing the last of the dishes. When Yanez finishes whatever he has to say, my three midsize thug friends head outside.

Yanez says something to Mr. Large Thug, then turns and disappears into the part of the house opposite from where they had their meal. Once he's out of sight, Mr. Large walks into the living room, sits on the sofa, and turns on the TV.

Outside, the Durango that followed Jar and me leaves, and sure enough, when I check the tracking app, the glowing dot is on the move again.

My original plan was to follow the Durango and wait until the owner of the phone was alone, at which point I would pay him a visit. But he's just a cog in the machine, and what I could get out of him likely would be less than satisfactory.

Yanez, however, is a different story. He's the big man, the one who likely ordered his men to keep track of Jar and me. Talking to him would be considerably more fruitful.

A light comes on behind a section of the big windows that, until now, has been dark. I already know it's a bedroom, from looking at it through the night vision setting on my binoculars. From the way Yanez is futzing around at the dresser, I'm guessing it's the master. After a few minutes, he disappears through a different doorway and another light comes on, this one in a smaller window I can't see through because the glass is textured. The master bathroom, I assume.

For the next forty minutes, the house tableau is pretty much unchanged, and the only person I see is Mr. Large in the living room, watching television.

The woman breaks the spell by exiting wherever she was—the kitchen, probably—wearing a coat and carrying a purse. She says something that gets Mr. Large's attention. They exchange a few words, he waves a hand, and she exits the house.

Her car is the Jetta, and she wastes no time pulling it onto the street and driving away.

And then there are two.

I study Mr. Large. He looks relaxed, like sitting on that couch and watching that TV is something he's accustomed to. I also get the sense he's not going anywhere anytime soon.

In the bedroom, Yanez finally reappears. He's wearing a dark robe and his hair looks damp. When he walks over to the window, I think he's going to shut his curtains but instead he stands there and stares out at the desert, somewhere to my left.

Eventually, without covering the windows, he returns to the bed, disrobes, and climbs in. He stretches a hand toward his nightstand and the bedroom lights go out.

A few windows away, Mr. Large is laughing at something on the television.

I wonder if his job is to stay awake all night and guard the place. Seems likely.

Speaking of wondering, why hasn't Jar gotten back to me yet?

I shoot her a message:

Yanez?

Seconds later, she responds:

Call?

Me:

Give me thirty seconds.

I scoot down the back side of the knoll, insert my wireless earbuds, and initiate a video chat.

When she answers, I see she's sitting in the backseat of a car. Music plays in the background, lo-fi hip-hop. I don't recognize the artist.

"We were in an accident," she tells me before I say anything.

"Are you all right?"

"I have not been injured," she replies. "I believe you call it a fender bender." She pronounces each word distinctively, instead of mashing them together and spitting them out fast like most Americans do.

The story I get out of her is, her car is one of six that bumped into one another in a chain reaction while crawling through traffic on the 405 freeway. Her driver is currently out of the car, dealing with the other parties and a couple of highway patrol officers.

"I am sorry I have not contacted you already," she says. "The accident has thrown me off, and..." She takes a deep breath. "And I forgot."

"It's okay. As long as you're not hurt. That's all that's important."

"I *am* hurt. I lost track of what I was doing. I do not lose track."

"Jar, relax. It only proves you're human like the rest of us."

From her frown, I know she doesn't like hearing this.

"Just let me know when you have something for me," I say.

"You do not understand. I already have the information, but I have failed to send it to you."

"I see. Well, could you tell me now?"

After taking another deep breath, she does.

If I tell you Yanez is dirty, you wouldn't be surprised, would you?

Well, he is.

Very.

His life on the other side of the legal line stretches back to his youth, when he was a member of a Phoenix-area gang. Unlike some of his other colleagues, he never went to prison. In fact, he extracted himself from the trappings of his misspent youth to become someone who—on the surface, anyway—looks like a legitimate businessman.

Don't get me wrong. Jar tells me his properties do bring in a lot of money in rentals and shared profits. But he also dabbles in some things that I bet would have impressed his younger self. Most of his illegal activities are centered around the trucking company he owns, through which he transports a considerable amount of counterfeit goods. Yanez hides much of his activities inside a Russian nesting doll set of shell companies, so few people are aware he's not exactly the good citizen he appears to be.

His cover-up scheme seems to be working, because he doesn't live like there's any real heat on him. If he was concerned about his well-being, he'd be ensconced in a walled-in compound, with half a dozen guys guarding him around the clock, instead of in a neighborhood where pretty much anyone could walk up to his front door and knock.

Or hike through a patch of desert to his back porch. You know, like what I've basically done.

Bottom line, his is a neighborhood of status, not protection. And I have a feeling Mr. Large is more a symbol of that status than anything else.

The other useful piece of info Jar passes on is that Yanez is a widower, with no kids. His wife died fourteen years ago, in her early thirties. Cancer. He either really loved her, or he enjoys the single life because he's never remarried. Whatever the case, it explains why he's sleeping alone.

"Maybe you should have your driver get you a new car," I say, once Jar is done filling me in.

"He has already called for one for me. There is a lot of traffic, so it is taking some time for it to get here."

"Sorry, Jar."

"I am sorry, too."

"Let me know when you finally get there."

With things quiet at the house, I decide it's time to move my observation post closer. I creep through the desert and avoid the motion-activated lights as I sneak all the way up to his built-in barbecue. From my new vantage point, I can hear occasional sounds from the TV. It's not enough for me to know what Mr. Large is watching, but from the boom of explosions, I'm guessing it's not a cooking show.

My plan is simple. If Mr. Large goes to bed, I'll remotely disarm the house's security system, disengage the lock on the French doors, and let myself in. Before I visit Yanez, I'll stop in on his bodyguard, hit Mr. Large with one of my tranquilizer darts, then proceed to the master bedroom. If Mr. Large appears to be planning to stay up for the whole night, there will surely be a time when he needs to use the toilet. I will employ the same plan then, adjusted accordingly.

Ten minutes later, Mr. Large picks up the remote and turns off the television.

I smile as he stands, and watch as he—

Heads for the French doors?

He opens one and steps onto the patio. A shiver rocks his shoulders as the night air greets him, but he doesn't retreat inside. What he does do is pull a packet of cigarettes from his pocket.

I have a pretty hard-and-fast rule: Do not ignore opportunities.

I will not be breaking that rule today.

Ever so quietly, I slip my dart gun out of my bag.

CHAPTER THIRTEEN

M r. Large lifts his lit cigarette to his mouth. I let him take a puff before I pull the trigger of my gun.

The dart catches him above his right hip. He remains conscious long enough to look down to see what happened before he drops to the ground.

His collapse is a little louder than I would like. I stay where I am and watch the windows of Yanez's bedroom.

No lights come on, nor does anyone suddenly appear in the living room. Even so, I don't move for a full minute, caution having saved my life on more than one occasion.

When I'm satisfied Mr. Large's fall has gone undetected, I walk lightly over to the patio.

I'm not a bad guy. As easy as it would be to do, I'm not going to leave Mr. Large lying out in the cold.

It takes a little extra effort to get him over my shoulder and lift him up—I mean, I don't call him Mr. Large for no reason—but I've had to deal with bigger bodies so I can't complain too much. Inside, I plop him down on his favorite couch, then roll my shoulder a few times to ease the strain.

Note to self: in the future, when knocking out people of a certain size, do so in a manner that has them falling onto a chair or some other convenient piece of furniture.

To make sure there isn't an unknown guest sleeping somewhere in the house, I search every room except for the master bedroom.

As I hoped, Yanez, Mr. Large, and I are the only ones here.

Outside Yanez's bedroom, I set my backpack on the floor, and from inside remove a hank of rope, a pair of box cutters, and my superhero mask, this last I put on. These items and my dart gun should be everything I'll need.

Before easing the bedroom door open, I turn off all the lights in the house and lower my night vision goggles. They're a little harder to see through when I have a piece of mesh between me and the lenses, but I'll make do.

Yanez is snoring as I slip inside. Though he seems to like sleeping with the windows uncovered, he's apparently less thrilled by the prospect of early morning sunlight because he's wearing an eye mask.

I cut a length of rope and tie slipknots on both ends, creating loops that would fit around two-liter soda bottles. I then lie on the floor next to the bed. There's nothing stored underneath. I shove one end of the rope across the wooden floor, and it stops just short of the other side. I walk around and pull out as much rope as I'll need. I now have loops on both sides of the bed.

Now comes the difficult part.

Yanez is lying on his back, on the right side of the mattress, everything but his head under his comforter. I carefully lift the blanket until I can see his arm. It's bent at the elbow, his hand resting on his hip.

Not ideal.

Hoping the other side is a better place to start, I return there and fold back the comforter until I can see his left arm. It's lying by itself, next to him, his hand turned so that his palm is facing the ceiling.

Much better.

By pressing down on the mattress near his hand, I'm able to move the left-end loop over his finger and palm then down around his wrist. Very carefully, I slip the knot until it's almost but not quite closed around his wrist. It's unnecessary for me to tighten it all the way. He'll take care of that himself. After I gingerly stretch his arm so that it lies straight out from his shoulder across the empty half of the bed, I tuck in the comforter from his waist down to the end of the mattress and then walk back around.

On the right side, I tuck the comforter in first, then lift the unattached end of the rope as far as I can without pulling on the loop already wrapped around his left hand. I have measured well. The length is pretty close to perfect.

I pantomime what I'm about to do a few times, to make sure I don't make a mistake. When I'm ready, I take a breath, grab Yanez's forearm, yank it away from his body, and slide the loop around his wrist.

Yanez wakes with a gasp, and reflexively tries to pull his right arm to his torso. Doing so jerks on the rope and tightens the slipknots around each wrist.

"What the hell?"

Not learning from his first attempt, he tries to remove the eye mask, and quickly finds out that's a no-go. With his hands back on the mattress, he rubs his head against the pillow to push the mask onto his forehead.

Once he can see, he looks at his wrists, and then around the room, where his gaze lands on my silhouette standing near the foot of his bed. He kicks out in an attempt to push off the comforter, but he can't get it untucked.

A string of swear words bursts from his lips. When he quiets again he stares at me, breathing hard.

I have not moved a centimeter since he first saw me.

"Who sent you?" he asks, without the slightest trace of fear in his voice.

I'm impressed. He didn't ask how I got in here, or where Mr. Large is. Apparently, the idea of something like this happening to him has been in the back of his mind.

"No one sent me."

A crease appears between his eyebrows. This is not the answer he expected. "Bullshit."

I find that sometimes in these situations, it's good to start off with a question that gets right to the heart of the matter. If it throws off your subject enough, he or she might respond in a way that is more revealing than anything they might say after they have a better understanding of what's going on.

Which is why I ask, "Why did you kill Naomi Bellows?"

"What?"

"Why did you kill Naomi Bellows?"

"Who the hell is Naomi Bellow?"

"Bellows. With an *s*."

"I don't know who you think I am, but I don't kill people."

"Maybe the name Saundra Moore is more familiar."

His expression is unchanged. "Who?"

I can't tell if he's really good at pretending, or actually hasn't heard the names before.

"How about Juan Sanchez?"

His eyes flare. "How the hell do you know about Juan? Are you the one who killed him?"

Now it's my turn to get a question I wasn't expecting. Blaming the inquisitor is not exactly a new tactic, but this doesn't feel like a tactic.

"No one knows he's dead," he goes on. "Not even the cops.

So that means you must be the one, you son of a bitch." He yanks again at the ropes and shouts, "Let me go, dammit!"

"*You* know he's dead," I say, my voice still calm.

"Because I found him! Stupid choice, making it look like he OD'd. That's one thing Juan would never do."

This is not going the way I expected, but things happen that way sometimes. I decide to follow him down the rabbit hole for a bit. "If you found him, then why didn't you call the police?"

"Because I knew they'd take the easy route and say he did it to himself. Why do you think?" The aggression flows off him in increasing waves.

"You thought it was better to let him rot in his home?"

His eyes narrow as they study me. "I know who you are. You're the asshole my men were following. You *are* the one who did it. You killed my nephew."

It's pretty hard to surprise me. Sure, I'll get an unexpected question here and there, but hearing something that stuns me into silence? I can't remember the last time that happened. Until now.

When I regain my voice, I want to be positive I understood him correctly. "You're Juan Sanchez's uncle?"

"That's right. And don't you think for one minute I'm not going to make you pay for what you did!"

"You're right and you're wrong. I am the asshole your men were following, but I had nothing to do with your nephew's death."

"Bullshit. My men saw you coming out of his place."

"They saw me coming out *after* he'd been dead for a few days."

"Yeah. It's called returning to the scene of the crime."

I stare at him like he's an idiot, because I'm beginning to think maybe he is. Unfortunately, he can't see my expression behind my goggles and mask. "Returning to the scene of the crime? That's what you're basing my guilt on?"

"Why do you think we were watching the place?"

"Hold on." I walk across the room, lift the night vision goggles off my eyes, and flick on the light. I grab a chair from a small writing desk, carry it over to the bed, and flip it around so that when I sit, I'm looking over the back. "You do know that returning to the scene of a crime isn't as common as it's made out to be. I mean, you're a criminal yourself. How often do you return to the scene of your crimes?"

"This is different! You killed him!" His muscles tighten, as if he's going to launch himself at me. This only pulls both sides of the rope, which in turn causes him to wince.

"Take it down a notch or you're going to end up dislocating your shoulders." I let him seethe for a few seconds before continuing. "Help me with the relationship here. Juan was your sister's son?"

His complexion turns a deep, angry red, my question seeming to stoke his rage. Through clenched teeth, he says, "My *wife's* sister."

The dead wife, he means. Which, as you can imagine, evokes a bit of sympathy from me. I wonder if she still talks to him. For that matter, I wonder if everyone who's lost a spouse or a lover still hears from them from time to time. Could be we're all so scared of being crazy we never mention it.

Who am I kidding? As much as that possibility would give me comfort, I have a feeling apparitions like Liz are rare.

"I hate to spoil your theory," I say, "but I had nothing to do with your nephew's death."

He scoffs. "Then what were you doing there?"

"I think the real question is, why the hell would you leave his body there for so long? You've heard about decomposition, haven't you?"

From his narrowing eyes and flaring nostrils, it appears I've pissed him off all over again. "Because I knew someone would come back."

It dawns on me what must have really happened. "You had just found him, hadn't you? Maybe an hour or two before I showed up. You were still trying to figure out what to do."

The confirmation is in his eyes.

"Here's the thing," I say, "I had no interest in killing him. All I wanted to do was talk to him."

A snort. "Yeah, right. And what did you want to talk to him about?"

"A train ride he took last month, from Tucson to Los Angeles."

My words knock the fire out of his eyes and replace it with befuddlement. That's not a word I use often, but it's accurate here.

"What train ride?"

"The one where he and two others made sure a fourth man —" I stop myself.

Holy crap. I pull out my phone.

"He and two others what? What the hell are you talking about?"

I hold up a finger. "Give me a moment."

"Give you a moment?" He's starting to sound pissed again.

"Shut up."

He scoffs and slams his head back against his pillow like an insolent child.

I send a text to Jar. Ten seconds later, the picture I asked for arrives. I pull it up on my screen and show it to Yanez.

"Do you know this man?"

He looks dismissively at my phone, but then his eyebrows knit together. "Is that Weakling?"

The picture is from the Carl Harrison fake ID card.

"That's a nickname?" I ask.

"It's what everyone called him."

"But his real name was David Weeks, correct?"

"I don't know. That sounds right. It was a long time ago. What does Weakling have to do with Juan? Did he kill him?"

"Weeks worked for you?"

"I asked you a question."

I'm tempted to remind him who's in charge, but giving him the answer might make him more cooperative. "No, he didn't kill your nephew. They knew each other, though, didn't they?"

Yanez says nothing.

"As hard as this might be for you to believe," I say, "you and I are on the same side in this matter. I want to know who killed Juan as much as you do."

"Why the hell would you care who killed Juan?"

"Because whoever killed him killed a friend of mine." I know, I've never actually met Naomi. Neither has Jar, for that matter, but she considers Naomi a kind of friend, even family of a type, and any friend of Jar's, as the saying goes. "I'm going to find whoever it is, with or without your help. But your answers might speed things up. Now, did David Weeks work for you? And did your nephew know him?"

Yanez stares at me for several seconds before saying, "Weakling drove a truck for me, but that was years ago. I don't know if Juan knew him but I guess it's possible. They could have met when Juan was working at the warehouse when he was a teenager."

And there it is. The connection.

"Does Juan still work for you?"

"Sometimes."

"What about since the first of the year?"

He thinks. "Uh-uh. Not this year. He's been busy with other things."

"You mean working for someone else? Do you know who that was?"

He raises his wrists a few centimeters. "Get these things off me. If we're on the same side, there's no reason to keep me tied up."

"I'll untie you after we're done."

"Then you're not getting any help from me."

"If that's the way you want to play it."

I get up, pull the chair out of the way, and retrieve my dart gun from the floor, where I'd set it before I tied up Yanez.

When he sees the strange-looking weapon in my hand, his eyes widen. "Hold on now! What is that?"

I point the gun at his torso. "Don't worry. I'm told it's painless."

From the look of horror on his face, I get the feeling Yanez might have dished out a lot of punishment over the years but has seldom been on the receiving end.

"Stop! Stop! You don't need to do that!"

"If you're not going to answer my questions, then you're no longer of any use to me. So, yes, I do."

"I'll answer, all right?"

I keep the gun pointed at him.

"I said I'll answer," he pleads.

"Then answer."

"Yeah, okay. I, um, I know Juan did do a job for someone back in January, but he didn't tell me who. Last weekend, he did call me and say he might be in a little trouble for what he did."

"What kind of trouble?"

"He wouldn't go into it. I only got the impression someone was giving him a hard time. He said he was going to try to take care of it, but it might help if he could drop my name, and he wanted to see if that was okay."

"Were the people who hired him bothering him? Or someone else?"

He shrugs and says, "I don't know," sounding frustrated and helpless.

"What did you say when he asked to use your name?"

"I...I said no. I told him to deal with his own problems. He did that sometimes, used his connection to me to get him out of trouble. I didn't like it."

"You don't know what happened after that?"

He shakes his head, frowning.

"I understand now," I say. "You started to feel guilty, didn't you? That's why you were looking for him yesterday, isn't it?"

He looks away, confirming what I said.

"Did he say what the job was he did in January?" I say.

"All I know is that they wanted him to deliver a package."

"*They*? As in more than one person?"

"It's the word he used so I assume yes. I-I also got the impression they weren't from around here."

"What do you mean by here? Goodyear?"

"Phoenix. I don't think even Arizona. Juan told me he had to fly out of town to meet them once."

This is news. "Did he say where he went?"

Yanez shakes his head. "But I did get the sense it was going to take at least a few hours to get there."

"When was this?"

"I don't know exactly. Not too long after New Year's, I think."

Which means before he took the train ride to L.A. on January 18.

"Had he already met with them when he told you this, or was the trip upcoming?"

"I'm pretty sure he said he was leaving the next day." Yanez becomes lost in thought again. "We talked on a...Thursday, I think. I remember him saying he'd be gone overnight and wouldn't be home until late afternoon on Saturday. We usually grab lunch together on Saturdays. He wanted to let me know he wasn't going to be able to make it that time."

"Did he mention what time of day he was leaving?"

"Morning. Maybe. Not one hundred percent sure about that."

"What about the airline he flew on?"

Yanez shakes his head. "He didn't say."

Having the name of the airline would have been nice, but it's not imperative. Knowing Sanchez took a (probable) morning flight on a January Friday prior to Naomi's murder should make it easy enough for Jar to figure out which flight he was on and where he was going.

Unless...

"Did he ever travel under an alias?" I ask.

"What? Like a spy?" Yanez snorted. "Not that I know of."

I head over to his dresser and remove the dart from the gun's chamber while my back is to him. Yanez does see me set the weapon down.

Upon returning to his bedside, I say, "Thank you. You've been helpful."

Not keeping the sarcasm out of his voice, he says, "Glad to hear it. Now how about untying me?"

"Soon."

Cue the return of Yanez's anger. "Come on! What the hell else do you want?"

"Nothing." I jab the dart into his thigh before he realizes my hand has even moved.

In the few seconds it takes the drug to kick in, he starts cursing at me again, but his protest doesn't last long.

When he's unconscious, I untie his hands, recoil my rope, and place it, the dart gun, the used dart, and the box cutters back in my bag.

I turn out the light as I exit his room, but I don't leave the house just yet. In the refrigerator, I find a can of sparkling water, and warm up some of the leftover chicken molé they had for dinner. After taking a seat at the dining table, I send Jar a text asking how things are going, then take a bite of the chicken.

Boy, is it tasty! Whoever cooked this knew what they were doing.

Before I can take a second bite, Jar video chats me.

I swipe ACCEPT, and am presented with a shot of a dark room, lit only by a flashlight and the screen of Jar's phone. She's in the center of the image, looking down at something out of frame. Behind her on one side is a pile of furniture, and on the other, the shadowy form of stacked boxes.

"You got in," I say.

"Of course I got in." Her eyes narrow. "Where are you?"

"Yanez's dining room."

"Then you have spoken to him."

"I have."

"And?"

I give her the highlights.

"He's Sanchez's uncle?"

"I know, right? Not what I was expecting, either."

"That does not mean he could not have killed him."

"True, but I believe him."

"Did Yanez know who hired his nephew?"

"Oh, I left out the best part. I mean, no, he didn't, but Yanez did say Sanchez took a flight out of Phoenix to meet with someone on one of the Fridays before Naomi died." I flip my phone to the calendar app. "Let's see. That would mean it was either the third or the tenth, or possibly the seventeenth, but I doubt that. Yanez said Sanchez was due back on a Saturday afternoon, which, if he had gone on the seventeenth, would have been on the day he took the train to L.A. That wouldn't have left much time to get to Tucson before the train left. Yanez didn't know the airline, but he thinks Sanchez left in the morning."

"I will look into it."

"How's it going there?" I ask. "Find anything?"

"Yes. That I am not the first person who has been inside for a look."

"What do you mean?"

She pans her camera around the room, shining her light so I can see what she's talking about. The boxes are not piled together as neatly as I first thought, and many have been opened. Spread across the floor are several things I'm guessing were inside one or more of the boxes.

Jar turns the camera back to herself. "There are also new scratches on the lock."

A sign it was recently picked. "Anything obvious missing?"

"How can I know that? I do not know what she owned."

"TV, microwave, maybe a computer. Could have been a thief, looking for something he could sell."

"There are two TVs and a microwave here. There is no computer, though."

While that doesn't completely rule out a random burglary, it does strengthen the possibility the previous visitors were associated with Naomi's killers. A computer is one of the likely things they'd have taken. "Have you checked the other—"

"Yes. Of course I have checked all units on this floor. None of their locks have been tampered with."

"Sorry, Jar. I doubt there's anything left for you to find. Looks like you made the trip in vain."

"Not true. I found this." She holds up a legal-sized envelope.

"Okay. What's important about that?"

"It is a letter from her bank. A confirmation of the rental of a safety-deposit box, starting on January 7. It made me think about the key."

The key I found at the bottom of Naomi's bag, she means. I'm the only one who's seen it, though I didn't really get a good look at it. It was small, which means it could very well be for a safety-deposit box.

"I'm surprised whoever searched the storage unit before you didn't take it."

"I do not think they found it," she says. "It was in a drawer, in the middle of a pile of advertisements from food markets and other places. I believe it is mail that arrived after the murder, and whoever cleaned out her apartment stuffed everything in the drawer."

And it was possible the other searcher thought it was all advertisements and didn't look through them.

"You still hunting around, or about finished?" I ask.

"I would like to perform another check. Be more thorough this time. It should take me no more than an hour. I will let you know what flight back I am on after I am done."

"About that—change of plans. Go to my place. I'm coming back there."

While we could pursue two or three leads in Arizona, most can be accomplished from afar. There are a few things in L.A., however, that I feel are more pertinent for us to look into.

After we say goodbye, I finish my molé, wash my dishes, and check to make sure Yanez and Mr. Large are sleeping peacefully.

I then use my phone to look for a flight home. Unfortunately, the last plane to L.A. has already left. There's a 6:40 a.m. Southwest flight I can catch, but I'd really love to sleep in my own bed tonight.

I do have a vehicle with a nearly full tank of gas, and at this time of night, I could probably cut the usual six-hour drive back to L.A. down to five or less.

I grab another water from the fridge and head back into the desert to the Subaru.

CHAPTER FOURTEEN

I t's 8:00 a.m. Sunday and I'm surprisingly awake. The drive from Arizona the night before was, as I'd hoped, smooth sailing. I arrived at my townhouse around 2:30 a.m. and was sound asleep not long after that.

I guess five-ish hours of shut-eye is my new normal.

I pull on a pair of shorts, a long-sleeve T-shirt and sneakers, and walk out to the living room, where I find Jar sitting on the couch with her laptop.

"Where are you going?" she asks.

"I thought maybe you'd like to go for a hike."

Her expression tells me she doesn't understand why I would think that.

"It's four weeks today," I say.

"Oh," she says.

Today marks four weeks since I discovered Naomi's body in Griffith Park.

"I would like that," she says. "Give me a minute to change."

It's warm enough out for us to take my motorcycle. At first, Jar's hold on me is tentative, but by the time we're heading north on the 110 freeway, her arms have slipped around me and her body presses snuggly against mine.

It warms me in ways I'm not sure I want it to, and yet I don't want her to let go. It's the memory of Liz and how she would ride behind me like this that's muddling everything up.

But she's been dead over a year.

I need to move on.

And yet I can't seem to.

And yet...

Jar's hands shift, and her arms tighten ever so slightly around me.

Be happy, Liz whispers.

A) That's not helping. And b), what the hell is that supposed to mean anyway?

And don't be stupid.

Now she's just getting mean.

Only she's not.

I'm not really as stupid as I'm pretending to be. I know she's telling me to move on and live my life. But if I do, does that mean she'll leave again and I won't hear her voice anymore?

Good thing Jar can't see me, or she'd wonder why my eyes are so watery.

I park in the same spot I did the morning I found Naomi. The warm weather means the hike up to the observatory is a lot more crowded than it was on that fateful day. Before we head up the rest of the way, I take her inside and show her the planetarium that Naomi never made it to. We then cross the parking lot and start up the trail that leads to the top of Mt. Hollywood.

Today the sky is a bit hazier, and while you can still see the ocean, it's more of an impression that blends into the sky than a distinctive body of water.

"We turn there," I say, pointing at the path that will take us over to Mt. Lee.

There are a few others going our way, though it's not nearly as crowded here as the way to the summit.

Jar and I have been talking most of the hike up, but it's been all small talk. I mean, as best as Jar can do at small talk. By unspoken agreement, when we turn off the Mt. Lee trail and onto the one from where I spotted Naomi's backpack, all conversation stops.

At basically the spot where I (and probably Naomi) went off the path now lives a makeshift memorial of bouquets and stuffed animals and cards, similar in many ways to one I saw last fall in Jenson, California. A few balloons lie in the brush, their air gone but their husks still connected to ribbons attached to the pile.

Jar's breaths come faster and louder as we near. She kneels in front of the display and reads several of the cards. When she stands again, a streak of tear divides her left cheek.

"Over there?" she says, nodding beyond the memorial.

"Yes."

"Show me."

I lead her through the brush to the top of the rocky chute, and we look down at where Naomi's body lay.

Jar is all but hyperventilating. I should say or do something, but before I decide what, she leans into me, wraps an arm around my back, and buries her face in my shoulder.

Before a month ago, I don't think I'd ever seen her truly cry. Now I've seen it happen twice, and it makes me so angry. Not at her. *Never* at her. But at those who took Naomi's life. At those who'd kidnapped her. And at those who had held Jar.

I probably should have brought her up here weeks ago, but at least now there's been time for the looky-loos to lose interest. So maybe the delay was a good thing. Who knows? If there's a handbook for this kind of stuff, I don't own a copy.

"Where was the backpack?" she asks once the tears have stopped.

I point to the spot.

Jar lets go of me, walks over to it, and kneels again. I follow.

There is nothing to see. Even the partial footprint that was nearby is gone.

"We need to get the SD card," she says. "And the key."

I couldn't agree more. Getting our hands on the SD card is one of the main reasons I wanted to come back to L.A. And though I'm still not sure how important the key is, we might as well grab that, too.

"I have an idea on how we might do that," I say.

She stares at the ground for a few more moments, and then stands. "Then we should get back to work."

We can't just walk into LAPD headquarters and ask to see the bag. In fact, *I* can't even set foot in the station.

Detective Hughes has probably all but forgotten about me by now, but if he sees me—and there's a chance he will—he'd remember and throw me in an interrogation room to find out why I want to see Naomi's stuff.

What we need is a surrogate.

We stop at one of my favorite restaurants, Thai Patio in Thai Town, but instead of eating there like we talked about on our hike up the mountain, we get our food to go and head back to my place.

I start working the phones as soon as we're home. As you may have gathered by now, the world in which I spend my professional time utilizes a lot of freelancers. You can find them all over the globe, but they tend to bunch up in certain places. Los Angeles—and the surrounding area—is one such location. I don't know everyone affiliated with the business who lives here, but I do know quite a few.

The first five people I call are all on projects out of town. Good for them. It's always nice to get work. Call number six is answered by a woman named Remy Chandler. I've worked with her three times in the past couple of years. I like her. She's competent and doesn't take herself too seriously so she's easy to work with.

"No, I don't have anything going until the end of the month," she tells me. "If you guys have a project, I'd definitely be up for it. You know I love working with you all."

"This isn't the whole team," I say. "You'd be working for me."

"You on your own now?"

"No, nothing like that. I just have a...personal job I'm dealing with."

"Personal?"

"Helping a friend."

"Then is this a favor? Or are you paying me?" There's no annoyance in her tone. She simply wants to know.

"I'm paying. I can give you your full day rate, but I should only need you for a few hours."

"A local job?"

"Yeah."

"I'm in. What's the gig?"

We meet Remy at three p.m. in a hotel room in Chinatown, not far from LAPD's downtown headquarters.

"You look perfect," I say as I let her in.

"Thanks," she says.

She's dressed in a gray pantsuit and a white shirt, her dark hair falling just above her shoulders. She looks a little like Kerry Washington if Kerry was playing Scully on *The X-Files*.

"Badge?"

She pulls a leather booklet out of a jacket pocket and hands it to me. Inside is an FBI ID, listing her as Special Agent Dora Kane.

"It'll hold up?"

"Wouldn't have brought it if it wouldn't." She looks past me into the room. "Who's your friend?"

I lead her over to the desk where Jar is working on her laptop. "Remy, this is Jar. Jar, Remy."

"Nice to meet you," Remy says.

"Thank you for helping us," Jar replies.

Remy looks at me. "I thought you were doing this alone."

"We're doing this alone," I say, gesturing to Jar and myself. "She's one of my colleagues."

"I am not as young as I look," Jar says.

Remy raises an eyebrow. "Did I say anything about your age?"

"Maybe not. But you were thinking about it."

This elicits a chuckle. "Busted. Sorry."

"Apology accepted."

"Have a seat," I tell Remy.

She takes the offered chair. I sit on the end of the bed and give her a more thorough brief than I did over the phone.

After I answer all of her questions, she says, "Great. I'm ready when you are."

Using my voice modulator, I call LAPD headquarters and ask for Detective Hughes. It was also a Sunday when I originally met him, but I'm hoping he has today off and all I will have to do is leave a message. I'm making the call because he was one of the main detectives on Naomi's case, and I want to make sure everything we're about to do looks on the up-and-up.

"Robbery-Homicide. Hughes."

So much for that idea.

"Good afternoon, Detective Hughes. This is Special Agent David Lamar, FBI Criminal Investigative Division."

"Afternoon, Agent Lamar," Hughes says with a touch of wariness. "What can I do for you?"

"Sorry to bother you on a Sunday, but I'm glad you're there. I have an agent in L.A. who I'm hoping you might be able to help out. Unfortunately, we're time strapped. She needs to fly back to DC tonight. I talked to Deputy Chief Freeman, who said I should call you." The deputy chief was three levels above him, not someone he would likely call.

"What kind of help is your agent looking for?" His suspicion isn't quite gone, but he is trying to sound more respectful.

"We're working on a group of homicides that may be connected. A recent case of yours has come to our attention, and I'd like it if Agent Kane could stop by and discuss it with you."

"What case would that be?"

"The Naomi Bellows murder last month, in Griffith Park. Name Saundra Moore."

"Bellows? We've already wrapped that one up."

"We're aware of that." I pause. "What I'm about to tell you is highly confidential. Only a handful of investigators are aware of it, and I need it to stay that way. Can I trust that you'll keep it to yourself?"

"Absolutely."

"I'm glad to hear that. Over the last twelve months, five people who were once in witness protection have been killed. Naomi is number six. Like I said, we're not sure if they're all connected yet, but there is a trend and we don't like it."

"We've already got our killer."

"You do, and we're wondering if you may have found ours, too. If you and Agent Kane can sit down for twenty minutes, she should be able to determine if your killer is someone we need to focus on or not."

A pause. "I guess I can do that."

As I hoped, letting him in on a secret and suggesting he might have already solved our problem has loosened him up.

"I was hoping to leave a little early today," he says. "Can she be here within the hour?"

"I'll call her right now. She's nearby, so I'm sure she can get right over there. Thank you, Detective."

I spend ten minutes running scenarios with Remy so she has ready options to work with, depending on how her conversation with Hughes goes.

"We'll be watching the whole time," I say as she gets ready to leave. She's wearing a camera, disguised as an American flag pin, that includes a microphone. "If it sounds like you might be having problems, I'll call you and you can say it's your boss."

"Well, technically you are my boss."

"Then it won't be a lie. If you feel like you're getting into trouble and I haven't called, cover the camera for a few seconds and I'll get the message."

Jar gives Remy a signal booster to put in her pocket, then hands her an Altoids mint container and a small washrag. The tin is not filled with breath mints, but with wax.

"Good luck," I say.

CHAPTER FIFTEEN

L ike flies on a wall—or on Remy's lapel—Jar and I watch on
Jar's laptop as our surrogate enters LAPD headquarters.

In a power move to remind her who's in charge, Hughes
keeps her waiting nearly fifteen minutes before he comes down
and gets her.

After they introduce themselves, Hughes says, "I understand you might have a few questions."

"If you don't mind, Detective, I think this is a conversation
best held someplace more private." I can't see Remy's face, but I
imagine she's giving him a humorless smile, meant to convey the
seriousness of the matter.

"Sure. Follow me."

He takes her upstairs into the same office he questioned
me in.

"This better?" he says.

"Much, thank you."

They sit across the desk from each other.

Remy says, "I'm told Special Agent Lamar briefed you on
why I'm here."

"Something about people in witness protection getting killed."

"That's correct, but after they leave the program. You are aware your victim was in witness protection several years ago?"

"Yeah, we found that out a few days after the murder." He sounds like he's being helpful, but his body language is all *this is a waste of time*.

Which is why Remy leans forward and says, "Detective, I don't know what you think is going on, but if you're concerned that I'm here to take your case from you, let me ease your mind. The Bellows case is yours. I'm only looking for information that might help with several *ongoing* investigations."

His mouth torques into a half smile, half sneer. "This isn't my first time dealing with you people, so I'm well aware of what you do. If you want to pretend what you said is true, fine. We can do that. But don't expect me to believe it."

"That's just great," I mutter. Have we made the wrong play here?

"I have no intentions of trying to persuade you," Remy says. "Honestly, I don't care what you think. I only need a little cooperation and then I'm out of here. If you don't want to give it, I'm sure my boss can run it up to the assistant director and have him call your chief. Is that what it's going to take?"

The corner of Hughes's mouth ticks once, twice, and then he exhales through his nose. "You want to know about the Bellows murder? No problem. I'll answer as best I can."

"Thank you."

For the next fifteen minutes, he gives her a rundown of the case, and how the LAPD came to the conclusion that Carl Harrison was the murderer. There's nothing here Jar and I haven't already read about in his files, but that's not the point of this conversation. Remy is simply putting Hughes at ease. In fact, I even detect a glint in his eye as the conversation goes on, which makes me think he's starting to wonder if Harrison *is* an oddly specific type of serial killer Hughes and his team will get credit for tracking down. (Never mind the fact Harrison didn't kill anyone *and* was already dead.)

When Remy has received as much information from him as she pretends to need, she says, "Was there anything left at the crime scene?"

Both Jar and I lean forward. Now we're getting to it.

Hughes has obviously moved on to other cases, because he takes a moment to think before he says, "I believe the victim's backpack was the only thing there."

"Nothing else?"

"No. Should there have been?" His voice has a touch of concern, like he's worried the lack of whatever she's looking for might torpedo any accolades he would receive.

Instead of answering him, Remy says, "Is the backpack still in your possession?"

"I'd have to check, but I'd assume so."

"Can you? If it is, I would like to see it."

After making a phone call that confirms the LAPD still has the bag, Hughes escorts Remy to the Metropolitan Detention Center a couple of blocks away, where the Evidence and Property Management Division is located. He leaves her in a small room with a table and two chairs and goes to retrieve the bag.

When he returns, he's carrying a cardboard box, on the side of which someone has drawn an X through the name BRAND and written BELLOWS above it in black marker.

On the table is a box of rubber gloves. After Hughes and Remy don them, the detective opens the box and removes the backpack.

Sorrow pulls at the pit of my stomach at the sight of the purple material, and for a moment, I'm taken back to that morning when I saw the blotch of color among the bushes.

"May I?" Remy says, gesturing at the bag.

"Be my guest."

She picks it up and turns it around, examining everything. When she looks at the side that would have sat against Naomi's back, she holds on to the shoulder straps and positions the backpack on the table so that it's facing Hughes, preventing him from seeing the other side.

I can't tell where Remy's eyes are focused, but I'm sure she's pretending to examine the back of the bag while her fingers do the real work of finding where the SD card is stored and working the hidden pocket open.

For a moment or two, I worry that the card is gone, but then I see a rectangle of black plastic slip into her hand.

With the dexterity of the pro she is, she deposits the card in her suit pocket and turns the bag again, leaving Hughes clueless as to what just happened. She unzips the large pocket and looks inside, then does the same with the smaller pocket before asking, "Was it empty?"

"No." Hughes reaches into the cardboard box and pulls out the two books I saw before.

Each is in its own evidence bag. He also removes three smaller bags. Remy arranges all five bags side by side so she (and we) can see everything.

The key is in the second from the left, but Remy does not go straight to it. Instead, she lifts the bag that contains the pack of gum and studies it as if it's important. "Has this been checked for prints?"

"Everything has."

"And?"

"We only found the girl's."

"May I open this?"

"Is it important?"

"It could be, yes."

"Just be careful."

"Of course."

She gingerly removes the gum from the bag and holds it like it might bite her if she's not careful.

After examining it and putting it back, she does the same with the pens.

When she picks up the Fonda Lee novel, that's my cue.

I make a call to Evidence and Property. "This is Detective Reese, Buena Park Police Department. I'm looking for Detective George Hughes. I'm told he's there."

"One moment." I'm put on hold, then, "He's in one of the evidence rooms."

"I really need to talk to him. Can you put me through?"

"Please hold."

After a few seconds, the line starts ringing.

On Jar's screen, as Remy is looking at *Jade City*, a wall phone rings at the other end of the room. Hughes looks over, pushes out of his chair, and walks toward it. The instant his back is to her, Remy removes the Altoids box from her pocket and puts the box on her lap.

The detective picks up the phone. "Hughes."

"Detective Hughes, this is Detective Reese, Buena Park PD." Once more, I'm using the voice modulator, but at a different setting from when I pretended to be Special Agent Lamar.

"Do I know you?"

"I don't think so, but I was told you could help me."

"I'm kind of tied up right now. If you give me a number, I'll call you back." He glances over at Remy as he says this.

"This should only take a moment," I said. "I believe you're familiar with a guy named Perry Wesson."

"Wesson?" On the screen, I see him turn away from Remy.

She immediately picks up the key bag and opens it. "Yeah, I know him. He's an asshole."

Earlier, before Remy arrived at the hotel, Jar and I looked through some of Hughes's recent cases and picked out the name of someone who'd been questioned about a homicide but ultimately deemed not involved. Why did we choose him? Because Perry Wesson is one of those people who spends his life treading the gray area between right and very wrong. Plus, he lives in Buena Park, which is close to L.A. but not too close.

"We brought him in last night for questioning on an attempted murder," I say.

"That's not surprising."

As I engage Hughes on his take about Wesson, Remy removes the key from the bag, opens the Altoids tin, and presses the key into the wax. When she closes the lid, the wax there makes an impression of the top side of the key. I wouldn't mind having the real key, but since it's listed on the inventory, its absence might be noted and it's not worth stirring up a hornet's nest. When Remy's done, she wipes the key off with the rag and returns it to its bag.

I let Hughes finish telling me about his questioning of Wesson, then say, "I appreciate you sharing that with me, thank you."

"Did he finally go off and kill someone?" he asks me.

"Still not sure. Could be it was wrong place wrong time, which, from what you've told me, seems to be a habit of his. Look, I've already troubled you longer than I intended. Thank you for taking my call."

"Not a problem."

"If I have any other questions, is it all right if I call you back?"

"Let me give you my cell number."

I don't write it down—I still have his business card at the townhouse—but I make him think I do.

We say our goodbyes, and I watch him hang up and turn back to the table. Remy has moved on to the accounting book.

"Find anything of interest?" Hughes asks.

She looks at the textbook for another moment before setting it down and frowning. "Unfortunately, I don't think your guy's the one we're looking for."

"You figured that out because of a bunch of stuff in a backpack?"

"Because of what's *not* in the backpack."

"What do you mean?"

"I'm sorry, Detective. Since I don't think there's a connection here, I can't share that information. I'm sure you understand."

He looks disappointed but says, "Yeah, sure. I get it."

They talk for a few more minutes, Remy apologizing for intruding on his day, and Hughes being surprisingly magnanimous by saying he's sorry it didn't work out.

Remy arrives at our hotel room twelve minutes later.

She pulls the data card and the tin of wax from her pocket and holds them out. "Who wants these?"

"Me," Jar says.

She takes them and hurries back to her computer.

"I can't tell you how much we appreciate your help," I say. "Thank you."

"Happy to be of service." Remy eyes me for a moment. "What are you guys up to?"

"A personal matter. Nothing important."

"Someone's paying you for this?"

As a rule, freelancers don't ask a lot of questions. But this situation is unusual, so it's understandable that Remy would like to know a bit more. She has, after all, put herself in a vulnerable position with the LAPD.

But it's also understandable that I'm not going to tell her. "Like I said, we appreciate your assistance."

"I watch the news. I saw the reports about Naomi's murder. I also remember the kidnapping." She looks at me, then at Jar, then back at me again. "One of you knew her, didn't you?"

I'm about to give her another non-answer, but Jar speaks up before I can.

"In a way, yes."

Remy cocks her head. "In a way?"

"It's a long story," I say.

"And the guy who they say killed her. You don't think he's the one who did it, do you?"

I smile. "Shall I transfer your fee to the usual account? Or is there someplace else you'd like it sent?"

Remy's eyes are focused on Jar, and she's made no indication she heard my question. Jar, for her part, is looking at something on her computer.

"Remy?" I say. "Your fee?"

There's a beat before she turns her gaze to me. "Keep it. I had nothing else to do this afternoon."

"But you don't need to do that. I told you I'd—"

"I said, keep it. You can pay me back if I need help someday."

I consider arguing the point further, but instead I nod and smile. "Thank you."

She removes the flag-pin camera and hands it and the signal booster to me. She then walks over and puts a hand on Jar's shoulder. I can see Jar tensing slightly, but she doesn't jerk away, nor does she look up.

"I hope you find the bastard who did this to her," Remy says.

"I do, too," Jar says.

So much for keeping it a secret.

Remy remains there, hand on Jar's shoulder, for another moment, then turns and heads toward the door. When she nears me, she pauses. "If you need anything else, you let me know."

"I will."

"I mean it."

"I know you do. Thanks, Remy."

She leaves.

"I like her," Jar says.

"She's good people." I join Jar at the desk. "So, what've we got?"

"I ran the serial number on the card. It's two years old and was purchased in an electronics store in South Korea."

Which coincides perfectly with Naomi's assignment there as an army communications specialist.

"Shall we see what's on it?" I ask.

Jar plugs a card adapter into the side of her laptop and inserts the SD card. When the menu comes up, she says, "Photos."

She scrolls through the files, which doesn't take long.

"That's it?" I ask.

"Yes. Seventeen photos."

"No hidden folders?"

She runs the card through a diagnostic program, then shakes her head. "Nothing else."

She opens the first shot. It's of a two-story house, clapboard style. Gray, or faded white, hard to tell. Whoever owned the place clearly did not prioritize maintenance. There are holes in many of the visible screens, and the rain gutter on the left side has broken free at one end and is tilting toward the ground like a long, mouse-sized waterslide. If not for the furniture I can see through the windows, I'd think the place has been abandoned. Then again, just because there's furniture inside doesn't mean it hasn't been.

Jar checks the meta data. "No location tag."

She brings up the next shot.

It's the house again but smaller in frame, the surrounding trees and bushes creating a green square in an otherwise brown landscape.

"That looks like it's in the desert," I say.

Sagebrush spatters the rolling terrain. No cactus, though, not as far as I can see. A dirt road runs from the house and extends past the lower edge of the picture.

Jar checks the data again, and again there is no information indicating where the shot was taken.

Two more photos are variations on the one we just examined. Photo number five is from an even longer range. The house is probably a kilometer or so away, the dirt driveway traveling over a hill and across a bridge spanning a small river, to where it ends at a two-lane blacktop road. This latter could very well be a highway, but there are no signs in the shot to identify it.

The banks of the river are green and crowded with bushes. Not a common sight in a desert, though I have seen something similar along the Colorado River between California and Arizona. This is way too small to be the Colorado, however. It looks maybe ten meters across at most. The Colorado is considerably wider than that.

The next shot is of a man. His tanned and weather-worn face makes it hard to tell his age. He could be anywhere from his late fifties to mid-seventies. His hair doesn't help, either. It's jet black and obviously dyed.

The shot is candid, the man facing the lens at about a forty-five-degree angle. He's squinting like the sun is too bright, and his lips are pulled away from his teeth in a sneer. He's wearing jeans and a khaki shirt, and is walking down a sidewalk alone. A business of some kind is on one side, and on the other, a couple of cars parked perpendicular to the street.

Jar zooms in on the nearest vehicle and focuses on the front license plate.

"Do you recognize what state this is from?" she asks.

Because of the way the cars are parked, only a bit of the plate is visible. The background is white-ish, and the only visible character—an 8 or a B...maybe—is either dark blue or black. "Could be California," I say.

"Only could be?"

I shrug. "The white looks...off. But that might be the exposure."

She studies her screen and lets out a low *hmmm*.

There are five more pictures of the man. Three are sequential to the first, but none provide a better view of the cars' license plates. The last two were taken on, I assume, different days from the other six. In one, the man is dressed in a white collared shirt, and in the other, a faded olive T-shirt. I guess he could have worn all three shirts on the same day, but he doesn't strike me as the kind of guy who enjoys doing a lot of laundry.

What he does strike me as is a person people tolerate but are never happy to see. It's just an impression and I'm not married to it, so I'll put a pin in it for now.

The twelfth photograph is of another building. Not a house but a business, at least on the ground floor. Painted on the window are the words HARDWARE & SUPPLY. Another word used to be above it but it's been scratched off. Maybe a name? You know, like Nate's or Jar's Hardware & Supply? Only a few more letters than either one of those. Whoever's place it was, it looks closed, as in permanently, because inside it looks empty.

Jar zooms in on the name. Whoever scratched it off didn't quite get everything. Specks of the old letters can be seen on the glass.

"You think there's any way you can piece together what it used to say?" I ask.

"With a little time, perhaps."

The final five shots are of a different man. He's bald, and though he's weather-aged like the other guy, he's not nearly as tan nor is he clean shaven. His beard is full and nearly all white. This, and the general look of the guy, gives me the impression his sixty-fifth birthday—maybe even his seventieth—was years ago. The pictures are not candid shots like those taken of the other man, as the bald man appears to be posing for the camera.

Unfortunately, nothing else in the images of him helps us identify the location.

"That is everything," Jar says.

"Who are these guys?" I wonder aloud.

"That is rhetorical, correct? Because I—"

"Yeah, rhetorical. No dates on the photos?"

Jar shakes her head. "Only the file creation dates. They are all December twenty-eighth."

"Of last year."

"Yes."

That was only three weeks before Naomi died. It doesn't mean the pictures are connected to what happened to her, but it would be a mistake to ignore the possibility.

I feel Liz suddenly beside me, staring intently at Jar's screen. Liz isn't saying anything, but I sense she thinks the men are important.

Silently I mouth, "If you have a lead, by all means share it."

"What?" Jar says.

Perhaps I wasn't as silent as I thought. "Nothing. I was, um, just thinking out loud."

"You mean like the other times," she says.

"What other times?"

"I have told you before. You do this a lot."

"I don't—"

"It is just the two of us, but sometimes it is like you are talking to someone else. Like you are wearing comm gear."

I laugh a bit more nervously than I would like. "No, I don't. And I'm not wearing any comm gear. I'm only—"

"Then who are you talking to?"

She stares at me, waiting, and I stare back, wondering how the hell I'm going to get out of this. In the end, I say what I believe is the truth. (Or what I hope is the truth.) "Myself. I'm talking to myself. It's a bad habit I've picked up in the last...since..."

Her face softens, saving me from having to say the actual words.

"I know you miss her." She puts a hand on my arm. "She will always be a part of you. Embrace that, or you will never stop fighting the past." When she lets go, she says, "And try to stop talking to yourself."

"Yeah. I'll, uh, I'll work on that."

CHAPTER SIXTEEN

W e return to my townhouse.
Jar sits at the dining table, trying to figure out where the photos were taken, while I'm on the couch with my own laptop, hunting for information in the police files that might help me with an idea I had. I finally find it in a transcript of an interview between a Detective Joon Kim and a woman named Cynthia Watson.

Note that this was conducted prior to the news that Saundra Moore was Naomi Bellows.

DETECTIVE KIM: Could you describe your relationship with Saundra Moore?
CYNTHIA WATSON: We were classmates and friends.
KIM: Close friends?
CW: Pretty close, I guess.
KIM: Would you consider yourself her best friend?
CW: No, I'm not sure she actually had a best friend here.

She just started fall semester. We had a class together and

hit it off, so we started hanging out sometimes outside of class. She was very, I don't know, I guess you'd say reserved.

KIM: What do you mean?
CW: Some people are easy to get to know, and others it takes a while. She was one of those who takes a while.
KIM: Did she have other friends?
CW: I can't say for sure. There were a few people she would talk to, but as far as I knew, I was closer to her than anyone else. I don't know. Maybe I was her best friend.
KIM: Do you know why she would have been in Griffith Park that late at night?
CW: The planetarium. She said she was going to a special late-night program they were showing.
KIM: With someone?
CW: I got the impression she was going alone.

This must be where the police learned about Naomi's plan to go to the planetarium. We know from the report, though, that she did not appear on the observatory's security video, nor is there a record of her buying a ticket for the event.

The rest of Cynthia's interview focuses on things she did with Naomi, which basically amounted to study sessions, watching movies at one of their places, and the occasional night out for a drink.

Talking to Naomi's friends is another reason I wanted to come back to L.A. They could give me some insight into what was going on with Naomi leading up to her murder. I was hoping the police had found more than just one friend, but it looks like Cynthia is it, and this transcript does not fill me with much confidence that I will learn anything new from her. I almost write the whole idea off, but then I discover a link to an audio file of the interview.

I click on it.

Something about Cynthia's voice makes me think she was giving the detective an edited version of the truth. It's in her pauses and the occasional change of tone that weren't evident in the transcript.

Perhaps there's a bit of hope after all.

Detective Kim has dutifully included the girl's address and phone number. I transfer the information to my phone and close my computer.

"I'm going out for a few hours," I say as I get up. "You'll be all right here?"

Jar looks up from her laptop. "Where are you going?"

"To see if I can talk to one of Naomi's friends."

"There was only one friend mentioned in the police report."

"Talk to her *friend*. Better?"

"Good idea."

"I'll pick up food on my way back. Any requests?"

"Papaya salad, *pet-pet*."

Cynthia lives in a complex called The Latitudes on Zelzah Avenue, directly across the street from the Cal State North-ridge tennis courts. Given the half dozen or so starter adults standing in front of the building, with book bags over their shoulders, it's a safe bet the place was designed with students in mind.

I find an open spot along the road and park.

The front entrance appears to be a fairly large lobby. I can see what looks like a reception counter inside, with someone sitting behind it. I'd rather arrive at the girl's room unan-nounced, so I turn down the street that runs along the south side of the building, looking for an alternate entrance. There are several, but the first one I try is locked. Since the others along this end are clones of it, I bypass them.

At the back of the building is a large, walled-in parking lot. It has an automated gate, but it's stuck in the open position because someone has moved the wheels at the bottom of the gate off the tracks. I have a feeling it was done by a resident, so his or her friends who didn't live there could park in the lot without a passkey. Whatever the reason, it benefits me.

As I step into the lot, a group of four students exits the complex and walks toward the parked cars. A few years ago, I might have been able to pass for one of them, but I'm at the back end of my twenties now and have lost that fresh-out-of-high-school look. Turns out I didn't have to be concerned about fitting in, at least not yet. Though a couple of the students glance my way, it appears to be more out of reflex than any interest, and they move on without saying a word. I'd like to think it's because I'm overestimating how old I look, but I have a feeling I could be a seventy-year-old grandpa and they would still ignore me.

The Latitudes consists of several buildings. I'm guessing the actual apartments are in the three largest. One is directly to my left, while the remaining two are at the other end of the property, one behind the other. There's a smaller building on the parking lot side, between the building next to me and the two tandem buildings. In front of it is an open area, beyond which I can see the backside of the main lobby building.

I walk through the gap between the small building and the nearest apartment structure, into the open area, where I find a giant swimming pool. With the sun already down and the temperature in the low fifties, no one's in the water, but several students are sitting on lounge chairs around the pool, talking and joking around. I go up to the group nearest me and ask if they can direct me to apartment 302K.

"That's in Kest Hall," one of them says. He points at the tandem building that sits at the front of the property, along Zelzah. "Third floor. Follow the numbers."

"Thanks."

I start to turn away, but another one says, "You're not going to be able to get in without a key."

I stop. "I didn't realize that. I was just supposed to meet my friend."

The first one stands. "I gotta get something out of my room anyway. I'll let you in."

Room 302K is on the street side of the building, directly across from the tennis courts. My knock is answered by a female voice shouting, "Just a second."

The door is opened by a woman in her early twenties. She's dressed in sweatpants and a GO LOVE YOURSELF pink T-shirt. She gives me a surprised look.

"Can I help you?"

"I hope so. Are you Cynthia Watson?"

"Yeah."

"I'm wondering if I might have a few moments of your time."

Her expression slides into side-eyed wariness. "You trying to sell me something?"

"Not at all." I glance both ways down the hall, making sure we're alone, and lower my voice. "I'm a private investigator. I'm working for Naomi Bellows's family. I believe you knew her as Saundra Moore."

Her eyes soften. "Oh, um, what do you want to talk about?"

My voice still low, I say, "I'd rather not discuss it out in the open like this. Is there somewhere more private we can go?"

She considers it for a moment, then says, "Hold on."

She shuts the door, and when she opens it again, she's wearing a sweater over her T-shirt and has pulled on a pair of sneakers. "Maybe one of the study rooms is empty."

The first study room we check is in use. The second, however, is unoccupied. She heads in and I follow. I close the door but leave a thumb-width gap to make sure she feels safe.

There are two tables in the room, and we take the one farthest from the door.

"I appreciate you doing this," I say.

"No problem."

"As I mentioned, I'm working for Naomi's family." I pause. "You don't mind if I refer to her as Naomi, do you?"

"No. That...that's okay. I mean, it was a shock to find out who she'd been before, but it actually explained a lot of things."

"What do you mean?"

"She was pretty reserved."

"Right, you mentioned that to Detective Kim."

She nods. "I knew there had to be something in her past that made her that way. I would have never guessed it was because of being kidnapped and held for all that time. Knowing that now, I'm surprised she was as grounded as she was."

Cynthia seems almost eager to talk about Naomi, which gives me the sense she hasn't discussed her friend's death with anyone else.

"Is that how you would describe her? As grounded?"

"She always seemed aware of everything going on around her." A quiet laugh. "Well, maybe not everything, but close. And she could talk about almost any subject. Intelligently, you know. She was pretty amazing."

"Her family will appreciate hearing that."

"What exactly are you doing for them?"

"They lost touch with Naomi when she and her mother

went into witness protection, so they didn't find out that Naomi died until the police found out who Saundra Moore really was and called them. The family hired me to make sure everything was as the police said it was, and also to find out what her life had been like. There are years of her life they don't know about. They want to remember her properly. I've come to talk to you because I'm hoping you can help them do that."

"I'll tell you what I can, but I don't know if it's much."

"Any little bit will help."

I ask her questions about the classes she shared with Naomi and the time they spent together, encouraging her to share a few anecdotes. Her stories paint the picture of a woman who was ardently self-reliant but also kindhearted. The kind of person who expected nothing from anyone but would have done anything for someone she felt was in need. The kind of person I would have liked to have known.

"When the police asked you if you knew of someone who might have wanted to harm Naomi, you said no. Has anyone come to mind since then?"

She frowns. "I thought the cops already knew who did it. That guy they talked about on the news. The one who'd been stalking her."

"Sometimes the police make mistakes. The family wants to make sure that hasn't happened with Naomi. If you know something that might not align with what the police think, it's all right to tell me. I won't say anything to them unless it pans out. And if it does, I would never mention your name without getting your okay first."

There is something. I can see it in how the corners of her mouth tense.

But whatever it is, she isn't ready to share because she shakes her head and says, "Sorry."

"That's all right. Maybe they did get the right guy." I pause as if I'm thinking about something. "I have to say, though, something doesn't feel right."

"About her murder?"

"Yeah. I don't think the police are hiding anything. I just think...never mind. It's not important."

"You think she was killed by someone other than the guy they found, don't you?" she asks.

I hesitate, and then nod. "It's mainly a feeling in my gut, but I trust my instincts."

"Who do you think did it?"

"That, I don't know. But I do know there are a couple things that don't add up about this Harrison guy. If I can prove someone else is responsible, I will." I smile. "You've been very kind to talk to me. Thank you."

At some point in the last few seconds, she's begun to chew the inside of her lower lip. "Can I...can I tell you something?"

"You can tell me anything."

Across the room, the door opens, and two women around the same age as Cynthia enter, carrying books. Their timing couldn't be worse, and I'm half convinced Cynthia will use it as an excuse to keep to herself whatever she was about to tell me.

The girls approach the other table but don't sit.

"Hey, Cynthia," one of them says. "Everything all right?"

There's no hiding the fact Cynthia and I have been engaged in a heavy conversation. We're sitting near each other, our demeanors serious.

"Everything's fine," Cynthia says. "Would it be possible for you to give us a few minutes?"

"Our study group is supposed to meet here now."

"We're almost done. I promise."

The other girl says, "Sure. We can wait outside."

"Thank you."

They leave, closing the door all the way. This doesn't seem

to bother Cynthia, which is another sign she's starting to trust me.

"Sorry about that," she says.

"It's fine. I hope my being here isn't going to cause you any problems."

"They probably think you're trying to ask me out."

"Do you want me to tell them that's not the case?"

A sneer. "Even if it was, they'd know you'd strike out. You and I don't play on the same team."

"I see. Well, then, let's move on, shall we?"

She studies me through narrowed eyes. "You're a decent guy, aren't you?"

The question catches me off guard. "I hope so. I mean, I-I try."

A smile.

"You were going to tell me something," I say.

She nods and says, "You didn't happen to find a FedEx envelope in her stuff, did you?"

The hair on the back of my neck tingles as Liz floats in over my shoulder, listening.

"No," I say. "Nothing like that."

She chews the inside of her mouth again.

"Should there have been an envelope?" I ask.

"I don't know. She probably threw it out."

"Was there something important about it?"

"I'm not sure." She lets out a decisive breath before saying, "She received it right after New Year's. I was with her when it arrived. Inside was another envelope containing a stack of about twenty or thirty sheets of paper, stapled together. She got really nervous when she saw it, or excited—I'm not really sure which. Maybe agitated is a better way to describe it."

"But you don't know what was on the papers?"

"No. Right after she pulled them out, she asked if we could

postpone our plans for a couple hours and that she'd meet me at my place. So I left."

"And she never told you what was inside?"

"Never."

"How did she act when you got back together?"

"She was quiet, more than usual. Her mind seemed preoccupied. I did ask if something was up, but she said no."

"How was she the next time you saw her?"

"Better, kind of. But she still seemed to be thinking about something, like it was always there in the background."

"Even the last time you saw her?"

"Yeah. Even then."

Cynthia is wrapped in an aura of sadness that seems out of proportion for the death of someone she's presented as being not quite a best friend, and I realize something I probably should have picked up on earlier. "You liked her."

"Of course I liked her."

"I mean more than as a friend."

She says nothing.

"Were you dating?"

She sits back. "I've told you everything I know. If you don't mind, I have a paper I need to get back to."

"I'm sorry. I'm not trying to upset you." This keeps her from immediately pushing out of her chair, but I know that could still happen at any second. "I didn't realize you were in a relationship with her. I'm sure her death hit you a lot harder than you've been letting on. I only wanted to say I'm sorry."

Tears gather in her eyes, and her lips tremble.

Tell her, Liz says.

"My girlfriend died a little more than a year ago," I say. "Most days are okay now, but it's taken a long time to get to this point. Some days...some days aren't as good."

"W-w-what happened to her?"

Tell her, Liz says again.

"She was shot."

"Oh, my God. Were you there?"

It's been a while since I've talked about this—since I've purposely thought about it—and I can feel my own eyes welling up. "I held her as she slipped away."

Liz's hand brushes my cheek without actually touching me.

"I am so sorry. Did they...did they catch who did it?"

"Yes."

I blink and look at her. She's leaning forward again, her hand covering mine on the table.

"I'm so sorry for your loss, too," I say.

A sad smile creases her face. "Naomi wasn't my girlfriend. I mean, I wanted her to be, but I don't know if she ever realized that. Or if she was even interested in girls. I just...I just really liked her."

I already know the answer to my next question, but it's something the person I'm pretending to be would ask. "Did you tell the police any of this?"

"No. I was still too shocked that she was dead when they talked to me that I didn't even think about it." She locks eyes with me again. "Do you really think they got the wrong man?"

"I do." I pause. "That FedEx package. You didn't happen to see a return address on it, did you?"

"No."

"But they delivered it to her apartment?"

"Yes."

"Any chance you might remember the date?"

She thinks for a moment. "I'm pretty sure it was on one of my days off, which are Sundays and Mondays."

"What do you do?"

"I'm a waitress."

"The perfect student job," I say. "So, a Sunday or a Monday, then?"

A nod. "In the afternoon, if that helps. Does FedEx even deliver on Sundays?"

"Sometimes." I look at the calendar on my phone. "You said she received it right after New Year's. Could it have come the week before she died?"

"I don't think so. It feels further back than that."

"That would leave only the fifth or sixth."

"Maybe FedEx can tell you who it came from."

"I hope so." Jar and I *will* get the answer from FedEx, but we're not going to ask. "Is there anything else you think might be important? Maybe something Naomi said."

"Nothing else comes to mind."

"Thank you. Really. The package is something no one knew about."

"I hope it helps."

"Me, too. I won't take up any more of your time. Thank you again."

As we stand, she hesitates, as if there's something she wants to say.

"Can I give you my phone number?" I ask. "In case you think of something I should know about."

"Um, yes. Sure."

She pulls out her phone, and I give her a number to one of my voicemail boxes.

As she finishes inputting it, she says, "Do you know what happened to her things?"

"From her apartment, you mean?"

"Yes."

"Everything is being held in storage until her family can figure out what they want to do with it."

"They're not going to keep her stuff?"

This is not a question I prepared for, but improvising is often a part of my job. "They might, but they're not in California so it would have to be shipped. Or they might sell or donate everything."

A worried look crosses her brow.

"Is there a problem?" I ask.

"It's just..." She takes a moment to collect her thoughts. "If they decide to sell or donate everything, there's one thing they should really hold on to."

"What would that be?"

"Naomi had a wooden box. About like this." She pantomimes something the size of a rectangular tissue box. "She kept her army things in it. Name tag, pins, things like that. I could tell she was proud of her service. I don't think the box is something that should be sold or given away."

"I'll let them know."

CHAPTER SEVENTEEN

I t's Monday afternoon, and Jar and I are on a flight to Eugene, Oregon.

Why Eugene? Because that's where Naomi's FedEx package was sent from.

We did give some consideration to staying in L.A. and trying to gain access to Naomi's safety-deposit box, but doing that would take time. And besides, the Fed Ex package isn't the only thing pointing us north.

Oregon is where Naomi was born, where she spent her preteen years. And where she was kidnapped and held prisoner.

Oregon was also the destination of the flight Juan Sanchez told his uncle Mateo about. Portland, to be precise. That trip happened on January 10 and 11, the Friday and Saturday a week before Naomi was killed.

But the most compelling reason, besides the mysterious FedEx package, is that Oregon is where the pictures on Naomi's SD card were taken. Jar figured that out while I was talking to Cynthia, by reconstructing the scratched-out name (Morgan) on the hardware store window and then conducting a Google search. There are apparently several Morgan Hardware companies and Morgan Supply companies in the world, but only one Morgan Hardware & Supply. It was located in Hayes, Oregon, and I say *was* because the store apparently is no longer in business.

Hayes, it should be noted, is in the eastern part of the state, maybe an hour's drive from Idaho. More importantly, it's only thirty minutes from Naomi's hometown of Willis, and forty-five from where she had been held prisoner near the town of Foster.

If it becomes imperative for us to see what's in the safety-deposit box, we can always go back to L.A. For now, Oregon is clearly calling.

Any doubts I had about Naomi's kidnapping and her death being linked have now disappeared. The evidence, circumstantial as it may be, is too great to ignore.

A part of me, however, wishes the evidence led us in another direction. I fear recent events are already triggering painful memories for Jar of her own captivity. She's tense and distracted. I hope when we land that will change.

There were no direct flights leaving Los Angeles when we needed to depart, so we end up having to fly all the way up to Seattle and catch another plane south to Eugene. By the time we touch down, it's nearly six p.m. and the sun has just set.

About those contacts we have all around the world who can supply us with gear. Not one of them operates out of Eugene. Which means instead of having a souped-up car filled with gadgets and weapons waiting for us in the parking lot, we pick up a no-frills Hyundai Sonata from Budget Rental and drive to the Residence Inn where we booked a two-bedroom suite.

There's no question about waiting around until morning to get started. Even if I wanted to, Jar wouldn't let me. But I don't want to.

The return address from the FedEx package leads us across the Willamette River to a two-story, box-like office building in a mixed-use area of businesses and homes. Except for a meter-wide strip of bright yellow around the top, the building is light gray. Between the windows on the first floor and those on the second is a sign that reads: WM. CAMERON BUSINESS CENTER. It's carved in stone to make the building look old, but the structure can't have been here more than a decade. On the grass out front is another sign, this one listing the six companies renting space inside.

Since it's after seven now, it's not surprising that even though the lobby is still lit, the first-floor windows on either side of the entrance are dark. That goes for the windows on the second floor, too. The unit we're interested in is 206, which means it's probably on the upper floor and toward the back.

I park in the lot beside the building and we walk over to the lobby door. I use my jacket-covered arm to push on the handle. It doesn't budge.

There's a call box on the wall, with a button for each suite, but we prefer to arrive unannounced, which has probably become obvious to you. Since the door lock is the electric buzzer type, Jar takes care of it, while I block her from the view of anyone on the street by pretending to be on my phone.

Suite 206 is indeed in the back of the building, near the stairs. The door is flush with the threshold so I can't tell if a light is on inside or not.

Unlike the other offices we've seen, there's only a discolored blank space on the wall where the plaque identifying the business should be.

Jar wands the door, checking for an alarm, and shakes her head.

From my pocket, I pull out two pairs of latex gloves, give a set to her, and don the other. I try the knob. Locked.

I remove what looks like a credit card from my wallet and pop out the lockpicking tools scored into it. I love these cards.

They're convenient, easy to carry, and never cause a problem with airport security. Yeah, metal picks last longer, but they're risky to travel with. I have a few boxes of these disposable picks in my storage locker back home, and always take several cards with me wherever I go.

The lock to suite 206 yields quickly, and we step inside.

The lights are not on, but we don't need them. More than enough illumination streams through the windows from street-lights and neighboring buildings. The suite, at least in its current configuration, is a single room.

A single, completely empty room.

There's not even a crumpled piece of paper lying on the floor. And either the walls were recently painted or the previous tenant never hung anything on them, because not a single nail hole is in sight. The carpet has been shampooed, too.

Before we left Los Angeles, we checked the website belonging to the sender of the FedEx box to confirm the return address was the one for this office.

Apparently, we should have looked into the business a little deeper, because what we're supposed to be standing in the middle of are the offices of Whitfield Investigations.

Jar pulls out her phone, and thirty seconds later shows me her screen. On it is the website for *The Register-Guard*, Eugene's local newspaper. The article she's brought up is head-lined: LOCAL MAN DIES IN CAR CRASH. I read the first couple of paragraphs.

Eugene resident Alex Whitfield died when his car skidded off Marcola Road into a tree. The accident occurred just after 11 p.m. on Friday night. Police suspect the car hit a patch of ice and Whitfield lost control.

Carla Whitfield, the deceased's wife, told investigators that her husband, a local private investigator, was meeting with a potential client, and had telephoned to tell her the client had not shown up so he was on his way home.

There's more, but nothing important.

The article is from Sunday, January 12, meaning the crash happened on Friday, January 10. Which was four days after Naomi received Whitfield's package on Monday, January 6—something we learned from Jar's dip into FedEx's database.

"I do not think it was an accident," Jar says.

"Neither do I," I say.

Sure, it wasn't a staged overdose like with David Weeks and Juan Sanchez, but it *is* another death connected to Naomi, and there's no way in hell I'd believe it's random.

But as much as I'd like to prove I'm right, we're not here to set the record straight about Whitfield's death. We're here to find out what he was doing for Naomi, and the only thing that has changed is the location of the files where that information will likely be.

Jar finds a number for his wife, Carla. Do I feel a little slimy about calling her with the intent of stealing one of her late husband's files? You bet I do. But I punch in her number anyway, because I know it's for the greater good.

The call doesn't even ring once before a prerecorded voice that might or might not be Carla's says, "Please leave a message." When the beep sounds, it's followed by a more generic voice saying, "Mailbox full."

I should be disappointed, but I'm relieved.

Jar and I both search the internet for anyone who might have worked for Whitfield. I find a news article from about a year ago, with a quote from Junabelle Staf, who is identified as a part-time employee of the PI. Jar finds the woman's phone number. Not a cell phone, but a landline.

I have Jar look up Junabelle's social security number. As I suspected, the woman is a senior citizen. She's seventy-one.

Prior to reporting income from Whitfield, she worked thirty-six years for a private investigator named Carl Vernon. Turned out when Vernon retired, Whitfield bought his business. Junabelle, in a part-time role, apparently came with it.

We brainstorm a plausible reason for contacting the woman, and I make the call.

Three rings, then, "Hello?"

"Yes, hello. My name is Tom McKrall. Is this Junabelle Staf?"

"Sorry, not interested." She hangs up.

Huh. Not quite how I mapped out things.

I call again and am sent to voicemail. I hang up before the beep and try a third time.

This time, she picks up again. "If you call again, I'm reporting you for harass—"

"Ma'am, I'm not selling anything. I'm calling because I hope you can help me."

"Help you with what?"

"I believe you worked with Alex Whitfield? I'm one of his clients. I mean, I *was* one."

"I don't remember your name."

"And I don't remember you. But I—"

"Then how would you even know to call me?"

"Because I know how to use the internet to find the name of someone Whitfield worked with," I say with a touch of annoyance. I take an audible breath. "I apologize. I didn't mean to be snippy. I just found out he died. My condolences. I'm sure it's been difficult."

A beat, followed by, "Thank you."

"Your boss was going to check on something for me. Said it might take him a bit to collect everything, but that he should be able to mail me what he found by the end of January. I've been out of town on business for a month and didn't get back until today. I expected a package to be waiting for me, but there was nothing. I tried calling the number he'd given me but it was disconnected. So I went by his office this afternoon and...well, you know, you aren't there anymore."

"When did you hire him?"

"Just before Christmas."

"The accident was only a couple weeks later," she says, the softening of her tone telling me she bought my story. "I'm sorry, but I don't think it's likely he was able to get to your case."

"That's what I was afraid of," I say, disappointed. "I don't mean to sound callous, but I would love to know for sure. Is there any chance you could check his files?"

"Unfortunately, I can't do that."

"Could you point me to someone who might be able to?"

"What I meant was, the files are gone. Someone broke into our offices and stole the computers. All of our work was on them."

I have little doubt Operation Cover Up Naomi's Murder struck again.

"That's awful," I say. "Did that happen before the accident? Or...?"

"A few days after, though we're not sure exactly when. The police think someone saw a story about Alex's death and took advantage of no one being at the office."

"Some people are just evil."

"You're right about that."

"What about backups of your data?" I ask. "Wasn't everything saved to the cloud?"

"Um, I *think* so. But I really don't know about that. You'd have to ask Alex's wife about that. She was handling those kinds of things."

"I see. Okay, well, I'm sorry to have bothered you."

"I could recommend another investigator, if you need someone."

"That's very kind. I think I'm going to take a little time to think things over and figure out what I want to do. I might call you back for that name later, if that's okay."

"Please do."

When I hang up, I realize Jar is staring at me.

"Someone broke in here right after Whitfield died and took their computers," I tell her. "She didn't know about backups. Didn't sound like she dealt with the technical side of things."

"There are a lot of tracks being hidden," Jar says, sounding as pissed off as I feel. "I can say it that way, yes?"

"I would say *covered*, but you're right. Whoever is behind this is definitely being thorough."

"But are they being thorough enough?"

I raise an eyebrow. "Think you can find something?"

"I assume that is a rhetorical question."

Jar and I are back at the Residence Inn, sitting at the table, looking at Jar's laptop. This is easier than us both trying to read off her phone.

Whoever raided Whitfield's office probably thought they did a good job, but at most it was cosmetic. I do have to give them props for deleting Whitfield's iDrive account, which eliminated his cloud backup. Not everyone would think of that. But where they messed up was with his email. They started the process well enough, by canceling his account with his email service provider. What they didn't take into consideration was that the account is on an annual subscription, saving Whitfield sixty-five bucks compared to the month-to-month option. So while his account was canceled, it wouldn't actually be deleted until the end of December.

Jar found twenty-seven emails between Naomi and Whitfield. From the brevity of each message, I get the sense that anything important was discussed over the phone.

For example, the first email Whitfield sent her reads:

Received your payment. Thank you. Will get things going.

AW

This went out back in October. Most of the other emails either acknowledge receiving phone calls or set up times when they could talk. But there are six emails of note.

Two, from December 28, contain the same pictures we found on Naomi's SD card. The date coincides with the creation date on the card's files. In one email, the pictures of the man who didn't know he was being photographed are grouped with those of the house sitting by itself in the desert. The other email contains the photos of the bearded guy paired with the images of the hardware store.

Whitfield was a man of few words, because there are only two in each message. At the top of the one containing the man in the candid shots, Whitfield typed Hank Morgan. And at the top of the email with the bearded guy and the hardware store is Gerald Morgan. I think we can safely assume that means Gerald owns or owned Morgan Hardware & Supply.

The next email of interest lists two addresses. At the start of each are initials, HM on one and GM on the other. Again, it doesn't take a genius to figure out HM is Hank, and he lives in the town of Raven, while GM is Gerald, who lives in Bend. Both communities are in Oregon, with Raven being no more than a half hour from Naomi's hometown of Willis. As we look at the pictures of the men, I can't help but think we are looking at two of her kidnappers.

Whitfield's last email to Naomi was sent on Saturday, January 4.

FedEx just picked up the package. Will be there Monday. When you decide what you want to do about this, let me know.

AW

As I said, there are six emails of interest. The two I haven't mentioned yet are both from Naomi. One is a response to Whitfield's final email, sent that following Monday.

I received the package. Thank you. I'll be in touch.

Naomi

Her last one to him was sent two days after that.

Mr. Whitfield:

After thinking about it, I have decided to handle things on my own for now, and will no longer require your services. Thank you again for your help.

Naomi

"Let's map this out," I say.

I find a piece of hotel paper and a pen in a drawer, then draw a crude calendar grid. After Jar tells me what day the first of January fell on, I write the numbers in the correct squares.

"Sunday, January nineteenth. Naomi's murder, sometime

after midnight." I write this in the square. "Same day, I find her body." I add this in, then back up one square. "Weeks takes train from Tucson with Sanchez and two others." I abbreviate this as *W train Tuc—>L.A., Sanchez+A&C*. Next I move a week and one day earlier, to the square for Friday January 10, and both write and say, "Whitfield crashes car." In the box for Wednesday the eighth, I write *Naomi sends final email-Whitfield*. Two days before that, on Monday January 6, I write *FedEx arrives 2 Naomi*.

I study the calendar for a moment, then point at the last thing I entered. "FedEx arrives on Monday..." I move my finger to the eighth. "Naomi decides on a different direction and ends her business with Whitfield on Wednesday..." My finger stops on the tenth. "Whitfield dies on Friday *and* Sanchez takes his trip to Portland..." It skips down to the eighteenth. "The fall guy is brought in from Tucson..." And finally moves to the next day. "Naomi is murdered...oh, and I forgot this." Over the squares for Wednesday the twenty-second and Thursday the twenty-third, I write *Weeks "OD."* I look over at Jar. "Tell me if I'm crazy, but I think whatever was in that package set things in motion."

"That docs appear to be the progression, but—"

"I know, it's a guess, and we would still need to prove it. There weren't any other emails? Something that hints at what was in the package?"

"Those were the only ones between them."

"Maybe the pictures Whitfield sent her or even whatever was in the package were things he received from someone else. Could be there's a message between whoever that person was and him."

"Yes, of course. I will check."

She spends twenty minutes sifting through Whitfield's emails, but when she finishes, she shakes her head. "If it is here, it is not obvious. I could read through each one, but there are a lot of messages and it will take time."

What she doesn't say is that we might still end up with nothing after she's done.

"Let's table that. We can always come back to it later. For now, we'll work with what we have."

"The addresses," she says.

I nod. "Let's get some sleep. We have some Morgans to visit tomorrow."

CHAPTER EIGHTEEN

J ar and I head east at first light.

Jar is a bit cagey this morning, like she doesn't want to tell me something. I try pushing her by asking things like, "Everything all right?" and "Get any new ideas while you were trying to sleep?" But I only receive a few yeses and nos and some mumbled answers I can't decipher. I eventually give up.

We reach Bend not long after nine a.m. The car's GPS leads us to the north end of town, on US 97. The address to Gerald's place indicates it's on the same road we're traveling, but so far the handful of houses we've passed are on side roads, not this one.

Turns out there's a simple explanation for this. Gerald resides in a place called Deschutes Memorial Gardens. If you didn't get it from the name, I'll be a little more direct. His gravesite is located near the back, tucked among dozens of others, and marked by a headstone.

"Is this what you didn't want to tell me?" I ask as we look down at Gerald's final resting place.

"I was not...I just..." She takes a breath and says, "Yes."

"Why not?"

"We were coming here anyway. It would not have changed anything."

Maybe she's tried to convince herself that's true, but I have a feeling the real reason is she fears one of Naomi's probable kidnappers might have permanently escaped punishment. Though she's broken her promise to not keep anything from me, I'm not going to call her on this. Instead I say, "Anything else I should know?"

"Gerald and Hank are cousins. Gerald was the oldest, by five years."

I thought they might have been brothers. Cousins doing bad things together is not unusual, though. Take the Hillside Stranglers, for instance.

"Please tell me Cousin Hank is still with us."

"As far as I can tell."

I look back at the headstone.

I'm guessing Gerald's passing isn't part of the trail of death we've uncovered. If it is, then this conspiracy goes a lot further back than January, because the date of death on his headstone is from three years ago. Which means those pictures of him had likely been found by Whitfield somewhere, not taken by him.

The only other info on Gerald's marker are his name and date of birth. There is something telling about his grave, however. Unlike others in the area, the grass creeping in at the edges of the headstone hasn't been trimmed in a long time. Maybe ever. I wouldn't be surprised if no one has ever visited him.

While we sit in the cemetery parking lot, Jar hacks into Deschutes Memorial Gardens' systems via their Wi-Fi network. The only next of kin listed for Gerald is—drumroll, please—Hank Morgan. According to a copy of the death certificate in the file, the elder Morgan died of heart disease.

It's been less than two days since Cynthia called me a

decent person, but I'm having a not-so-decent thought right now. If Gerald was indeed one of the men who had kidnapped Naomi, I hope his death was long and painful and debilitating.

I'm pretty sure Cynthia would forgive my lapse.

One thing about finding Gerald Morgan lying in a graveyard is that we're now free to move on to our next destination, putting us a full day ahead of where I thought we would be.

Before we head east, we stop at an ACE Hardware store and pick up a few items we didn't bring with us on the plane. We don't know exactly what's ahead of us, so it's best to be as prepared as we can be. I'm not talking about weapons per se (though I do grab a couple of utility knives, which I know from experience can do plenty of damage in a pinch). I mean more everyday items like rope and duct tape and zip ties.

When most people think about the desert, Oregon is not a place that immediately comes to mind, but that's exactly what the southeastern part of the state is. Miles and miles of nothing but dirt and sagebrush, with outposts of civilization small and few and far between.

It takes us about three hours to reach our next destination.

What's smaller—a town or a village? My guess is a village, but whatever the answer is, it describes Raven, Oregon.

The only business in town appears to be a gas station/market/hardware store/café called Lottie's. I know this from the signs in front of the place as we drive by. The only other structures are a couple dozen houses. It's like a slightly larger yet more condensed version of Crestville, Arizona.

A kilometer past the last house, I pull onto the shoulder. Across the highway from us is the mouth of a dirt road. Also on the other side is a stream that the map tells me is called Black

Horse Creek. I've never been here before, but I have seen this spot on a photo from Naomi's SD card. The dirt road bridges the creek and travels over the hill just behind it, and in the valley on the other side would be the less than well maintained two-story house belonging to Hank Morgan.

It's obvious now that Whitfield had used a drone to get the shot he sent to Naomi. Which is exactly what I wish we had right now, because it'd be impossible to drive down the road to get a look at the house without being noticed.

"We'll come back here after dark," I say. "Let's go see if we can find a motel."

As I turn us around, Jar checks for someplace we can stay.

"No motels in Raven. The closest is in…Foster." She says this last part with a bit of surprise, like she forgot the town associated with Naomi's captivity is in the area.

I'm worried about the negative effect staying there might have on her, so I say, "What was that town we drove through? About forty-five minutes back or so? Burns, was it? I thought I saw a few motels there. Maybe we could—"

"Foster is closer. We should stay there."

This is going to sound weird, but about five miles before we reach Foster, I begin feeling a sense of oppression, like weights are being set on my shoulders, the load increasing the closer we get to town.

A glance at Jar makes me think she's feeling something similar. She's staring out the windshield as if she's a coiled snake, ready to strike.

Foster is, in a word, underwhelming.

Everything is brown—the businesses, the homes, the bushes, the dirt, and the hills surrounding it. Even the trees look covered in dust. I'm not going to lie, tiny Raven seemed like a glowing metropolis of optimism compared to where we are now.

The trip from the city-limits sign to the parking lot of the Gray Coyote Inn across town takes four minutes and twenty-one seconds. This is mostly due to the unnecessary stoplight in the middle of the "business district."

I chose the Gray Coyote only because it looks about a decade newer than the town's other inn, the Foster Desert View Motel, which is right next door. That's not saying much. The Gray Coyote has to be at least seventy years old.

I secure two adjacent rooms with a connecting door, along the arm that faces the highway. The rooms have been updated since the place was built. Granted, the renovations likely happened a few decades ago, but the motel is far from the worst place I've ever stayed.

After Jar examines her room, she comes into mine and says, "I want you to take me there."

She doesn't need to explain what she means. It's been on both of our minds since we knew we were coming to Foster.

I nod, and we head outside.

Our rental car is not the right vehicle for what we want to do. So we make inquiries at the motel office and are directed to a garage a few blocks away, where we're able to rent a Honda CRF150R motorcycle and a couple of helmets.

With Jar giving me directions, we head west out of town. Not once does she refer to any notes. Though she's never been where we're going, she knows the route. And probably has for years.

About seven kilometers outside town, she says, "It should be coming up."

I slow the bike.

"There, I think."

She points past my arm, at the right side of the road. At first, the spot looks no different than the rest of the desert we've passed. But as I let the Honda roll to a stop, I see what can best be described as the ghost of a path, leading away from the highway.

As I follow the old road into the wilderness, Jar adjusts her hold on my waist to compensate for the rougher terrain. The path curves between hills, crosses several dry washes, and dips into a wide valley.

Jar squeezes me tighter at the sight of the gray concrete wall half a kilometer away, sticking up from the otherwise undisturbed desert.

It's no surprise the path leads directly to it. I stop the bike about ten meters away and we sit there for several seconds, neither of us moving.

The wall is all that's left of a home that was here so long ago that probably no one remembers what it looked like.

When Jar releases me and climbs off, I engage the bike's kickstand then follow her. I don't try to catch up, though. I stay a few steps back and let her have as much time alone as she needs.

Naomi's kidnappers had picked the perfect spot. The police never looked here because they had no idea the ruins of the building hid a still intact basement. As far as they were concerned, the wall marked another failed desert homestead, nothing more.

After Naomi had freed herself from her prison, after the investigation learned what little it could from the burned-out room, a demolition crew was sent in to collapse the ceiling and fill the basement with dirt. In the ten-plus years since, the dirt has settled, creating a depression that goes down almost a meter at the center.

Jar shakes slightly when she steps into the depression. I can't imagine the tremors that would have rocked her body if she could've gone into the enclosed space. I would have tried to stop her, but I'm sure I would have failed.

Do I sound overprotective? Sure. But none of us want the ones closest to us to hurt. I know I don't.

She seems to be aimlessly wandering around, but when she stops and points at the ground, I realize there was intention in her steps. "Her cell would have been right here," she says.

I'm not sure what triggers me but I'm already on the move as she finishes speaking. Even then, I barely reach her before she becomes overwhelmed.

I turn her so her face is in my chest. She's not crying, but she's shaking like it's minus thirty degrees and her breaths are shallow and quick.

A part of me wishes I didn't bring her out here, but we couldn't have avoided making the pilgrimage. As much as it tortures me to see her in pain like this, she needs to be here. Needs to go through this. Both to help her eventually find closure for her feelings about what happened to Naomi, and also—dear God, I hope—to release all she's been holding in about her own stolen youth.

When the tremors ease, I lead her to the edge of the depression and we sit, our legs stretched over the filled-in basement.

Jar whispers something into my shoulder.

"I didn't catch that," I say, my voice as soft as I can possibly make it.

"I...I am so sorry," she whispers. "I did not mean for that...I do not know what..."

Finally, the tears come. Not just hers, but mine, too.

I hug her tight and whisper into her hair, "I told you before, there's nothing about any of this to ever be sorry for," then I repeat the word *nothing* a few times before I kiss the top of her head.

She hugs me even tighter, pressing her face into my neck.

In a tearful, jagged voice, she whispers, "Thank you."

Don't ask me how long we stay like that. I have no idea. All I know is that it's dark when she wipes her eyes and we stand up and hug again.

We stay like that for a while, too.

After a stop at the motel to pick up a few things, we head back to Hank's house in the car.

When we drive through Raven, it looks larger than it did during the day, but that's only because of the lights on in most of the homes. Soon enough, we're surrounded by complete darkness again.

The highway remains empty all the way to where the dirt road to Morgan's place begins. I know from both Whitfield's photos and Google Maps' satellite view that the road is, in essence, a half-mile long driveway to the house and goes nowhere else. Which means, even though it's night now, we still can't drive the vehicle in without risking being seen. But thanks to the satellite image, I know we don't have to.

Another thirty yards down the highway is an area with a bit less sagebrush than elsewhere. I'm able to slowly drive the car into the desert and park it where it shouldn't be seen by anyone passing by.

We grab our things, head back down the highway, and jog over to the dirt road. There's enough starlight that we don't need a flashlight to guide us as we hurry across the bridge and follow the road up the hill. A glow of light greets us before we reach the summit, and we creep the rest of the way up.

"Looks like he is expecting someone," Jar says.

She's not joking.

Floodlights are attached to every side of Hank Morgan's house, lighting up the yard surrounding the building in a white glare. Additional lights illuminate the detached garage and parking area. It's like a prison, only without the barbed wire and chain-link fence. As far as I can tell, no lights are on inside the house.

Morgan clearly does not want anyone approaching his place unseen. I don't believe he gets a lot of visitors out here so it seems like overkill. Or possibly the work of someone who fears for his life. He can't have been living this way since Naomi escaped all those years ago, can he?

"He is not making this easy for us," Jar says.

"No, he isn't."

I raise the binoculars for a closer look. Power lines come to the house from poles by the backside of his property. If I had the correct tools, I would be able to disable the lines, but I don't. I continue to scan and quickly realize that robbing him of power would not be as simple as cutting some wires. Sitting next to the house is a large generator.

I move my gaze across the front of the house, and stop again.

"Can you bring up the photo Whitfield took of this place?" I ask Jar. "The close-up one."

She finds the shot on her phone and shows it to me.

"No lights," I say.

She looks at the image and cocks her head. "You are correct."

There are no floods in the picture, so they were installed after it was taken. Though we'll probably never know when the photos were shot, my educated guess is no earlier than October, when Naomi hired Whitfield. Could have been as late as December 28, the day he sent her the jpegs.

What prompted the new security?

I switch my binoculars to night vision and aim them at the first-floor windows, looking for signs someone is home. Furniture only. No people.

There are two windows on the second floor. I check the one on the left first, and see the end of a mattress and what's probably a dresser along a wall. Again, the room is deserted.

I move my gaze to the other upper window.

Bingo.

While I can't see a face because of the angle, I do see part of the body of a man sitting near the window. I also see a rifle lying across his lap.

He's obviously waiting for something.

But what?

I hand the binoculars to Jar. "Top left window."

She looks for a few seconds and says, "I do not like this."

"Let's take a look around back."

The floods are aimed so that nothing can get within fifteen meters of the house without being lit up, so we descend the hill and circle through the desert, beyond the halo of the light.

As we come around the back side of the house, Jar touches my arm, stopping me.

"Do you see that?" she whispers. "Near the ground. There and there and there." Each time she points at a different spot in the yard.

I pull out the binoculars.

"What is going on with this guy?" I mutter.

The backyard is crisscrossed with monofilaments, some parallel to the house, some perpendicular, all sitting not far above the ground. Trip wires would be my guess, likely created from fishing lines and connected to either an alarm or something more nefarious. The former, probably, because unless the filaments have been strung extra taut so that only a human or large animal can set them off, the lines must get tripped all the time by rabbits and coyotes and other wildlife.

Whatever the case, it's clear Morgan does not want anyone getting close to him.

We continue on until we're behind the middle of the house. I examine it through the binoculars. There are only four windows, two on each floor, and like those on the front of the house, no light shines from any of them. I flip back to night vision and look for people standing guard in the windows but they're all empty.

Back on normal vision, I scan the garage. Something connected to the wall, next to the floodlight there, catches my eye, and I increase the magnification.

A camera. If I wasn't looking at it from this angle, I would have missed it in the glare.

Which makes me wonder...

"Wait here," I whisper, and retreat several meters the way we came.

From there, I train the binoculars on the house, near one of the floodlights on the back, and grimace. Mounted to the wall, in a similar spot as the one on the garage, is another camera.

I return to Jar and tell her what I found.

"Shield me," she says.

I move between her and the house, to hide the light from her phone's screen. The top of her head rests against my chest as she taps away.

"He has Wi-Fi," she whispers a few seconds later.

"Security?"

She snorts softly. "Not nearly as good as he thinks." The next half minute is filled with only the sound of her fingers working the screen, then she says, "The cameras are wireless. Motion sensor activated."

"Can you disable them?" If the cameras remain off, Morgan will think no one is there.

"I just need to rewrite a small bit of the code so that he is not notified the cameras have shut down. Two minutes, please."

"Take three if you need them."

"I do not."

She ends up not even needing the full two.

Once the cameras are disabled, we pull on our superhero masks. Jar is using the spare of the pair she gifted me. It's the same as mine, but instead of the mesh over the eyes being deep blue, hers is black like the rest of the mask.

Staying low, we move toward the light.

The house is surrounded by a two-meter-wide strip of open dirt between the desert brush and the mostly neglected back-yard grass. The first trip wire is half a meter inside the strip, at ankle height.

I point it out to Jar and then step over it.

The next line comes right after the dirt strip meets the ragged lawn. From where we are now, it's harder to see where the other wires are. The floodlights illuminate the yard like it's daytime, but their glow radiates toward us, making it harder to see the glints off the lines like we could from our slightly elevated position farther back.

To counteract this, I pull out my flashlight and hold it by my knee, angling it so its beam hits the ground a meter in front of us. The light reflects off a monofilament just ahead.

I use this method to get us all the way to the house without alerting Morgan.

Jar wands the nearest window to check for an alarm, and shows me her phone. He does have an alarm, and it's on. The problem for him is that it's a straight-off-the-shelf brand, the kind a layman would buy. It's loaded with bells and whistles that jack up its price, which in turn creates the illusion it's a robust system, but it's useless against people like Jar and me. Then again, most security systems are.

Jar exploits the flaw in the alarm's software, and deactivates all of the sensors while leaving the system itself on.

I give the window we're next to a nudge, but it's either locked or stuck in place. After checking the other back window and receiving the same result, I lead Jar around to the side of the house that faces the garage. There, three wooden steps lead up to a door.

I place a toe on the bottom step and give it a gentle push. The whole thing wiggles so I immediately stop and signal to Jar not to touch it.

I move to the wall beside the steps and examine the door hardware. Like the rest of Morgan's security measures, the knob and the deadbolt above it are new. I reach up to see if it's unlocked, but the doorknob doesn't turn.

Though I could probably get the lower lock undone, there's no way I could unlock the deadbolt from this low. I look around and spot a small pile of bricks by the garage. Working quickly and quietly, we each grab two bricks at a time and create a platform, four bricks wide by five tall, that will put me at eye height with the deadbolt.

I pull out the lockpicks I used at Whitfield's office and undo the two locks.

Even with all the precautions we've taken, we need to assume Morgan knows we're here and is waiting just inside for us to come in. After Jar moves behind me, I turn the knob and give the door a little push to test the hinges. No creaks or whines, so I shove a little harder and duck back around the side of the house, letting the door swing open.

I hear nothing from the other side. No intake of air, no shuffling of feet, no sound of movement at all.

Jar taps me on the shoulder and hands me her phone. She's

attached one of our gooseneck cameras to it. This one's about half a meter long, and like the others in our collection, can be twisted in any direction so we can look through holes and cracks and around corners.

I bend the gooseneck ninety degrees near the camera end and slip it around the edge of the doorway. Jar has preset her phone to night mode, allowing us to see that the room beyond the door is a mudroom that opens into a kitchen. Morgan does not appear to be in the immediate area.

I help Jar through the doorway. She disappears into the house for several seconds. When she returns, she mouths, "Clear."

Getting myself inside without touching the stairs is trickier. But this is where the yoga classes I take pay off. I stretch a leg over the threshold, grab the side of the doorway, then swing up as I pull myself inside.

We sneak into the kitchen, past a sink full of crusty dishes and a refrigerator that looks like it's from the 1950s. When we reach the end of the room, Jar points at her ear then at the ceiling near the front of the house.

I cock my head and hear a faint, rhythmic knocking sound. If I'm not mistaken, it's coming from right below the spot where we saw the man—presumably Morgan—sitting. I'm guessing he's either rocking in his chair or moving his foot. Either way, it basically confirms he's on edge.

Jar, still in the lead, guides me out of the kitchen and into a wide central hallway that all the rooms on the first floor appear connected to. It turns out, this is also where the stairs are located.

We're about halfway to the staircase when Jar stops and very slowly pulls her foot back. She points at the board in front of her and motions for me to avoid it. This is one of the advantages of her going first. Her light weight allows her to find loose boards before the wood can moan and reveal our presence.

When we reach the stairs, however, it is my turn to take point.

I pull out one of the collapsible batons I always travel with and extend it. I have two of them, and have given the other one to Jar, which she has also extended. Because of the lack of supplier contacts in this part of the state, our only other weapons are the utility knives from the hardware store.

I head up, placing my feet at the edges of each tread. Jar waits at the bottom, watching past me for any movement. When I reach the top unscathed, she starts up.

Once we're together again, we check the rooms at the back of the house, the bathroom in the center, and the front room opposite the one the man is in. As I hoped, he's all alone in the house.

I move to the final doorway. The man is still sitting at the window, staring outside. His hair looks right for Morgan, but I still can't see his face. It's his foot that has been making the sound we heard downstairs. Heel planted on the floor, his toes are tapping the hardwood planks, in the kind of unconscious action people perform when they're waiting for something to happen.

In deference to the cold air streaming through his open window, he's wearing a down jacket over what appears to be a blue cable sweater and a pair of jeans. Most of his rifle is hidden by his torso so I can't tell what kind it is. I can see only a portion of the stock. On a small table nearby is a metal army ammunition box, its top open and moved out of the way for easy access. Beside it sit three grenades. The only other item of note is an open laptop computer on the bed behind him. I can't see the screen, but I'm guessing it's what he uses to monitor his cameras.

His bouncing foot slows. Worried he might have sensed my presence, I pull out of sight.

His chair groans as he shifts his weight. Is he looking at the door? Does he suspect he's no longer alone? Another groan, then after a moment, the tapping of his toes resumes.

I relax, but only a little.

He's clearly sensitive to changes around him, so I'm concerned that if Jar and I try to sneak into the room or even rush him, he'd realize we're coming and be able to get a shot off before one of us reaches him. I prefer to try something a little less risky.

I lead Jar to one of the back bedrooms and into the closet, where I whisper in her ear my idea, then ask, "Doable?"

She nods, pulls out her phone, and gets to work. When she's ready, she touches her screen.

There is a delay of approximately five seconds before we hear a trill of chimes from the man's laptop. The loud scrape of his chair against the floor signals he's stood up. In my mind, I see him check his computer for the feed of the camera Jar just remotely triggered, but he'll see nothing that could have set off the motion sensor. If he wasn't so clearly on edge, I would bet he writes off the alarm as animal related, but from his hurried steps a second later, I know he's not willing to do that tonight. I tense as I hear him bound into the hall and enter the back bedroom across from us.

For the next minute, all is quiet, as he presumably scans the backyard looking for signs of an intruder.

When he moves again, I have the fleeting fear he's decided to return to his post at the front window. But no. He does what I've been hoping for and hurries into our room. My hand is on the closet door, ready to open it, but I want to give him a few seconds to settle in at the window so I force myself to count to ten.

As I reach seven, I hear something.

Only it's not the man.

It's the sound of an engine, coming from the front side of the house.

The man hears it, too, because at the same time I register the motor's growl, he races out of the room back toward his perch.

I lead Jar out of the closet and into the front room directly across the hall from the one the man is in, so we can see what's going on. The window here is closed and mostly covered by a curtain. We walk up to either side of it and pull the cloth away just enough to peek through the glass.

There are actually two vehicles coming down the hill toward the house. What we heard was the one in the lead—a large pickup truck, with a powerful diesel engine that seems to make the ground shake. The other is a Dodge Charger, the kind of muscle car police forces sometimes use for high-speed chases.

Two new floodlights pop on, illuminating the area in front of the property that the truck has entered. The floods aren't motion activated, because part of the area they cover is ground Jar and I walked through earlier and we didn't set anything off. So, they must have been turned on by the man.

The truck doesn't stop until it reaches the split rail fence that encloses Morgan's front yard.

As the driver's door opens, the voice of the man in the house blares from a speaker that must be attached to the front of the house. "Get back in your truck. Turn around. And get out of here!"

There's no way the driver could have failed to hear him, but he climbs out anyway.

"Evening, Hank," the man yells, his voice deep and resonant, confirming the man Jar and I are stalking is indeed Morgan. "Told you we'd be back."

Something's familiar about the guy at the truck. I raise my binoculars for a better look.

"And I told you to stay away!" Morgan says. "Now go and don't come back again."

Well, look who we have here. It's Man A from the train ride to Los Angeles.

I give Jar the binoculars and motion for her to look at him.

"Oh, no need to worry about that," Man A shouts. "We're not coming back. Mr. Dean is tired of waiting. He wants to talk to you. *Tonight*. He has been very patient, but you've run out of time to think about it. Come on out."

Jar lowers the glasses and gives me a look that tells me she recognizes him, too.

"You have until the count of five," Morgan announces. "If you are not back in your vehicle and driving out of here by then, I will shoot you."

"I don't think you understood me. You're coming with us."

"One," Morgan says.

Behind the truck, the Charger stops and one of the back doors opens.

"Two."

"Stop wasting time," Man A yells.

"Three."

"Hank! Put the gun down and get your ass out here."

"Four!"

The driver turns to the open door of his truck. Before climbing in, he says something in the direction of the Charger.

Just as Morgan starts to say, "Five," a deep *whomp* radiates from the back of the Dodge.

I see something fly across the yard, then hear it smash through a downstairs window. After a moment, a hissing sound comes up the stairway.

Jar and I share a look. There's no need to say anything. We've been tear-gassed before and know what it sounds like.

A second *whomp* is followed by a canister hitting the side of the house, right next to the window where Morgan is. Morgan opens fire on the car, but before he can get more than a few shots off, a third *whomp* fills the air.

This time, the canister is on target and sails into Morgan's room.

"I'll get him," I say to Jar. "You get towels and water."

She rushes to the bathroom as I hurry toward Morgan.

While my mask might help disguise me, it is decidedly not gas-proof, so I leave my eyes open only long enough to spot Morgan scrunched against the front wall, on the other side of a billowing cloud of gas. His arms are over his head and he's already coughing.

Eyes squeezed shut, I hold my breath and rush forward. When I think I'm close, I reach out and swing my hand side to side until I grab on to his arm.

"What the—" he yells. "Let go of me!"

I yank him to his feet and away from the window, then manhandle him into the hallway. He coughs as he squirms in an attempt to break free, but his strength is no match for mine.

"Hold still and keep your eyes closed," Jar says, her voice muffled by a towel she's shoved between her mask and mouth. She splashes water on my mask, wipes it off with a cloth, then lifts the mask and repeats the process with my face. When she finishes, she puts a new cloth soaked with water across my mouth and lowers my mask over it.

"You'll have to hold it," she says.

I put my free hand over the part of my mask covering the cloth.

"Now open your eyes. Slowly."

I part my lids, braced for the sting of the gas. When this doesn't come, I open them all the way.

"I'm fine," I say.

She tries to put a wet hand towel over Morgan's face, but he twists his head back and forth so she can't.

"Do you want us to leave you here for those men outside to find you?" she says. "They do not seem to have your best interests at heart. If you stop struggling, we will get you away from them."

His head stops moving, but I have a feeling it's more out of confusion than any belief we're here to save him.

Jar puts the towel over his eyes and mouth. "Hold it. It will help block the gas."

Morgan coughs, unintentionally emphasizing her point, and puts both hands on the towel.

"Come on out, Hank!" the driver shouts from the front yard. "It's only going to get worse for you if you stay inside!"

Whomp.

The window of the bedroom Jar and I were in shatters as another smoking canister bounces into the house.

Jar heads down the stairs, holding a third damp towel across her face. I follow, guiding a blind and reluctant Morgan beside me.

The gas from the first canister has been seeping slowly into the central hallway. It's not too bad yet, but I feel a bit of its sting at the edges of my eyes.

"Back window," I say to Jar.

The side door is not an option, because the Charger is far enough back that anyone inside it would see us. We hurry into the back of the house.

"Hank! Get your ass out here right now!" The voice is muffled by the house now, but there's no missing the impatience. If they brought gas, I have to believe they have masks, too. Which means it won't be long before they come through the front door.

"Wait here," Jar says. She goes left, through a door that leads to the other back room. She returns a few seconds later and beckons me to follow.

The room was probably designed as a dining room, but Morgan has been using it to store boxes of God knows what. The only thing that matters to us is the window facing the backyard. It was closed when we checked it from outside, but it's cracked open now.

Jar races over and shoves it up as far as it will go, then rips through the tattered screen on the other side and jumps out.

"Your turn," I say to Morgan.

"My turn to what?" His voice is weak and scratchy from the gas, but still has a hint of defiance.

I lead him to the sill, pull one of his hands away from the towel over his mouth, and put it in the opening. "It's a window," I say. "Climb out."

Whether out of instinct or stupidity, he lowers the towel and tries to open his eyes. The moment they part, he starts to cry out.

I slap a hand over his mouth. "Shut up, keep your eyes closed, and climb *out*."

"But they hurt," he whines behind my fingers.

"Fine. Then we'll leave you here. Sorry to have troubled you."

I push him to the side, like I'm going to climb out.

"No. Please! Take me with you."

He's more scared of the others than people he doesn't know. That's telling.

"Out the window, then."

I help him over the sill, and Jar makes sure he doesn't fall on his way to the ground.

As soon as she moves him to the side, I follow, then pull the window closed in hopes it will hide our escape, at least temporarily.

Jar and I each grab one of Morgan's arms and we run straight out from the house, not worrying about trip lines or wireless cameras.

With every step, I'm sure the truck is going to swing around the back of the house and see us, but we make it out of the lit area and into the dark desert unseen.

More shouting comes from the other side of the house, and while the words are indistinct, I have a feeling Man A has lost what little patience he had left.

"You lead," I whisper.

Jar guides us in a wide arc around Morgan's property. When the front of the house comes into view, we see that the truck is now sitting right in front of the steps to the porch. Three men are standing around, each wearing a gas mask. The door to the house is open, so it's a fair guess more of them are inside. For a second, I wonder if any of them is Man C.

We head for the hill, moving on a line roughly paralleling the dirt driveway. I take a few backward glances as we go to see what's going on. The men at the house have spread out and are searching outside. If any of them is a halfway decent tracker, he'll find our prints and figure out where we've gone, but so far none of the men have ventured into the sagebrush.

Right before we reach the top of the hill, we hear a car door closing. Pausing, Jar and I look back in time to see the truck reverse out of the yard and speed toward the dirt road. The Charger, however, does not follow, and I can see three men still searching the property.

"Down, down, down," I say and push Morgan to the dirt as the truck nears the hill.

I crouch low enough so that those in the vehicle won't see

me, but I can still see the road and watch the truck's headlights race up the slope past our position.

When it reaches the summit, I nod at Morgan and mouth to Jar, "Watch him."

I sprint to the top of the hill and crouch again. The truck descends the other side and crosses the bridge over Black Horse Creek. When it reaches the highway, I expect it to turn west, toward Raven and the rest of Oregon, but instead it goes east.

Huh. There are only two or three more towns between here and the Idaho border.

The truck goes past the spot where I left our rental car without slowing, and soon its taillights disappear behind another hill.

I glance back at the house. The search is ongoing. I have a feeling the men left behind have been ordered to stay until they find Morgan.

If so, it's going to be a long night for them.

CHAPTER NINETEEN

W e can't take Morgan to our motel. The Gray Coyote's paper-thin walls will not contain shouts for help, and there *will* be shouts.

Luckily for us, we know someplace where we won't be disturbed.

"Why are you helping me?" Morgan asks. "Who are you people?" He's lying in the backseat of the rental, pressing the now not-so-damp towel over his eyes.

"Mr. Morgan, you're out of danger. That's the only thing that should be important to you right now."

Am I lying about the danger part? Depends on how you look at it. In the short term, not at all. It's absolutely true we rescued him from what was shaping up to be a very bad situation. In the long term? I guess we'll see, won't we?

When we go off road, I have to drive the rental extra slow so that we don't get hung up or stuck. This doesn't prevent us from bouncing around a lot, and we jostle for nearly twenty minutes before we reach our destination.

After we stop, I turn and look into the backseat just in time to see Morgan remove the towel from his face. He grimaces, his facial muscles tightening as he peels open his eyes enough to let a little of the world in. But his peek doesn't last much more than half a second, as he immediately shuts his eyes again and sucks in a pained breath.

"Still stings?" I ask.

Looking like he's sure he's going to die, he whines, "I think my eyes are hurt bad. I need a doctor."

"Nah, probably nothing a good washing out won't take care of. We can do that for you."

"Yes. Yes, please. Wash them out! Hurry."

"Give us a moment to get everything ready. Just relax until we tell you to move."

I hit the button that pops open the trunk, grab my mostly full bottle of water from the cup holder, and Jar and I climb out. From the back, I retrieve our gear bag, then meet Jar on the dirt that now fills the basement where Naomi was held hostage.

She points at a chunk of concrete lying on the ground at the edge of the depression. "How about that?"

The block must have come from a part of the house that's long gone, because it's too thick to have been a piece of the disintegrating but still standing wall.

"Perfect."

I hand the bag to Jar and push the piece of concrete toward the wall.

As I near it, Jar says, "Half a meter to your left," anticipating where I'm headed.

I glance up and see the reason for the suggested course correction. In the wall, there are several holes through which we can string our rope near the place she's directing me to.

I push the rock until it butts against the wall and take a step back. "Good?"

"Good."

Back at the car, I open the rear door and say, "You can come on out now."

Morgan exits with his eyes still shut. I guide him to the concrete block and turn his back to the wall.

"There's a seat behind you. It's a little low but you should be fine."

"It feels like we're still outside," he says.

"Do you want your eyes cleaned out or not?"

"Yeah, I just—"

"Then sit."

He lowers himself onto the block.

While I was off collecting him, Jar strung one of our ropes through chest-height holes on either side of where he is now sitting. Another rope is laced through holes below waist level. They're a little farther down than I would have liked, but they'll work. One end on each rope has been tied off in a loop.

"Lean forward," Jar says. "And turn your head to the side so you are facing the sound of my voice."

Morgan does as directed.

"I am going to open your right eyelid and pour some water over your eye. Do not try to fight it."

Morgan takes a ragged breath. "O...okay."

With her forefinger and thumb, Jar separates his eyelid. Right away, he winces and tries to blink a couple of times, as if he wants to shut it again.

"I said, do not fight it."

"Sorry," he says. "It...it stings."

"That is what we are trying to stop."

The blinking ends, but I doubt the urge to shut his eye has gone away.

Jar pours water from my bottle into his eye. Normally, I would advise against using it in case there has been any backwash. But with this guy, I have a feeling I'll regret not having spit in the bottle a few times first.

When Jar finishes, she steps back. "You can blink now."

Morgan's lid flutters rapidly.

"Better?" she asks.

"Still a little sting, but not so bad."

"We will do the left now," she says. "Please turn the other way."

While she repeats the process with his other eye, I activate my audio recording app and place my phone in my pocket, microphone up so it will have no problems capturing our voices.

When Jar finishes, she says, "Sit up and close your eyes again so I can make sure there is no more on your face." She wipes his face with one of the towels we took from his house. "Keep them closed for a minute, to let the water dry."

Jar makes it sound like if he doesn't he could end up in pain again, but it's only misdirection. While he's jamming his lids together, I take the chest-high rope and thread the untied side through the loop on the other end, while Jar does the same to the one at Morgan's waist.

On my signal, we pull them tight.

Morgan slams against the wall, my rope pinning his biceps to his sides, and Jar's trapping his butt against the concrete block.

"Hey!" he yells. "What are you doing?"

He curls his forearms and tries to grab the rope around his chest, but the angle is bad. Though he can get his fingers around it, he can't give it more than a weak pull. After we secure the lines, Jar grabs a zip tie off the ground from where she set it. At the same time, I grab Morgan's hands and pull them down so she can put the tie around his wrists, like handcuffs.

"Let go of me!" Morgan shouts. "Stop it!"

Jar grabs another tie and attaches it around his ankles as he continues to protest.

If he keeps wiggling around, he's liable to get loose. The ropes are good but just the two aren't enough.

I hold out my hand to Jar and say in a very clear voice, "Knife, please."

After she slaps the utility knife into my hand, I extend the blade and place it against Morgan's neck. It's funny how quickly something like that can cause a person to freeze.

"Stop fighting it, understand?" I say.

His eyes widen even more. "You son of a bitch. You tricked me! The gas, the threats—those were just distractions to get me to go with you. But *you* work for him, too!" He looks around. "Where is he?"

While he makes his accusations, Jar goes behind the wall and slips two more ropes through the same four holes. Morgan twists his head as he hears one of the lines drop against the wall next to him.

"What is that? What are you doing?"

"Mr. Morgan, I will say this only once. Face forward and shut up. The only time you speak is if you have been asked a question. Every time you break that rule, I will remove a piece of you. Do you understand?"

He glares warily at me, as if he thinks I would never follow through with that but can't be one hundred percent sure.

Jar comes back around to our side and secures the two ropes diagonally across his torso, shoulder to waist, like straps in a race car. She then uses more rope to tie his legs to the block, and his forearms to his lap.

When she is done, she takes a step back, looks him over, and nods.

Morgan can move around all he wants now, but he's never going to break free on his own.

The look in his eyes reveals he knows he's in serious trouble, but he tries to put on a brave face by saying, "If he wants me dead, fine. It's not like I can do a lot about it now, is there? So, go ahead. Don't keep me waiting."

I gesture around us. "How does it feel being back here?"

The gap between his brows narrows. He glances past Jar and me into the darkness, then looks to either side.

I flick on my flashlight and point it at the wall. "Maybe this will help."

The ropes prevent him from turning his whole body, but he can angle his head enough to see what I'm lighting up.

There's a moment when he doesn't understand, but when I move the light from the wall to the ground where the basement was, his expression changes.

Up until this moment, we could not eliminate the possibility that Morgan had nothing to do with Naomi's captivity, but from the sneer that now grows like a cancer on his face, I know without a doubt we have found one of her kidnappers.

He chuckles and looks as if he's suddenly in control of the situation. "Trevor thinks bringing me back here is going to scare me? He's even dumber than I thought."

One of the most effective interrogation tools is to simply say nothing and let your subject fill the void. Humans abhor silence when in the company of others, and will say things they wouldn't otherwise just to hear the noise.

Morgan has already given me the name Trevor, who—and I don't think I'm going out on a limb when I say this—is probably the Mr. Dean that Man A from the truck was yelling about. That's some decent actionable intelligence already, and we haven't even started yet.

Morgan holds out for about twenty seconds before giving in to the inevitable. "He is going to kill me, isn't he? He's finally decided I'm too much of a liability, huh? Well, screw him. I did what he wanted. I've *always* done what he wanted."

When we still don't respond, confusion and doubt begin to erode what remains of his confidence.

"Is Trev here?" Morgan says. "He could at least give me the respect of doing this himself."

I give it a few beats, then say without emotion, "No one else is coming."

As if a switch has been thrown, he yells in frustration and thrashes wildly, pulling at the ropes and trying to stand up. But there is no one within miles to hear him, and our restraints hold tight.

Eventually he runs out of energy and droops forward, panting through his teeth. When his head tilts up again, his eyes lock on me. "I never told *anyone*."

"About Naomi, you mean." This from Jar, and though her tone sounds detached, I know a tsunami of emotion is hiding right below the surface.

A flash flies through his eyes. He is definitely talking about Naomi.

"Just kill me," he says. "For God's sake, just...do it." His tone starts off strong, but it fades at the end.

He's at the breaking point. I would love to take credit, but we haven't been working on him nearly long enough for that to happen. If I had to guess, it's the multiple visits from Dean's men that has pushed him to the edge. We're simply the proverbial last straw.

I lean toward him. "You're right. Mr. Dean does want you dead, but not quite yet."

His lips move, but I can't hear anything.

"Speak up."

His mouth freezes for a moment, then in a whisper he says, "He knows I never told anyone about them. He knows I never told anyone about them. He knows I never told anyone about them."

Again and again he repeats this, like a mantra or spell that he thinks if he says enough times, it'd shield him from harm.

It's the word *them* that sends a chill through me. It's clear he means Dean, and while it's not as obvious who else he's referring to, there's only one other player in this drama it must be.

I take a few steps away and place my flashlight on the ground, pointing the beam at Morgan, then motion to Jar.

We walk into the desert toward the car. I expect Morgan to yell out, wondering where we're going, but a glance back tells me he's still lost in his miserable thoughts and probably doesn't even know we've gone.

When we're far enough away that he won't hear us, I whisper, "Trevor Dean."

Jar pulls her phone out and begins searching for information. While I wait, I turn my gaze to the sky to calm my soul. Because if I don't, I'll end up killing this guy and that's not going to help us.

We are in a dark part of the country, where light pollution is nonexistent, and the heavens are teeming with stars.

For a time when I was young, I wanted to be an astronomer. I don't know how many times I talked my parents into taking me to the Griffith Observatory. The thing I remember most was sitting in the planetarium, staring at the stars projected above us. (The real stars are better, of course, but growing up in L.A., the planetarium shows were the closest I could get to seeing what a true night sky looked like without taking a two-hour trip into the Mojave Desert.) I'd get lost among the points of light and wonder how many planets circled them, and how long it would take to get to the farthest one, and most of all, if there were children on those other worlds looking at the stars and wondering the same things I was.

I'm not exactly sure why astronomy fell off my radar. Probably had something to do with me deciding my future was playing third base for the Dodgers. But that sense of wonder has never left me, and it's especially strong when I stare at a sky like the one above me now. Did Naomi share a love of the stars, too? Is that why she was going to the planetarium that night?

"Nate," Jar whispers.

I let my gaze linger for a moment longer, enjoying a last moment of peace, before I look at her. She hands me her phone.

Liz materializes beside me, and we look at the screen together.

On it is a picture of a man and a woman, smiling at the camera. They're standing in front of a white backdrop, with the letters BCBI watermarked across it in black. The man is wearing a black suit, and the woman a stylish red dress. It's clearly a photo from an event of some kind. From the touch of gray at the man's temples and the wrinkles around his eyes, he looks to be in his early fifties. His date, however, appears to be a good two decades younger.

For a moment or two, I think I've met the man before. But no. While he may have a familiar face, I don't know him.

"Scroll down," Jar says.

Below the picture is some text.

This past Saturday, local businessman Trevor Dean (pictured above with his wife, Lorna) received the Boise Council of Business and Industries' Community Excellence Award, for his work as head of the Fredrick Dean Foundation. The foundation was founded in 1986 by his father, Matthew, who named it after his own father. It is most known in Boise for its after-school training program that helps high school juniors and seniors prepare for their futures. Matthew Dean started the program to combat what he said at the time was "an absence of structure for the young people of our city." Trevor Dean took over both his father's business, FM Dean Management, and the foundation when his father retired several years ago, and has overseen the expansion of the foundation's program to more than forty high schools statewide. At the same time, his company, which is the parent organization to several tech start-ups, auto dealerships, and franchise restaurant locations, has continued to thrive. The award was presented at the council's yearly...

"You're sure this is the right Trevor Dean?" I whisper.

It's him, Liz says.

"There is no other one in the area," Jar says, then adds after a pause, "The truck that left Morgan's home. You said he turned left."

I did. Toward Idaho. Toward *Boise*.

The picture, Liz whispers.

I scroll back. That sense of familiarity hits me again.

Yes.

I'm not sure what she means. Does she think I actually know this guy? Because I'm positive I don't. I concentrate on his wife for a moment, to see if she might jog my memory, but I don't sense even a hint of familiarity with her.

"Second wife?" I ask.

"Yes. His first died sixteen months before he married this one."

"Natural causes?"

"She fell off a boat and drowned."

It's an interesting detail, but it seems tangential at best to what we're dealing with here.

Jar nods toward Morgan. "If he and his cousin were Naomi's main captors, then this man..." She looks at the screen. "What if he is the third one she did not see much? You heard

Morgan. Dean did something to Naomi and he doesn't want anyone to know. It is him. It has to be him."

It's him, Liz says.

Jar is not one to usually make leaps without concrete proof. Liz believes her, though, and if I'm honest with myself, I do, too.

But we need to connect the dots. "I'll see if I can get him to open up more."

She frowns.

"What?" I ask.

She takes a long look at Morgan, then turns back to me. "Let me question him."

My gut reaction is that's not a good idea. She may not have lost her cool when she said Naomi's name to him earlier, but that doesn't mean she'll be able to maintain control the next time they interact. And if we make a mistake, Morgan will stop talking. We are so close to the truth here. We don't want to screw that up.

You're not being fair to her.

I blink. I'm not, am I?

Jar may be young, but she is a professional who's proven more times than I can count that she deserves my trust and support. She knows what's at stake here as much as I do.

"All right," I say. "You take lead."

"Thank you."

We return to Morgan, who has barely changed positions in our absence.

"Sit up," Jar says.

It takes a moment before he lifts his head and leans back against the wall.

She stares at him, saying nothing. Though he can't see her eyes through the mask, it's not long before he begins to fidget and his lips start silently moving as if he's reciting the same words from before.

She lets this go on for about fifteen seconds, then slaps him hard across the cheek.

"Stop it." Her voice is the same monotone she used with him before.

Morgan tries to move a hand to where she hit him, but of course he can't. He settles for stretching his jaw while looking warily at her.

"Who did you talk to?" she asks.

"I told you already. I didn't talk to anyone."

"You told us you did not talk to anyone about *them*. But you did talk to someone. Who was it?"

"I don't understand. What do you mean?"

"Who?"

"No one. I-I-I talked to no one. That's what I said."

"What about the private investigator from Eugene?"

"I...I don't know any.... What investigator in Eugene? I-I-I don't even remember the last time I was *in* Eugene."

He is lying, and boy, is he trying hard to cover it up. Too hard. I was an idiot to even hesitate letting Jar talk to him. She's pushing all the right buttons.

"He has your contact information and other notes," she says. "His records are very detailed."

"Then...he's...he's...lying." He sputters this out as if the words are popping into his head one at a time. When he speaks again, he's more fluid but just as dishonest. "Why would I ever talk to someone like that? I have no reason to. A private investigator? No, I wouldn't—"

Jar slaps him on the other cheek to even things out.

"Do you even understand how this works? Your lies will make what happens to you long and painful, while your truthful cooperation will be rewarded with a swift and compassionate conclusion. Which will it be?"

A breath escapes his mouth as he lolls his head back and stares at the sky.

"You talked to him," she says.

Morgan doesn't respond.

"To Alex Whitfield."

Though Morgan is still leaning against the wall, his gaze has jumped from the sky to Jar. "I never went...to Eugene. I told you."

"I did not say anything about going to Eugene. Whitfield came *here*."

He closes his eyes and his lips start moving again, only the pattern is different from before.

"Mr. Morgan!" Jar snaps.

His eyes spring open and his head jerks away from the wall. He stares at her for a few seconds before saying, "I didn't know who he was. Not at first. Honest. I didn't know."

He takes a stuttered breath, and then the story spills out.

CHAPTER TWENTY

W e were wrong.

From the first moment we learned Saundra Moore was really Naomi Bellows, the possibility of her childhood kidnapping being the reason behind her murder had always been simmering in the back of our minds. Since finding out about Juan Sanchez's connection to Oregon, discovering that the state was also the location in the photos on the SD card, and that Naomi's FedEx package had been sent from Eugene, the idea that her captivity and subsequent escape had been the reasons for her murder had only strengthened. And when our investigation led us to Hank Morgan, one of her kidnappers, any remaining doubt evaporated.

And yet, we were wrong.

Yes, her kidnapping and captivity are part of the picture, but they are not *why* she was pushed off the side of a mountain.

The true reason she died is so much more devious. So much more immoral.

So much more repulsive.

When Morgan finishes telling us the story, it affects me to the point where it takes all of my willpower not to choke the life out of him on the spot. But while there is plenty of blame to place on him, Morgan is not the main evil here.

That honor belongs to the pillar of Boise society, Trevor Dean.

And with minimal effort on Jar's part, we now know where he lives.

———

One of the standard items in my go bag is a small black case that passes as an insulin kit for the diabetes I don't have. One of the vials does contain insulin in case I need to prove it, but the other two are filled with Beta-Somnol, my drug of choice for putting people to sleep. (Temporarily, not permanently.)

Depending on the dose, the recipient could be out for a couple of hours to nearly a day. The dose I give Morgan should keep him dreaming well into tomorrow afternoon. I'm sure he'll be stiff, having been tied up the whole time, but I'm more than okay with that.

I really wish I picked up a can of spray paint when we were at the hardware store. I would love to paint something like HERE SITS HANK MORGAN, CONFESSED KIDNAPPER OF NAOMI BELLOWS on the wall above him. Unfortunately, I have to settle for writing on his forehead with a sharpie. The reduced canvas only allows for NAOMI BELLOWS'S KIDNAPPER. It's not quite as elegant as the sign I made for the Valley Heights Rapist, and there will be no pop of confetti, but it will do.

Our plan is to call the sheriff's department and report where he is. But we won't be able to do that for at least twenty-four hours, which leaves us with a little logistics problem since we can't leave him out here on his own for that long.

After a few phone calls, I reach a freelancer I know named

Shawn Darby who lives in Seattle. She doesn't bat an eye when I tell her what I need her for. What can I say? Babysitting a guy tied to a wall for a day or two is not even close to the oddest thing we have to do in our business.

"I'll pack a tent and my yoga mat, make a retreat out of it," she says. "Should be able to get there by about three a.m."

———

It's a three-hour drive to Boise, which would put us in town a little before one a.m. There are three of us in the car. Me behind the wheel, Jar beside me on her computer. And Liz in the backseat, furious and silent.

Unlike Jar, whose mind is occupied by doing the research we need for what lies ahead in Boise, I'm stuck staring at the empty road and hearing Morgan's words play over and over and over in my head.

He has not told us everything, because he thinks we work for Dean, so there are holes in the information he assumes we already have. But what he *has* told us should be more than enough to help Jar fill in the rest.

Three things I will note right now:

One, Hank and Gerald aren't the only cousins in this mess. Trevor Dean is a younger cousin to both of them. His mother is sister to their fathers. It's a cousin trifecta of ruthlessness, if you will. A family whose reunions are probably best avoided.

Two, Hank has no idea Naomi and Whitfield are dead. He is no longer one of Dean's confidants, and until recently, hadn't heard from his cousin in months.

And three, I've already alluded to this, but to be clear, Naomi did not hire Whitfield to help her find her kidnappers but find them he did.

I stop just over the Idaho border to fill the rental's tank. As the gas is pumping, I make a call to someone I trust, and ask if he knows of any suppliers in the Boise area.

"There's one who's pretty good," he says. "Max. She's a woman. A little rough around the edges, but she's got a good selection of gear."

"Does she mind getting calls in the middle of the night?"

"You'll have to ask her that yourself."

He gives me the contact number and the code phrase that will identify me as reliable, and I make the call.

"Yeah?"

"I'm looking for Max."

"You got her. Who's this?" I don't know if my friend meant it this way or not, but the little-rough-around-the-edges description perfectly describes her gravelly voice.

"I'm a friend of Carl Ridley's," I say, speaking the first part of the code phrase. "He said I should look you up when I'm in town."

"And when would that be?"

"Sometime in the next hour or so."

"Stop by. I'll give you the lowdown on all the hot spots."

The address Max gives me takes us to a Jackson's Food mini-market and gas station off I-184, in the middle of Boise.

Parked beside the building is the big old 1970s-era Cadillac I was told to pull in next to. No one is in the car, but as I exit our sedan, a woman comes out of the market, carrying a bag of chips and sucking on a straw sticking out of a giant soda cup. Her hair is white but she doesn't look much older than forty, so it's either prematurely that way or bleached. She's wearing a black coat and a pair of blue sweatpants with BOISE STATE printed on one leg.

"You Ridley's friend?" she says to me.

"I am. You Max?"

"That's me. You got a name?"

"Nate." I nod back at my car. "She's Jar."

"Jar? Like—"

"Like Jar."

She looks past me and shrugs. "All right, Nate. Welcome to Boise. You want to ride with me or follow?"

"Follow will probably be faster."

"Suit yourself." She takes another loud sip of her soda and heads for the Caddie. "Try to keep up."

Unlike Victor in Phoenix, Max doesn't seem to care if we know where her operation is located. For the record, it's in a Stow-'n'-Go public storage facility that I get the sense she owns.

She takes us to the middle unit of the middle row, a spot conveniently hidden from view of both the street and the surrounding businesses. Jar and I get out of our car and meet her at the unit's door as she's unlocking the padlock. When the door rolls out of the way, I see the room is actually three units wide. Shelves built from square wooden posts and thick sheets of plywood are stationed throughout. On them sit identical opaque plastic storage bins, none with any indication of what's inside.

When Max turns back to us, she looks at Jar and says, "Nice name."

"Thank you."

I'm pretty sure Max was being sarcastic, but if Jar realized this, she's decided to ignore it.

Max's gaze moves to me. "So, what da ya guys need?"

We leave twenty minutes later. Max didn't have everything I

would have liked, but she had enough choices for me to improvise a gear kit that I believe will be sufficient for our needs.

We really should call it a night. I'm not going to lie—I'm exhausted. But there's one more thing I'd like to do before we sleep.

Boise might be the largest city for a couple hundred miles but it's not *that* big, and twelve minutes after we leave Max, we're driving down a quiet road on the far east side of town.

"There it is," Jar says. She points at some lights near the top of a hill just ahead and to the left.

We drive by at a leisurely pace. The lights come from the only house on the entire hill.

Trevor Dean's house.

The place is hard to see in the dark, but that's okay. Jar found pictures of it on a real estate website so we know what it looks like, inside and out. What the photos don't fully convey is its actual size. The house is a massive, sprawling structure, four levels high, including the basement. The side facing us bulges out in an elegant windowed arc that makes me think more art museum than residence. The hill is high enough that anyone looking out those windows would have an amazing view of the entire city.

In Los Angeles, a home like this would easily sell for well over thirty million dollars. But this isn't L.A. The real estate website says the property was last purchased eight years ago for three point two million, and gives a current value of seven million. If that doesn't make it the most expensive house in Boise, I'd be shocked.

Next to the road, at the base of the south end of the hill, is a black metal gate, closing off a driveway that runs up to the mansion. There's a camera mounted on a stone pillar to the left of the gate, angled down to catch visitors, and an intercom box next to the gate for them to announce themselves.

A hundred meters past the driveway, on the west side of the street, three new houses are being built. Not monoliths like Dean's place. Just your basic two-story family homes, with no more than five meters between them. Cozy. The kind of places where kids can talk to one another from their bedroom windows.

I pull in behind the partially finished buildings and roll to a stop. There are no other vehicles, but we wait for several minutes, the car idling, to see if a night guard will show up and ask us what we're doing here. But the construction site remains quiet, no sign of life anywhere.

Yes. This will do just fine. We can leave the car here without anyone being the wiser.

But that is for later. Now it really is time to get some rest.

CHAPTER TWENTY-ONE

When I wake, the curtains of my hotel room are glowing from sunshine. According to my phone, it's almost 8:23 a.m. I could have sworn I set my alarm for seven, but when I check, I see that I set it for seven *p.m.* That goes to show how tired I was.

Still, since Jar gets up early, she should have woken me by now.

I shuffle over and open the door between our rooms, but her room is as dim and quiet as mine. I tiptoe in.

She's lying on her bed, fast asleep, her computer beside her.

I wonder how long she stayed awake after we checked in. Could be she's been out for only an hour or two and I should let her sleep. Or maybe she was as tired as I was and has been this way for a while.

I can't bring myself to disturb her yet, so I return to my room and carefully close the door.

After a quick shower, I throw on some clothes and head down to the coffee shop in the lobby, where I pick up a few pastries and two iced lattes.

Back upstairs, I reenter Jar's room with one of the coffees

and a chocolate croissant and carry them over to her table. As I'm setting them down, I hear her stir behind me.

"Nate?"

I turn. She's looking at me as if she has no idea where she is.

"*Sawadee krap*," I say, greeting her in Thai.

She blinks, then looks around and grabs her phone. "Eight forty-five?" Her gaze flicks back to me. "Why did you let me sleep so late?"

"Uh, why did you let *me* sleep so late?"

She sits up, still a bit disoriented.

"How long did you stay up last night?" I ask.

"I do not know. No more than an hour, I think."

Which means she had at least five hours of sleep. That might be her most ever.

"Here." I hand her the latte.

She takes a sip through the straw. And then another. And then sucks the rest down without taking a breath. "I will need more of this."

───────

Today is a day of preparation, because tonight we are going to finish this, and we want to make sure there will be absolutely no problems.

We owe Naomi that.

I owe Jar that.

Jar remains at our hotel, finishing the research she wasn't able to complete last night and preparing the technical side of this evening's activities.

As for me, I'm on scouting duty.

My original plan, if I'd risen in time, was to start with following Dean from his home to his work, but I have a feeling he's already left. So I head straight to his office and do a drive-by.

FM Dean Management is located in a four-story office building the company owns near downtown. Several of the company's subsidiary businesses also have offices there. Places such as Dean Fleet Rental (which I'm guessing works hand in hand with his automotive dealerships), Travonics (a moderately successful app developer), Hilltop Systems (an IT services company), and Dean Home Security (a growing home alarm monitoring company, currently serving customers in Idaho, Washington, and Oregon). I would bet anything that the person Dean asked to delete the Amtrak footage from the San Diego-to-L.A. train works for one of these last three companies. Which is also a reason he would have limited the person's involvement to the bare minimum so the person wouldn't see the footage of Weeks as Harrison, and wonder why Dean would want to delete it.

On the next block, in a two-story building also owned by FM Dean, is the main headquarters for the Fredrick Dean Foundation. Both buildings are no more than a fifteen-minute drive from Dean's house.

All very nice and convenient.

I don't see Dean anywhere, but I didn't expect to. He's likely already in his office, probably on the top floor. I'm only here because you can often get a sense of a man from the things he owns. For example, a sign on the side of the four-story structure proclaims it as THE TREVOR DEAN BUILDING. There's also a sign on his foundation's building, this one saying THE FREDRICK DEAN FOUNDATION, and below it in smaller letters—but not too much smaller—TREVOR DEAN, CEO.

The sense of the man is coming through loud and clear.

I pick up some food for later, then head east to the road

below Dean's house. I can't leave the car at the construction site because things are hopping there right now. But that's okay. I don't mind walking a bit today, so I park on a side street about half a mile away.

From the trunk, I take the backpack we picked up from Max. While it's built to carry the specific set of items it holds, there's still room for me to add a few things, like microcameras, a signal detector, and just in case I run into problems, a dart gun. The gun isn't next gen like those Victor had, but it's perfectly serviceable.

I walk along the road, back toward Dean's house. Around the quarter-mile mark, I veer off onto a trail leading east that I discovered on a Google satellite image before I left the hotel. The area is dotted with copses of trees and open fields that continue all the way to Dean's hill.

(I wonder if he actually calls it Dean Hill. It wouldn't surprise me if he's petitioned for that to be the official name. Wait, not Dean Hill. *Trevor* Dean Hill. Wouldn't want to get himself confused with his forefathers now, would he?)

The path winds due east for a few hundred meters before turning northeast, taking me toward the back side of the hill. Before I get there, I stop at a group of four trees that are the closest along the trail to Dean's driveway. I attach the micro-camera with the best zoom lens to one of the tree trunks and hide a signal booster on the ground nearby. After checking the feed on my phone to make sure the camera is aimed the way I want it, I target a narrow area along the driveway, and activate a setting that will vibrate my phone anytime something passes through. I continue on my way.

Behind the hill is a brook small enough to jump across, and I find a place to sit, under the shade of several trees growing near the bank. The spot is off the trail a bit, and the trees hide me from view of anyone walking by.

From the backpack, I extract a palm-sized drone and its controller. The small aircraft is painted sky blue. There are two alternate shells in the bag that can be attached over the blue. One is gray for cloudy days, and the other black for night. Since it's clear today, the drone is fine as is.

I fire up the controller and turn the drone on. The spinning propellers create no more than a quiet hum, thanks to the device's whisper technology. If I were buying this instead of renting, it would cost several thousand dollars more than the equivalent-sized loud ones I could get for less than fifty bucks online.

I check that the camera is working properly, then sync it with my phone through the controller so that it records everything it sees.

And then I send it aloft.

To make sure I don't make stupid mistakes later, I spend the first few minutes getting used to the controls. When I'm satisfied, I guide the drone to the area above the house.

As I scan the home, I pay particular attention to the courtyard outside the front door, the walkways around the house, the French doors to the lagoon pool area, and the door at the south side of the building that provides easy access to a garden with a gazebo and an empty fishpond. One of these will be our way in.

I make a second pass of the place, this time looking for cameras and outside lights. There are plenty of both.

I focus next on the wide circular driveway in front of the house. It kind of reminds me of a drop-off area in front of a fancy boutique hotel. Parked there are two cars—one a BMW 525i and the other a Mercedes G-Class SUV. Off to the side is a garage, big enough to comfortably fit four cars. Its doors are closed so I can't see inside.

About fifteen minutes into my observation, a woman exits the house, holding a small dog. A few steps behind her are two men, one wearing a blue jacket and the other a gray sweater. I zoom in as far as the lens will go. I don't recognize the men, but the woman is Lorna Dean, Dean's second wife. And, for the record, the dog is a Chihuahua.

The woman and the dog get into the Mercedes, and the other two climb into the BMW. They leave together, the Mercedes in the lead. My sense is the men are bodyguards.

Dean and Lorna don't have any kids, but he does have two daughters from a previous marriage who could be in the house.

And what about a cook? Or a maid? Maybe a few of each? If there are servants, and I can't imagine there aren't, I wonder if any of them live on-site. If the Deans used an agency to hire their staff, we should be able to find that out.

I shoot Jar a text so she can add that to her to-do list.

Her reply:

Already checked. Two maids every day. Job description states they prepare meals, too.
The first arrives at 7 a.m., the last leaves at 9 p.m. No one lives on-site.

Okay, so Jar doesn't need to add it to her list. Fine.

Good to know there are no live-ins.

I recall the drone and change the battery. I have four, each with enough power to keep the small aircraft up for more than half an hour. I don't send it right back up, however. I'll do that later. For now, I need to take care of a few tasks on foot, so I repack everything and return to the trail.

In the field near the north end of the hill, double lines of trees stretch all the way from a small grove of evergreens near the trail to the base of Dean's knoll. When I reach the tree lines, I turn and walk along them toward the slope, moving carefully from one pair of trees to the next.

When I'm halfway to the end, I pull out one of Jar's little goodies from my bag. It's a Wi-Fi detector that will pinpoint the direction a signal is coming from. I turn it on, hit the scan button, and continue walking.

An icon on the small screen rocks back and forth, letting me know the device is hunting for signals. It stays that way until I'm about a dozen trees from the hill, when the icon is replaced by a list of two acquired Wi-Fi networks.

One still uses its factory default network name, while the other is called TLDHUB7NE.

The location data tells me the second signal is coming from Dean's place, but I already figured that. I mean, TLD? Trevor Lorna Dean? Seemed pretty obvious.

I continue walking until I reach the last set of trees. At the top of the hill is the northeast corner of the house. Which is probably why the network name ends in NE. The HUB7 can be explained by the size of the house. Lots of hubs would be needed to ensure coverage everywhere.

The signal is strong enough here that I could connect my phone to it and watch a movie without any playback issues. It's not my phone, though, that I'm planning on connecting.

I pull out two items from the bag. One is a square box about the size and width of my palm. The other is also a box but it's rectangular and thicker, like a brick that's been sawed in half. It has a connecting wire protruding from one end. Both are black, their shells made of plastic.

I use an app on my phone to connect the square device to the Deans' network. In essence, it will act as another hub, but it won't show up on any programs they might use to monitor their network. Next, I plug the wire from the rectangular box into the square box, and then hide them in some bushes near the trees.

I text Jar.

Yes on wi-fi. And you should now be connected.

The rectangular box is a satellite phone that only sends or receives computer signals. Through it, we now have access to the Deans' house.

I work my way back to where I flew the drone from and have a seat. After checking the camera that's watching the driveway, I pull out the food I picked up and enjoy my lunch.

The vibration of my phone wakes me.

I sit up with a start, my back scraping across the tree behind me. I don't remember falling asleep.

I check my phone and turn off the alert. It went off because a car has passed through the targeted area on my driveway-focused camera. I also note, with a bit of relief, that I was asleep for less than twenty minutes.

I unpack the drone and send it back into the sky. By the time it's high enough for me to see anything, the car that set off the alarm is pulling to a stop near the courtyard entrance. I keep the camera focused on the area as I move the drone closer.

It's not the Mercedes SUV or the BMW. It's a Tesla Model S.

When it stops, the front doors on both sides and one in back on the passenger side open.

The drone is close enough now for me to see faces.

The driver is Man A, and the person who was sitting next to him is none other than Man C. Out of the back climbs the big prize.

Trevor Dean.

Until proven otherwise, I will assume the two men with Dean are his bodyguards. Which makes four guards between him and his wife. Jar and I will have to plan our activities as if all four (or their replacements) will be present tonight when we pay our visit.

Dean walks toward the front door with the other two several steps behind, just like what happened with his wife and her escorts, only in the other direction.

When they reach the house, Dean begins to open the door, but whips around and yells at the other two. Most of his anger seems to be directed at Man A.

No, the drone doesn't have a microphone, and I can't hear Dean from where I am, but from his body language it's obvious he's royally pissed off.

I have no idea what's going on in his business world, so something there could have provoked his outburst, but because his ire is aimed at Man A, I can't help but feel the tirade has probably been going on all morning, and has everything to do with Man A's failure to bring back Cousin Hank last night.

Man A tries to get a word in, but every time he opens his mouth Dean's anger increases.

Here's what I think. Dean's been in cover-his-ass mode since he realized in early January he had a problem. First to go was Alex Whitfield. Then Dean's real target, Naomi. After that, it was all cleanup. David Weeks to give the cops a killer they couldn't talk to. Juan Sanchez to eliminate a loose end he could never trust from outside Dean's organization. And his own cousin Hank Morgan, in a not yet successful mission to rid himself of the man who knew Dean's secrets and, in Dean's eyes, had been responsible for everything flaring up again. There's at least one more body—whoever died in the fire that burned down Weeks's trailer, so I wouldn't rule out the possibility of others we don't even know about.

It pleases me to see Dean so agitated, though his being on edge means we'll need to be extra careful in our approach this evening. I'm fine with that. I want him on edge. I want him to feel anxious. I want him to suffer, even if only a little bit, with every single breath.

Besides, his worry will be focused on what his good-for-nothing cousin will do.

What poor Trevor won't be expecting is us.

When the berating comes to an end and Dean disappears inside the house, I recall the drone and pack it away.

I've seen all I need to see here.

CHAPTER TWENTY-TWO

I t's 11:35 p.m. when the lights in the Deans' master bedroom go out.

Jar and I are in the field behind the hill, sitting against the trees I used for shelter in the afternoon. We have been here since 10:15 p.m., and I have been flying the drone on recon since a few minutes after that.

The drone is wearing its black shell now and is almost impossible to see, even for us whenever I fly it back in to change the battery. It's been doing a yeoman's job and has confirmed that the same four bodyguards are still on duty.

Because of the tongue-lashing I witnessed earlier, Jar did some research into the guards, and answered one of the few remaining open questions in our investigation. Man A's name is Ryan Long, and he's a native of Phoenix, Arizona. When he was a teenager, he worked a couple of summers for Mateo Yanez's trucking company, where he would have crossed paths with Juan Sanchez and, quite possibly, David Weeks, too. The dots have been connected.

Long is now the head of Dean's personal security team, which is undoubtedly why he's still on duty. I'm guessing the other three men are the best of Dean's other security team members. Why else would they have been chosen to protect Dean and his wife on a day when Dean is afraid Cousin Hank will strike back for the attack on the man's house?

Though Jar also learned the name of Man C and the two other guards, I continue the established naming theme for the still unlabeled guards and dub them Man D and Man E.

Two of the guards, Long and Man E, are stationed in the courtyard—Man E close to the driveway, Long at the front door. Man C is walking around the lagoon pool, and Man D is at the back of the house, pacing in the gazebo.

Until a few minutes after eleven, light and the occasional movement could be seen through the windows of the massive living room along the arc, on the opposite side of the house from where we are. After the lights went out, others came on in the master bedroom, one floor up.

And now those lights are out, too.

I recall the drone, replace the batteries, and send it back into the air.

Then, without a word, Jar and I lower our masks, don our backpacks, and head to the line of parallel trees that will take us to the hill.

The guard at the gazebo is wandering back and forth across the platform, like a bored child. We watch him via the drone, and every time his back turns to us, we move a little closer.

When we are within ten meters of the structure, I hand Jar the drone controller, extract my dart gun, and move the rest of the way in on my own. Except for where the stairs are located, a waist-high railing extends all the way around the platform. Between the railing and the gazebo are vertical panels with decorative shapes cut out of the centers but are otherwise solid. I hide behind one of them.

The guard's shoes clack softly against the wood planks as he walks toward me. When he reaches the railing, he pauses like he's always done and turns to amble away.

I rise to my full height, aim the dart gun, and pull the trigger.

"Wha—" is all the guard manages before he falls to the gazebo floor with a thud.

I'm confident we are far enough away that the other guards didn't hear anything, but I drop back out of sight anyway in case anyone comes to check.

Jar joins me a half minute later. "All clear," she whispers. She used the drone to monitor the others.

I find a Beretta APX pistol in a shoulder holster under the guard's left arm and toss it into the bushes. After retrieving the dart and zip-tying his hands and ankles, we rope him between two of the side wall posts so that he's stretched across the center of the gazebo, his hands and legs pulled in opposite directions.

One down.

The area containing the lagoon pool and outdoor living room is nearly as large as that of the house. And in an extravagance worthy of a fine resort, a rock feature at one end of the pool boasts a slide that shoots through a tunnel on the way down to the water, and a waterfall that hides a six-stool full bar.

Man C is near the shallow end, opposite the rocks. Perhaps skittish from Dean's lambasting that afternoon, he appears more attentive than his buddy at the gazebo.

On previous passes, we observed him doing a loop from where he is currently, past the empty lounge chairs flanking the middle of the pool, and around the rock feature before working his way back to the shallow end.

Jar and I are in the bushes behind the rocks next to the wooden shed that houses the pool's pumps. Man C's path passes between the rocks and our position.

We watch the monitor on the controller, and I'm happy to see the guard does not appear to be deviating from his routine.

As he nears the path that will bring him to us, I scoot back a little to make sure I'm out of the way. Jar has takedown honors this time.

A steady pace of crunching footsteps precedes his arrival. Once he has moved by us, Jar slips onto the path and raises her gun. A split second before she lets her dart fly, her target pauses. Maybe he senses she's there. If so, he never gets the chance to turn around and find out.

The dart hits him in the thigh, and as he reaches down to pull it out, he just keeps going in that direction until he's sprawled on the path.

I throw his weapon into the pool, and Jar and I tie him like we tied his friend, the only difference being we use trees as anchor points instead of gazebo posts.

Two down.

The courtyard is the trickiest location.

With Man E at one end near the driveway and Long back by the front door, there's no way to take out one of them without the other seeing it.

Which means a more creative solution is needed.

We sneak back to the patio and hold a hushed conversation about our options. I come up with a pretty decent plan but Jar's is better so we go with that.

She returns to the corner of the courtyard where we were, while I quickly make my way around the house and approach the courtyard from the other side. I can't get any closer than the garage, because Man E is positioned right at the front of the courtyard on this side.

That's okay, though. This spot will work just fine.

I click my comm mic twice, letting Jar know I'm in position. She gives me a double click in return, then after a pause, adds a third to indicate she's ready to go.

I click once in confirmation and lift the drone controller.

I fly the drone low and slow over the top of the house toward the courtyard. After it clears the roofline, I guide it about four meters over the pergola that runs along the east side, and then bank it out to the center of the open area and let it descend to eye level.

I don't see what happens next because I'm already on the move. I do hear Long's surprised yelp when he sees the drone and I have no doubt he's reaching for his gun.

I race down the sidewalk, my dart gun raised. As Jar predicted, Man E is no longer looking at the driveway, but has turned toward the front door in response to Long's voice.

I pull my trigger and hit Man E in the back with a dart.

At the other corner, Jar rushes into the courtyard toward a hopefully distracted Long. I come around my corner a second later and the moment I see him, I fire again.

My dart hits him in the shoulder, but Jar's shot reaches him first, hitting him in the abdomen and taking him down.

I stop next to Man E and take only long enough to check that he's unconscious and not just dazed. Then I meet Jar at the door, where she's already done the same with Long.

We move to either side of the entrance and wait to see if anyone responds to the disturbance. When we're confident no one is coming, we cuff Man E and string him between two decorative cast-iron benches along the non-pergola side of the courtyard.

As for Long, we have something special in mind.

After looping a rope around his zip-tied hands, we attach the other end to the top of the pergola, so that his arms stretch upward at about a forty-five-degree angle. We tie his legs to the opposite end in a similar manner, creating a kind of human V that leaves only his ass on the ground.

You may think it's a little much but if you ask me, he's getting off easy.

Four down.

We're at the door and Jar has her phone open.

Thanks to having access to the Deans' Wi-Fi network all afternoon, she assumed control of the house's security system hours ago. With a tap on her screen, the alarm is deactivated, and with another, a command is sent for the electric deadbolt to open.

Normally this would trigger a soft trill of chimes to inform anyone nearby of the lock's change of status, but she has turned that function off and the only sound we hear is that of the bolt slipping free.

Even this can be dangerous, however, for there's a wild card we still have to deal with.

I open the door wide enough for a foot to fit through, then drop a piece of what I'm hoping is our secret weapon on the ground, just outside the threshold. At the same time, Jar adds a couple more pieces in a progression away from the door, then she and I crouch out of sight behind the planters on either side of the entrance.

Faint, rapid clicks on a hardwood floor, growing louder and closer until they stop maybe a meter from the door.

Another click, hesitant, then a few more, followed by Lorna Dean's Chihuahua sticking its head out the door. When it spots the piece of cheese I dropped, it steps over the threshold and eats it. After it finishes, it moves on to the next one, going farther outside. The third piece is a good meter and a half away from the door, and after the dog walks over to it, I lean over the planter and pull the door closed.

The dog performs an impressive jump turn and starts to yip, but Jar, her mask pushed off her face, holds a larger piece of cheese toward it. The dog is momentarily confused, unsure if it should bark at us or accept the offering. It chooses the food, though eyes Jar almost as warily as it eyes me.

Jar makes some comforting sounds and keeps her movements slow and small as she holds out a fragrant oatmeal cookie. With this, she's able to lure the dog closer, and establishes enough trust that it allows her to pet it. From there, it's only a minute or so before Jar is able to pick up the dog.

"Her name is Ariel," she whispers, after looking at the tag on the dog's collar.

"Nice to meet you," I say.

She growls at the sound of my voice.

As I raise my mask, Jar says to Ariel, "It is okay. He looks scary, but he is a friend."

I'm pretty sure it's the additional piece of cookie Jar offers the dog rather than her words that tempers the animal's behavior, but whatever the case, Ariel goes back to ignoring me for now.

This afternoon, during our final planning session, we discussed options on how to deal with the Chihuahua. She's an alarm system that we couldn't just hack into and turn off. Luring her with treats seemed like the best idea. But figuring out a way of getting her under control only addressed the first part of the issue. We still had to come up with what to do with her, if and when we had her under control.

The easiest thing would have been to drug the treats to knock her out while we take care of business. But while both of us have no problem doing that to people, the idea of doping a dog made us uncomfortable. Another idea was to leave her outside, in the fenced-in area around the pool, but we worried the cold night would not be kind to her.

That left only one option.

With Jar holding Ariel against her chest and feeding her bits of cookie, I open the door again. The only sound I hear is the distant hum of what is probably the heater.

We enter and go left, toward the part of the house away from the bedrooms. At the back of the giant living room, we take the stairs to the basement two levels below. From there, we go down a hallway to the last door on the right and enter the Deans' home theater.

This is not some random room with a few couches and a large TV. This is an actual theater, with three tiered rows of five overstuffed chairs each, a snack bar area complete with a soda dispenser and a popcorn-making machine, and a projection screen that takes up the entire north wall. According to the real estate website, a small platform with a digital projector on it lowers from the ceiling.

The website also mentions the room is soundproof, making it the perfect place to stow a dog. But since this is also the room we will be using for our evening festivities, we won't be leaving Ariel alone yet.

While Jar starts setting things up, I head back into the house.

From her research this afternoon, we learned that Dean's daughters both attend college at Washington State University in

Pullman, Washington. Given that school is in session and today is Wednesday, they should be there. Meaning, in theory, the only people home are Dean and Lorna. My task is to see whether that's true or not.

I sweep the basement level and then proceed one floor up, where five of the six bedrooms are located. The daughters' rooms are easy to identify from the abundance of personal items. Neither room looks like it's been used in months. The other three bedrooms are more generically decorated and, like the girls' rooms, are not being used.

I move up to the next level, the one where the entrance is located. This is the public space—living room, dining room, kitchen, game room, smaller television room (at least in contrast to the theater), and home office. There are probably some interesting things to find in the latter, but we already know all we need to know. We'll leave the honor of searching through Dean's papers to someone more official.

The house's top level is half the size of the other floors and contains only three main rooms: a space that probably qualifies as a seventh bedroom but is currently being used as Lorna's overflow closet; an open, stone-floored lounge area at the top of the stairs; and the master suite.

The door to the suite is open halfway. I step inside and scan the space.

The room is unsurprisingly gigantic, like you-could-almost-fit-the-entire-upper-level-of-my-townhouse-in-it gigantic. A king-sized bed is off to the right, facing the windows and sitting free of any walls. I can just see the tops of Dean's and Lorna's heads. I'm guessing they're not exactly the cuddling type, because there's enough space between them for two other people.

A nightstand presses up against the bed on each side, and along the near end, where most beds would have a headboard, is a settee. Other furniture in the room include dressers and a large makeup table and chairs and, to my left, a whole living room setup of couches and tables and another TV. I don't see a bed for Ariel, but I do see a set of movable steps near the foot of the bed that would allow her to climb onto the mattress.

There are three doors other than the one I'm standing in. With another hat tip to the real estate website, I already know one leads into a bathroom and the other two into separate walk-in closets. The closet doors are closed, but the bathroom's is open and a dim light shines from inside.

I take one last look around and head back to the theater.

When I enter, I find Jar sitting in the center chair in the front row, with Ariel in her lap between her and her computer, and our equipment in position.

"How much longer?" I ask.

"Checking angles. Almost done. The house?"

"Everything's good."

She continues working on her laptop for about half a minute, then closes it and helps Ariel onto the floor. After depositing the computer on the chair at the far end of the middle row, Jar walks over to the door to join me, Ariel following. The dog is still not sure what to make of me, but at least she's not growling. We'll move her again when we come back, but at that point we won't need to worry about anyone hearing her bark.

Jar bends down and scratches the dog's head. "If you are good, I will bring you a few more cookies."

"You're going to spoil her."

"So what if I do? I like her."

She pets the dog again before we slip out the door and head upstairs to the master suite.

It's time for the main show.

CHAPTER TWENTY-THREE

I approach Dean's side of the bed, while Jar does the same on Lorna's.

My first task is an easy one. I point the Glock 9mm we obtained from Max at the man's head. It's unloaded—no bullet in the chamber, and the magazine is in my pocket. (If I really need to shoot, you'd be amazed how quickly I could insert the mag and fire one off. But I won't need to.) My intent is only to terrify Dean if he wakes up before we're ready for him.

Jar's current task is more involved.

In her hand is a small metal bottle, about the size of an air freshener aerosol can, but instead of a spray cap attached to the top, it has a plastic face mask that could cover someone's nose and mouth. The mask is on a hinge that allows Jar to position it however she needs it.

When she turns the dial, a hiss emanates from the bottle as its contents flow out. She positions the mask above Lorna's mouth and nose, without touching the woman's face. Though Lorna is already asleep, we want to make sure she stays that way. The anesthetic will help with that, but it's only the first of two steps.

After she's given Lorna enough of the gas, Jar pulls the bottle back and turns off the valve, then injects the woman with an eight-hour dose of Beta-Somnol.

In a way, we're doing Lorna the favor of giving her one last good night of sleep before she learns how evil her husband is. Of course, he may have already told her everything, but I doubt it. It's a past he's been trying to hide since long before he married her.

As soon as Jar is done, she returns the syringe and gas bottle to her backpack, which is in the hallway with mine, and joins me on my side of the bed.

Considering Dean's state of mind, it is a fair assumption that, even with bodyguards, he would feel the need to have a weapon nearby. Which is why Jar checks the area around us.

Sure enough, in a clip on the side of his nightstand, she discovers a .40-caliber Smith & Wesson pistol. But that's not all, folks. Near the top, on the same side of the stand, and designed to look like it's part of the molding, is a button that likely sends out a help signal. We could disable it, but it would take more time than it's worth, especially when all we have to do is pick up the stand and move it out of reach. Which is exactly what we do.

Jar checks the bed frame and the mattress to make sure Dean hasn't hidden anything else. She gives me a thumbs-up and moves down the bed until she's just past the man's feet. There, she pulls out her own unloaded Glock and takes a similar aim to mine.

She's ready, and so am I.

With my free hand, I grab Dean's pillow and rip it out from under him.

His head drops with a thud against the mattress. He coughs and blinks and looks around bewildered, until his gaze falls on me.

Like he's practiced it a thousand times, his hand shoots out for his panic button while his eyes remain focused on my gun. When his hand touches nothing but air, he looks over and stares at the space where his nightstand used to be.

When he turns back to me, he asks, "What are you doing here? What do you want?"

I motion with the muzzle of my gun for him to sit up.

He doesn't move.

Jar taps his foot with her gun, causing him to gasp and jerk his legs toward his chest in surprise, realizing I have not come alone.

I motion with the gun again.

This time, he pushes the comforter out of his way and swings his legs off the mattress. He's wearing nothing but a pair of underwear. Though he was in good shape once (we've seen pictures), years of success have brought too much food and excess living, leaving him with a belly that flops on his thighs and a chest in need of some artificial support.

Jar and I take two steps back, and I motion for Dean to stand up.

"I have an alarm," he says. "The police will be here any moment."

Jar puts her gun in her waistband, retrieves her phone, and points the screen at Dean. She methodically flips through the camera feeds from his system, ending on the one of his body-guards tied up in the courtyard.

The message is clear. No one is coming, and the guards he hasn't even mentioned won't be of any help, either.

After she puts the phone away and raises her gun again, I repeat the motion to stand.

"Just tell me what you want," he says. "I'm sure we can work something out."

I hold up five fingers then start lowering them one at a time.

As the third touches my palm, Dean puts a hand on the mattress and starts to push up, but he abruptly stops and looks over at the other side of the bed, as if he just remembered he doesn't sleep alone.

I slap him on the back of his shoulder with the gun, hard enough to sting.

He twists back around and rubs the spot. "What did you do to her? Is she dead?"

I grab his bicep, yank him to his feet, and shove him toward the open door.

He stumbles before regaining his feet. When he glances back and sees the gap between us, he twists back around and sprints for the door.

Well, not really *sprints*. He's an overweight, out-of-shape, fifty-three-year-old man, so it's more of a lopsided, accelerated walk than anything else.

Jar gets behind him ahead of me.

While there's no question she can take him down before the exit, she slows enough to let him leave the carpet-covered bedroom for the stone-floored hallway before she extends her baton with a flick of her hand and throws it at his ankles.

Dean trips and flies forward, like a diver jumping off a cliff, and belly flops onto the unforgiving floor.

He sucks in air as we turn him over, the wind knocked out of him. The blood pouring from his broken nose is probably not helping.

I give him a minute to get his breathing under control before I haul him to his feet.

Jar throws him a towel she took from the master bathroom while he was on the floor, and he holds it to his nose.

A wave of my gun gets him walking, and he gives us no more trouble as we escort him down the stairs to the theater.

I forgot all about Ariel, until Jar holds up a hand for Dean and me to wait a few steps from the entrance. She crouches down next to the door and pushes it open. Before she can grab the dog, Ariel scampers around Jar's hands and turns like she's going to run down the hallway. But the moment she sees Dean, she freezes and starts to growl.

Perhaps it's the bloody towel covering his mouth and nose that triggered her reaction, but I prefer to think she knows a monster when she sees one.

Jar scoops her up and carries her toward the bathroom down the hall.

While she gets Ariel situated, I push Dean into the theater and guide him toward the front row.

"Please," he says, "I need a doctor. My nose. I'm bleeding. I'm—" He stops when he sees one of our two camera-and-tripod setups, this one at the far side of the screen. "What is that? What's it doing there?"

The only answer he gets from me is a hard shove in the back. When he reaches the center chair, I grab his shoulder, turn him, and push him into the seat.

"For God's sake, just tell me what you want," he pleads. "I'm sure we can work something out. I have resources."

Jar rejoins us and quietly moves down the second row of chairs until she's directly behind Dean. On the armrest of the seat nearest her is small black case we also picked up from Max. Jar picks it up and opens it.

Dean, unaware she's there, continues to negotiate a way for us to let him go free, most involving cars and money and promises he won't say a thing about tonight to anyone. Why do deviants and scum always think they can buy their way out of trouble?

I let him go on for a bit, then I raise the barrel of the gun to my mask, like a finger to my lips. He clearly understands the gesture, but all it does is make him change tactics.

"You'll never get away with this," he says, his face hardening. "The police *will* catch you. And you will spend the rest of your lives in prison for what you've done to me!"

Jar chooses this moment to plunge the needle of the prepared syringe into his shoulder, near the base of his neck.

He winces and turns, yelling, "What the hell? What are you doing?"

But he's too late. The hobbler has already been injected, and is working its way into his system.

Jar returns the syringe to its case and takes the seat at the far end of the second row, where she left her laptop.

Dean looks back at me. "What was that? What did she give me?"

I can see he wants to get up, so I remind him about the gun pointed at his face. He seethes in his chair, probably plotting how he'll make both of us pay for *what we've done* to him.

I let him stew until enough time has passed, then I give his foot a kick. It flies sideways into his other foot, which accompanies it in a small arc off the floor, neither resisting the force I applied to them at all.

Dean's face turns pale. "Wh-wh-what happened? I-I didn't feel that." He pauses as he looks down at his legs. "Why won't my legs move? Oh my God, what did you do to me?"

I press my gun's muzzle into his chest, high enough that he should still be able to feel it. When I have his attention, I raise the barrel to my mouth again, repeating my earlier gesture.

He swallows nervously, his gaze flicking between his legs and my mask. "Am I going to die?"

I move the gun away from my lips and nod, then I hold it against them again and shake my head.

He shuts up.

I walk to our camera at the side of the screen and click it on. It's zoomed in tight on Dean so that he's framed from the middle of his chest to just above his head. And while it's not shooting him straight on, he's in three-quarters profile so the camera will see enough.

Our second setup is two rows directly behind him, aimed so that it will record the back of his head and everything he sees on the screen before him. Jar has a remote for this one, and as soon as I move out of the frame, she turns it on.

A tap on her laptop's space bar dims the lights.

Behind us, Dean's HD projector—which has been lowered from the ceiling—whirls to life, and on the screen an image of Naomi Bellows appears.

It's the last school picture she took before she was kidnapped. Her smile is carefree and innocent. A state I fear she never achieved again.

"W-w-what is this all about?" Dean stammers. "Who-who-who is that? Am...am I supposed to know her? Because I-I don't."

There's not an intelligent person on the planet who would believe anything he just said.

Jar types on her computer and hits ENTER.

From Dean's impressive sound system comes our surrogate electronic voice. "You know who she is. You have always known."

I can see Dean's mind whirling, as if he's searching for a way to deny the words. But he knows there's nothing he can say that will refute the truth. In an act of desperation, he shoves himself out of his chair, topples to the ground, and claws at the carpet as he tries to pull himself out of the room.

I walk over to camera one and hit the pause button. After Jar does the same with camera two, I saunter over to Dean, who has barely crawled a chair's length, and crouch down in front of him.

"Get out of my way, asshole!" he growls.

I do not comply.

He pulls closer and tries to reach for my gun. I easily evade the attempt, and tap him on the side of his head with the barrel.

His head drops, cheek on the carpet, as he teeters in the gray zone just this side of consciousness. He's not getting out of this that easily, though. I grab him under the shoulders and haul him back to where he was.

I've come up against some adversaries who, if they'd tried the stunt Dean just did, would have impressed me with their never-quit attitude. But Dean could never do anything that would impress me.

After zip-tying his arms to the chair, I give him a few wake-up slaps to the cheeks. Finally, the dazed look in his eyes begins to disappear. When he's back with us, I tousle his hair like he's a good doggie and give him a thumbs-up.

I restart camera one and return to my place against the wall.

The picture of Naomi appears on the screen again.

Thundering from the speakers, our voice says, "Say her name."

Dean's head shakes back and forth, like a bobblehead flicked from the side. "I...I...I don't know what—"

A horn blares and he jerks hard against the seat back.

I suggested using the sound of the buzzer from *Jeopardy!* but Jar prefers the blare of a tugboat horn. It is loud and deep and bone jangling. An excellent choice.

"Say her name."

"Go to hell! I don't know what this is...this is all about, but I-I-I-I'm not talking to you about anything!"

On the last part of our drive from Oregon to Boise last night, Jar and I talked through the script for this evening. What we came up with was a kind of choose-your-own-adventure presentation that, depending on Dean's responses, could go in various directions. We decided to start by giving Dean a chance to come clean.

And as we were sure would be the case, he has failed to take advantage of our kindness.

Jar tees up instruction number two, and the voice says, "Then we will talk for you."

A clip from a YouTube video plays. It was shot at a fundraiser for the Fredrick Dean Foundation. This particular segment features Trevor Dean speaking to the attendees.

"I can't tell you how much we appreciate your love...and your money." A laugh from the crowd. "The work we've done over the last several decades has had a huge impact on our community here in Boise and the entire great state of Idaho. The only things I'm prouder of than the work we do at the foundation are my daughters. The Dean Foundation changes lives for the better. *Your* donations change lives for the better."

The clip freezes and fades away as a picture of a high school senior class takes its place. The students are crowded together on a football field, looking up and waving at the photographer, who must have been standing at the top of the bleachers. Of the four hundred thirty-seven students, only twenty-three are people of color. The image zooms in, until only one of twenty-three fills the screen.

Because the photo was never intended to be blown up this big, the image is blurry, but there's enough detail to make out the person is a girl. We stay on this for a moment before a new photo replaces it.

It's the same girl. Her senior picture, sharp and crisp.

Monica Bellows, Naomi's mother. She's young and beautiful and has no idea how quickly her life will change.

The voice again. "Monica Bellows was seventeen when she signed up for the Fredrick Dean Foundation After-School Training Program. From a broken family, she was hoping to learn skills that would give her a chance at a better career and future than she had been heading toward."

The picture changes, this time to one of Dean, at least twenty years younger and in much better shape.

"When Monica was accepted into the foundation, you were thirty-one and one of its program directors. A year later, you would be married to your first wife, Diana, and another year after that, the two of you would welcome your first daughter together. But at the time Monica started her training, you were only engaged to Diana and not as faithful as your future bride probably thought you were."

"Stop this!" Dean yells. "Stop it right now! If you're imply-ing...I don't...I don't know that woman." He pauses before repeating "I don't know that woman," only this time as a whis-per, as if he's trying to convince himself.

Dean's picture fades away, and the screen goes black.

I can hear him breathing harder and harder until finally he yells, "Let me the fuck out of this chair!" He wiggles his shoul-ders side to side, as if doing so will free them. "Dammit! Let me out!"

In the darkness, the voice says, "Three months after being accepted into the program, and a month before she would have graduated, the foundation found a job for Monica, in the small town of Willis, Oregon. Six months after that, Monica's daugh-ter, Naomi, was born." The younger picture of Naomi reap-pears. A baby photo would have been better, but Jar couldn't find one. "*Your* daughter."

"Bullshit, bullshit, bullshit! You think I'd have a daughter like—" He stops himself, then just repeats, "Bullshit."

Dean is not a typical asshole. He's a racist asshole. He didn't actually finish the sentence, but there's no question where he was going with it. His penchant for white supremacy was one of the things we learned from Cousin Hank. Not that Morgan used those words exactly, but it was bubbling below everything he told us.

"You thought hiding Monica in Oregon would be enough," our voice says. "You paid your cousins, Gerald Morgan and Hank Morgan, who both lived in the area, to keep an eye on her and her daughter." The Morgans' pictures appear on the screen. "But it continued to haunt you, did it not? And you worried the truth would get out. That is why, eleven years ago, you decided Naomi needed to disappear."

Dean stares open-mouthed at the screen, the blood around his nose and lips glistening from the glow of the projection. But before he can think of anything to say, Cousin Hank's voice fills the room.

"Me and Gerald did everything Trev asked for. Everything! No one else was as loyal as we were. We're his *family*, but now he doesn't even care about that, does he?" The projection cycles through pictures of the cousins, Naomi, news stories of the kidnapping, and the solitary wall in the desert marking the location of the hidden basement. "We hid his black bastard for him where no one would ever find her. Who else would have done that? No one, I tell you. No one. We even got the grave dug up in the hills, away from everything like he wanted. I mean, he's the one who said he didn't want anyone to see her again. But every time he came to check on us, we'd ask if it was time and he'd say not yet. I don't know if it was cold feet or what, but what I do know is that it's his fault she got away, not ours. We kept her there for *fourteen* months. *For him!* And he couldn't make up his damn mind. It's his fault, not ours. His."

Morgan did not give us precise details about why the kidnapping happened when it did, but he gave us the gist. And Jar plays that next. "Trev had everything in front of him. He was important. What was she? Another lowlife colored bitch who'd end up on food stamps. If Uncle Matthew found out about her, he'd've sold the company before he gave it to Trevor. But because of what we did, what *I* did, that didn't happen. And now he wants to get rid of me?"

This might be the first time I've ever seen someone go white as a sheet while growing angry at the same time.

"Lies," Dean says, sounding like he's trying to convince himself. "He's lying."

A video of a news report plays next, from a Portland television station about Naomi's escape, then the screen goes black again.

Hank Morgan's words are not lies. Public records confirm Dean assumed control of the foundation and his father's company during the fourteen months Naomi was being held. A big decision like his father's to step down would have likely been made a year or two before that. Which means Dean would have known it was coming, and wanted to make sure his past "mistake" didn't come back to ruin his ascension.

A picture of Gerald Morgan fades in, and Cousin Hank's voice comes through the speakers again. "That guy, the PI, he doesn't know we had anything to do with the kidnapping. It was Gerald's stupid kid. He took a DNA test on one of those family history sites. The girl took one, too, and then hired the PI to track down her relatives. None of this has anything to do with what we did to her. So I didn't do anything wrong, see? The girl just wants to know who her father is."

And that is why we were wrong. This was never about the kidnapping. This was about a girl searching for a connection to her roots.

There is one aspect of all this that Jar and I don't know the truth about yet. Why didn't Monica ever point the finger at Dean? It would seem that, as the father, he'd at least be someone of interest she'd tell the police about. But she never did. Nor did she list him on Naomi's birth certificate, or ever tell Naomi who her father was.

I have what I think is a strong theory for why none of that happened. And I'm hoping we're about to find out if I'm right.

An image of Naomi's birth certificate replaces that of Gerald. The projection pushes in on the blank space where the father's name should be.

Letters spelling out TREVOR DEAN appear in the box, in the same font and size as that of the other information printed on the form.

Cousin Hank's voice repeats, "The girl just wants to know who her father is," several times, becoming more and more of an echo on each successive play.

Our narrator then gives voice to my theory. "The reason her mother never told her it was you was because she never knew."

I stare at him, not wanting to miss any of his reaction. There is no denial on his face, no confusion. There is only guilt.

I want to question him about this, but that is for someone else to do. If I had to guess, I would say there was a party, with lots of teens and booze and a back room somewhere, where a passed out young woman was raped by an adult who should have been there to protect her.

The electronic voice says, "Because of the DNA test, Naomi was able to put the pieces together and figure out you were her father. She reached out to you, not knowing the person you really are and what you had done. Maybe you would have been, at the very least, tolerant of her if your father wasn't still alive and serving as chairman of the board. You may think of it as your company, but you would've still had to answer to him for this. You would have had to explain to your daughters why they had a half sister, born a year after you and their mother were engaged. You remember their mother, don't you? The woman you drowned in the Sea of Cortez?"

The blood drains from Dean's face, and his lips move, as if he's talking to himself.

When Jar had first told me about Diana Dean's death, I doubted it had any bearing on what we were doing. That changed after we learned what was really going on. This afternoon, Jar did some investigating, and while her work was by no means thorough, what she found was enough to convince both of us the drowning had been no accident.

Seeing his reaction, I nod at Jar. She cues up one of the optional pieces of dialogue and hits Play.

"Though you may have been too scared to kill Naomi while your cousins held her captive, your experience with Diana allowed you to shed your fear. So when Naomi showed up again, you knew what you had to do, and you knew you could do it."

The terror on his face underlines his guilt, as his lips continue to move. I can hear a few words now: *don't* and *else* and *choice* and *understand*. But no matter how he tries to rationalize this for himself, it is not going to end well for him.

Next up on the hit parade are highlights from the footage we obtained from the Tucson Amtrak station, while our voice says, "David Weeks was your fall guy. He was found by Juan Sanchez, who was recruited by his childhood friend Ryan Long, one of your bodyguards. Weeks was then escorted from Phoenix to Los Angeles by Sanchez, Long, and one of your other men on the night Naomi was killed. But Weeks was not the one who murdered her. He was not there in time to do that. You, on the other hand, flew to L.A. on the morning before the murder."

The train footage disappears, and a new short clip from an airport gate security camera plays, showing Dean boarding a flight. It's generic enough to be from anytime, but it's not. A check with security at Boise Airport will reveal the clip is from the boarding of a flight to Los Angeles on the morning of January 18.

The clip is replaced by one from a rental car agency, showing Dean getting into a black Toyota Prius. This is followed by footage from a security camera at a Los Feliz Shell station, across from one of the Griffith Park entrances. The video is time stamped 10:40 p.m. on January eighteenth, exactly fifty minutes before the special planetarium presentation was scheduled to start. Even though it's night, there's more than enough light to see a Prius sitting at a nearby stoplight with Dean behind the wheel. When the light turns green, the car turns onto the road into the park.

The next clip is from the same camera. The time has jumped ahead to 10:54 p.m. The car that turns into the park is the same Hyundai Accent hatchback the police found in the observatory parking lot the next morning. Naomi's Hyundai Accent hatchback. While it's not easy to tell who is behind the wheel, it's her.

A last clip. Same camera. Time 1:42 a.m. The Prius again, leaving the park, with Dean inside.

And to finish everything off, a final picture. This from the police files. The daughter of the rental car driver, lying dead at the bottom of a rocky chute in the Hollywood Hills.

CHAPTER TWENTY-FOUR

ere's my guess as to what happened.

Naomi contacted Dean, scaring the hell out of him. As much as he might not have liked to admit it, he was not yet out of the shadow of his father. So he formulated his plan to be done with her forever, in a way he was sure could never be tied back to him.

When he found out she lived in L.A., he told her he would be in town on business and maybe suggested they meet. The planetarium show offered him the ability to lure her to a place with a lot of area to get lost in. Maybe he told her he'd been given the tickets by a client. Maybe he told her it was something he'd always wanted to do. Whatever the ruse, I doubt he ever purchased tickets.

When they met, he had been all charm and affection. At some point, he suggested a walk. It was more important to talk than to see the show, he said. And why would she have thought anything was wrong? He was her father and he seemed nice, and they were getting along. Besides, if there was trouble, she knew how to fight from her time in the army. But why would she need to?

Just off a trail on the back side of Mt. Lee, he might have made a comment about the view. She turned and looked out at the San Fernando Valley, unprepared for when he grabbed her by the neck and shoved her over the side.

I don't think she had her backpack with her. It was probably still in her car. But it was perfect for his purposes, because he wanted to make sure she would be found sooner than later. So he went down to her body and took her keys, then hiked back to her car to find something that would catch a passerby's attention. My attention.

He's not the most in-shape person in the world, so a second trip up the mountain to stage the backpack tired him. Which explains why he didn't leave the park until after 1:30 a.m.

Am I right? I don't know, but I'm sure I'm close.

It doesn't matter, though.

We don't need a confession.

We don't need explanations of what happened.

We don't need to hear Dean's voice again.

The police can get it out of him, if they want, but we already have more than enough evidence to lock him up forever.

A lifetime in prison seems too kind, though, and I can't help but want to walk over and deliver the final justice myself.

He's not worth it, Liz says.

I know.

You and Jar found him. That's what's important.

I know.

Naomi says thank you, and so do I.

I take a deep breath, then turn off camera one and walk over to Jar.

She clicks the remote, killing camera two, and opens the hypodermic kit. As much as I would love to jam the needle in, the honor should be Jar's.

She walks over and stops directly in front of the man who

killed Naomi Bellows and holds up her left hand, showing him the needle.

"What is that?" Dean asks, his voice weak and strained.

She looks at the syringe, then at him again, and moves the needle out another ten centimeters or so to the side. His gaze follows it, unable to look away.

"Wha—"

Jar smashes her other fist into his jaw, whacking his head against the chair back.

This was not in the script, but I have to say I approve of her improvisation.

Dean's head lolls forward, his eyes drooping. When he tries to look at her, she hits him again, knocking him out. Only then does she stick the needle into his arm.

After delivering the Beta-Somnol, she glares at him, no doubt a part of her wishing she could do the same thing I was contemplating.

After several seconds, I say, "Jar."

Her eyes remain on Dean.

"Jar."

Not a twitch.

"Jar."

Finally she looks at me.

"I don't know about you, but I'd rather not stay here any longer than we have to."

She closes her eyes for a few moments, then nods and returns to her computer.

While she checks the video files of Dean watching the presentation to make sure we are never seen or heard, I pack up the gear. We finish at about the same time, and she uploads the movie to the temporary website she's created, where it joins, among other things, a copy of the full-screen version of our presentation.

I do a final check of Dean's restraints, look around to make sure we haven't forgotten anything, and we exit the theater.

Ariel is pleased to see Jar.

"It would be nice to take her with us," Jar says.

"It would," I say.

Jar smiles wistfully, knowing as I do that we can't.

We take the Chihuahua back to the master bedroom and put her on the bed with Lorna. The dog circles around a few times, then lies down next to the woman's shoulder, without displaying any of the repulsion she showed Dean.

Fourteen minutes later, we are on the road.

———

I call Shawn Darby from a truck stop outside of Boise.

"It's done," I tell her.

"Go the way you hoped?"

"It did. How's everything there?"

"The old guy got a little mouthy once, but we had a...talk, and he's been pretty much staring at nothing ever since."

"He still breathing?"

"Last I checked."

"Go ahead and dope him up and get out of there. I'll send the notification out in about thirty minutes. Unless you think you need more time than that."

"Nah, that'll be plenty."

"Thanks, Shawn. We appreciate the help."

"This kind of thing I could do any day of the week. Feel free to call me again."

"Careful what you offer."

There's a 24-hour restaurant inside the truck stop's main building, where Jar and I take a table and order an early breakfast. When we're done, I send the email notification.

It will appear to come from a generic address within the FBI's Criminal Investigative Division. The subject line reads: IMMEDIATE ACTION NEEDED ON NAOMI BELLOWS MURDER--NEW SUSPECT DETAINED.

The message starts with a concise description of the case against Trevor Dean, plus instructions on where to find him and Hank Morgan. At the bottom is a link to the temporary website Jar made, where the recipients will find more detailed notes, the videos she uploaded, all the evidential video clips in longer form than what we showed to Dean, and all the other pieces of evidence we have collected.

It's not the first time I've sent an email like this, so it is a well-crafted, thorough report.

As far as recipients go, I have always taken the viewpoint I can't send emails such as this to only the local authorities, since the subject of my report might have friends in the police and/or area government.

This is certainly true in Trevor Dean's case. To ensure there's no cover up, tonight's email is addressed to the Boise Police Department, the Idaho State Police, the Oregon State Police, the Malheur County Sheriff's Department (also in Oregon, where Cousin Hank is currently hanging out), Detective George Hughes of the LAPD and other members of the Robbery-Homicide Division, the deputy director of the FBI, and US Marshal Renee Faust.

If I left anyone out, I'm sure someone will let them know.

After the email is off, Jar and I head west toward Portland, Oregon, where we'll catch a plane bound for Los Angeles.

CHAPTER TWENTY-FIVE

I t's the last Tuesday of February, and Jar and I have been back in L.A. for five days.

News about the arrest of Trevor Dean for the murder *and* kidnapping of Naomi Bellows years earlier has made the national news. Unfortunately, it hasn't held on to the top spot for as long as I would have liked, due to weightier topics fighting for the big headlines. A presidential primary for one, but mostly a virus that has been gaining traction throughout the world over the last couple of months. There are a few more than fifty cases here in the US right now. I'm not sure what, if anything, that's going to mean for us, but I can understand why it has some people on edge. I've been up close and personal with a bad virus before, and it's not something I'm anxious to do again.

At least the truth about what happened to Naomi is out there. And someday, hopefully soon, Dean and those who helped him will be found guilty and receive the sentences they deserve. That goes for Morgan, too. In fact, I wouldn't be opposed to them having a family reunion as cellmates. That would never happen, but it's a fun daydream.

This morning, Jar and I are standing in front of the Pacific

Sierra Bank in Granada Hills. With us is Cynthia Watson, Naomi's friend from college.

"We should go in," I say to her.

She takes a nervous breath. "I don't know. Maybe there was a mistake."

"There's no mistake."

She grimaces as if she doesn't believe me, but when I start toward the entrance, she follows. She still thinks I'm a PI, and I've introduced Jar as my assistant.

Once we're inside, I lead us to an unmanned window at the far end of the counter, away from the regular tellers. I catch the eye of a Hispanic woman in her forties, sitting at one of the desks.

With a smile, she comes over and says, "Good morning. How may I help you?" Her name tag identifies her as Delores Chavez.

Cynthia says, "Yes, um, I, um..." She looks at me, her gaze pleading for help.

"We've come to open the safety-deposit box of Cynthia's friend," I say. "She passed away recently."

"Oh, I'm so sorry to hear that. What was her name?"

"Saundra Moore," I tell her. It's the name the box is under.

"Do you have the key?"

Cynthia holds up the key Jar gave her. It's not the original. That one's still in the backpack in an LAPD evidence locker, part of a now reactivated investigation. This one looks exactly like it, though. We took the wax impression to a friend of ours, who made a temporary key of hard plastic that he then used to cut a new one, out of his stock of blank Pacific Sierra Bank safety-deposit box keys that we'll just say he happens to have lying around.

"Great," Delores says. "I will also need a death certificate and an ID. Do you have those?"

"We do," I say. "But I don't believe the death certificate will be necessary."

"Unfortunately, we will need the certificate to open the box."

I motion to Cynthia. "Not if she's already authorized to use the box."

The woman blinks, then looks at Cynthia again. "You're an authorized user?"

"I've been told I am, yes."

"Told?"

I smile. "Cynthia, why don't you give her your ID and she can check?"

After Cynthia does this, Delores turns skeptically to her terminal.

We already know she'll find Naomi added Cynthia to the account the day she opened it. We can't know exactly why Naomi did that, but at a minimum she must've been very fond of Cynthia.

Delores's eyes widen. "Oh. You are authorized. I'm sorry for, um, any confusion." She smiles meekly, and after Cynthia signs on a digital screen, says, "If you would follow me."

Once we've retrieved the box from the safe, we're led to a private room with plenty of space for the three of us.

"Just push this button when you are finished, and I'll help you put the box back," Delores says, pointing at a black button on the wall next to the door.

"Thank you," I say.

A smile and she's gone.

Cynthia takes a step back from the box.

"You should open it," Jar says to her.

Cynthia's eyes widen. "Me?"

"She was your friend," I say. "It's only right."

Cynthia nods solemnly and approaches the waist-high counter where the box is sitting. She stares at it for a moment before releasing the latch and lifting the lid.

A breath catches in her throat.

From inside she lifts out a rectangular wooden box. She looks at me. "This is the box I was telling you about."

By the time she opens it, her eyes have filled with tears. Inside, the box is lined with dark purple velvet and filled with the decorations and dog tags Naomi wore while she was in the army.

Jar and I checked Naomi's storage unit for it over the weekend. When we didn't find it, I had a feeling Naomi had put it here, which is the main reason I wanted Cynthia with us. I'm glad I was right.

"It's yours," I say.

Her gaze darts to me again. "What?"

"It was decided that the box should stay with someone Naomi was close to."

"But...really?"

I nod.

She shudders as she tries to control her emotions. "Thank you."

The ones who decided Cynthia should have the box were Jar and me, of course. Perhaps it wasn't our place, but it felt right. As for Naomi's other property, I guess everything could go to Dean's daughters, Naomi's half sisters, but that will be decided by someone else.

"May I?" I say, gesturing to the safety-deposit box.

"Oh, yes. Of course." Cynthia moves out of the way, holding the wooden box tight to her chest.

Naomi stored two other things in the metal box, a nine-by-twelve-inch mailing envelope and a FedEx envelope. I pull out the mailing envelope first since it's on top. It's addressed to Naomi, with a return address for someplace called Your Life Discovered.

I remove the sheath of paper from inside. It's a report on DNA results for the test Naomi took. I leaf through it and stop when I see a section labeled RELATED TO YOU. Some people are listed by their full names and others by abbreviations. According to an explainer paragraph, abbreviated names are people who have requested privacy. They can apparently be contacted through the Your Life Discovered website, where they can decide if they want to reveal themselves or not. There are handwritten check marks by all but one of the names. None of those are familiar to me, and if I had to guess, I'd say they are all people from Naomi's mother's side of the family. The one without a check has a question mark next to it. That name reads: AARON MORGAN. Gerald Morgan's son.

The FedEx envelope is from Alex Whitfield. Inside are three separate documents. One is a copy of the DNA report for Aaron Morgan. I wonder if Aaron gave it to Whitfield willingly or the PI obtained a copy by less direct means. The second is a report comparing Aaron's and Naomi's DNA and confirming they are indeed related and likely second cousins. And the last is a list of Aaron Morgan's relatives, with their probable relationship to Naomi.

Is Trevor Dean on the list?

Yes. Yes, he is.

TREVOR DEAN — FATHER 97%

This last report is the reason Naomi let Whitfield go. He had found her father. That was all she wanted from him. Contacting Dean was something she'd do herself.

"We'll make sure the right people get these," I tell Cynthia as I put everything back in the envelopes.

She nods. We've told her the papers are important to Naomi's estate, but not why. She's been fine with that explanation so far and shows no signs of increased interest now.

And I'm not lying about getting them in the right hands. After we scan each page, we'll send digital copies to the same people we emailed last week. The originals we'll FedEx to Detective Hughes.

I double-check to make sure we've missed nothing in the safety-deposit box. I then close it and tell Cynthia, "Go ahead and press the black button."

After goodbye hugs, Jar and I watch Cynthia drive off. It's been an emotional morning for her, and I so hope the box helps her find some peace.

It's usually after I think something like this that Liz shows up and says, *It will.* But the last time I heard from her was at Trevor Dean's house, when she passed on Naomi's thanks.

I don't know why she's been gone so long, and I'm not sure what to do about it.

It scares me to think this might be it. That I'll never hear her voice again.

"Are you all right?" Jar asks.

I force a smile and rub my eyes, pretending they aren't watery. "Sorry. It's just..."

"I know. Not easy."

"Yeah."

She slips her hand into mine as if doing so is part of our daily routine. But she's never done that before. She then leans against my arm. "I have never known anyone like you," she says, each word brimming with importance. "I have never trusted anyone like I trust you. But I...I do not know how to thank you for what you have done for Naomi. And...and for me."

I slowly turn to face her and wrap my arms around her back, hugging her to my chest. "You thank me every day by being my friend. Everything you just said are the same things I would say about you." I look down at her and she looks up, our faces separated by the width of a hand. "You are my closest friend, and I never want that to change."

We stand there for several moments, eyes locked as we gain strength in each other's embrace.

"You said before that I am welcome to stay with you anytime," Jar says.

"I did. I meant it, and still do."

"I do not..." She takes a breath. "I do not want to go back to Bangkok on Friday."

"Then stay."

"I am not sure I want to go back to Bangkok...at all."

A motion causes me to glance behind Jar, and for a second I see Liz standing nearby, smiling.

When she disappears, I look back down and repeat, "Then stay."

ABOUT THE AUTHOR

Brett Battles is a *USA Today* and Amazon bestselling and Barry Award-winning author of over thirty-five novels, including those in the Jonathan Quinn series, the Night Man Chronicles, the Excoms series, the Project Eden thrillers, and the time-hopping Rewinder series. He's also the coauthor, with Robert Gregory Browne, of the Alexandra Poe series.

Keep updated on new releases and other book news, and get exclusive content by subscribing to Brett's newsletter at his website brettbattles.com, (scroll to the bottom of the webpage). You can learn more about his books there, too.

And around the internet:

facebook.com/Author-Brett-Battles-152032908205471

twitter.com/BrettBattles

instagram.com/authorbrettbattles

Made in United States
North Haven, CT
21 December 2024

63225910R00205